He was too old in experience.

As far as the world was concerned, he'd lived a lifetime compared to her.

He had to stop thinking of her in such a personal way. More than that, he had to get her out of his place now, before he did something he would regret for a long time to come.

He didn't want to lose his job. He liked working here. He had hoped to remain here as long as he wanted. When he got bored he would move on. That was the way he liked it—no ties that bound, no one to worry about but himself.

Until he'd seen Lindsay, that is.

He wanted her. No use denying that any longer. But he wanted a lot of things he couldn't have. Lindsay was just another in a long list.

"Good dialog, provocative chapter endings that literally force a page turn, and a streamlined writing style..."
    —*Library Journal* on *One Summer Evening*

Also available from MIRA Books and
MARY LYNN BAXTER

HARD CANDY
LONE STAR HEAT
A DAY IN APRIL
AUTUMN AWAKENING
TEARS OF YESTERDAY
ONE SUMMER EVENING

Watch for the newest contemporary romance from
MARY LYNN BAXTER
May 2001

MARY LYNN
BAXTER
SULTRY

MIRA®

MIRA®

ISBN 1-55166-588-3

SULTRY

Copyright © 2000 by Mary Lynn Baxter.

All rights reserved. Except for use in any review, the reproduction or utilization of this work in whole or in part in any form by any electronic, mechanical or other means, now known or hereafter invented, including xerography, photocopying and recording, or in any information storage or retrieval system, is forbidden without the written permission of the publisher, MIRA Books, 225 Duncan Mill Road, Don Mills, Ontario, Canada M3B 3K9.

All characters in this book have no existence outside the imagination of the author and have no relation whatsoever to anyone bearing the same name or names. They are not even distantly inspired by any individual known or unknown to the author, and all incidents are pure invention.

MIRA and the Star Colophon are trademarks used under license and registered in Australia, New Zealand, Philippines, United States Patent and Trademark Office and in other countries.

Visit us at www.mirabooks.com

Printed in U.S.A.

ACKNOWLEDGMENT

Special thanks to my friend Dr. Laura Horne
for coming to my rescue with her medical expertise.

One

Summer 2000

"Okay, how badly is he *really* hurt?"

Lindsay Newman tried to keep the tremor out of her voice, but she couldn't. Her father, a retired heart surgeon, had been injured in an automobile accident. She was afraid the truth concerning his condition had been kept from her.

"Like Tim told you on the phone, it's not serious." Peter Ballinger frowned, knitting his thick, dark brows together. "Cooper's not serious. He's going to be all right."

Lindsay peered at her friend Peter long and hard, trying to pick up on any hint that he was lying to her. Her efforts proved futile. Underneath his bland but handsome facade, his conviction didn't appear to waver. It was then that her insides seemed to turn loose. Before they had been tied in tiny knots. Now she could breathe and function like a human.

"Ah, here are your bags."

Lindsay looked on as Peter motioned for a bellman to tackle the three pieces of large luggage, all the while continuing to breathe deeply. She couldn't believe her trip to London with a couple of friends had ended on such a frantic note.

She had been gone almost four weeks when her brother Timothy called and told her about their father's accident. She had taken the first plane out. Yet it seemed like an interminable amount of time had passed since she'd boarded that jet at Heathrow and arrived in Garnet, Mississippi.

It wouldn't be long now before she actually saw for herself that Cooper was not in jeopardy; the limo was waiting to take them straight to the family estate.

"So were you having a good time?" Peter asked once the luggage was loaded and they were on their way.

Lindsay didn't answer for a moment, still irritated at having seen Peter at the airport instead of her brother. However, she knew why Tim hadn't come. A doctor himself, he was most likely by Cooper's side, which was where he belonged.

Still, seeing Peter hadn't been to her liking. Although he professed to love her, she knew better. He wanted her; she wouldn't deny that—although she suspected it was the family money he wanted more.

Peter was from a family rich in lineage, but short on cash. She thought that a rather ironic situation, since he was a banker, banking being considered a "suitable" position for a Southern gentleman.

And Cooper was urging her to marry this stuffed shirt. She had met Peter at a charity function and ended up dancing with him several times. He'd asked her out the following week, and she'd gone.

Even though she saw him quite often after that, she never considered him anything other than a friend, someone to go out with, no strings attached. He'd been fun, harmless and at loose ends.

Peter, however, had other ideas, especially after he met Cooper. They formed an instant rapport, and Cooper saw him as the perfect match for his daughter.

From then on, Peter turned into a man with a mission, becoming more of an aggravation than an asset. Unfortunately, that hadn't changed, and she was getting fed up.

"Lindsay?"

Shaking her head to clear it, she faced Peter once again and gave him an aloof smile. "Sorry, I'm having trouble concentrating."

"I understand," he said in his smooth voice. "Now that you're back, what are your plans?"

"I think that should be obvious," Lindsay said with a slight sting in her tone. "First of all, I'm going to see to Daddy."

His perfectly shaped mouth stretched into a thin smile. "Of course."

His words were not without their own sting, and she knew why. While Peter respected Cooper and saw him as an ally, he also resented her father because of her attachment to him.

"I gather you don't want to talk about us."

There is no us, she was tempted to say, but didn't. "No, Peter, I don't."

"Dammit, when are you going to think of yourself? Do something for yourself?"

Lindsay's irritation burgeoned into anger. Nonetheless, she managed to hang on to her control, though her voice was cold as icicles. "I'm happy with my life the way it is, thank you."

Once she'd said that, Lindsay turned away, hoping he wouldn't see the flush that covered her features, a tell-all that she hadn't exactly told the truth. But the demons she was wrestling with weren't any of his business.

Other than clenching his jaw a bit tighter, Peter showed no emotion. But he dropped the subject and didn't try to break the silence that fell between them. Finally the driver braked the limo inside the gates of the mansion grounds.

For a second Lindsay didn't move. It was good to be here. She loved this old home. Her gaze roamed over the huge flower garden set amidst the perfectly manicured grounds of this fine old Mississippi mansion, one that had been in the family for generations. However old it might be, it was in mint condition, having been refurbished and redecorated on several occasions.

One day this estate would be hers. Tim didn't want it, she knew, having been given several acres of adjoining land where he and Eve had built a lovely home of their own.

"Thanks for meeting me," Lindsay said, once they were standing outside the vehicle.

Peter nodded, then leaned and grazed her cheek with his lips. "Any time."

Before Peter made it to his car, Lindsay was inside and dashing up the stairs.

"Lordy, child, is that you?"

Lindsay stopped for a second at the top of the

circular stairway and whipped around. "Oh, hi, Dolly. I was wondering where you were."

The housekeeper's round face broke into a huge grin. "I was comin' to the door as fast as I could get there. Only you were faster." Dolly's grin fled as she placed her hands on her equally rounded hips. "You don't look so good. You've lost weight."

"Don't hover, Dolly. I'm okay. After I see Daddy, I'll give you a hug."

"The tea cakes will be coming out of the oven about then. Meanwhile, you skedaddle. He's waitin'."

The instant Lindsay entered the master suite, her brother rose to his feet, met her halfway and gave her a brief hug, which she returned. Then her eyes sought the man who was in the bed, propped against massive pillows.

"Oh, Daddy—" Her voice broke as she crossed to his bedside, grasped his hand, then bent and kissed him lightly on the cheek.

"Ah, hell, I'm fine. Don't fuss so." Cooper cut his eyes over at Tim. "If I had my way, I'd be on the golf course right now."

"Dream on," Lindsay muttered, looking toward her brother, then back to Cooper. "I have to say, you don't look like you've been run over by a truck."

"I don't feel like it, either."

Lindsay scrutinized him. If not for the brutal-looking circles under his eyes, circles that heretofore hadn't been there, and the purplish spot on his right cheekbone, no one would have known he'd just experienced a life-threatening trauma. Dr. Cooper Newman was still a striking figure.

Blessed with deep-set, piercing green eyes, a thick head of silver hair, and a tall lean frame, he was downright good-looking. When he was dressed for success, no one would guess he was in his middle sixties.

"Well, he has a concussion to prove it," Tim said in a firm tone.

Lindsay's gaze shifted back to her brother, who did not have anywhere near the commanding presence Cooper had. Yet in all fairness, Tim, who looked like their mother, Emily, had no trouble holding his own.

Perhaps if he didn't wear glasses and have a mustache, there might be more of a resemblance between father and son, Lindsay had always thought. At thirty—four years her senior—Tim was tall and fine-looking in his own right, with light brown hair and dark brown eyes, the same as hers—eyes they had inherited from their mother.

"What about his heart?" she asked into the silence, her voice anxious.

"My ticker's ticking right along," Cooper snapped before Tim could answer.

Lindsay raised her eyebrows at her brother. "Is it?"

"So far, so good. Other than what's visible, and the fact that his muscles have to feel like he's been in a war zone, he came out of the fiasco relatively unscathed."

"Thank God for that."

Cooper made a strange noise. "Would you two stop talking about me as if I'm not here?"

Lindsay cut her gaze back to Cooper and smiled. "You haven't even said you were glad to see me."

"There was no need for you to come home," he muttered darkly.

"I disagree. That's precisely what I should've done."

"Dad's right, you know," Tim said. "You could've remained in London. I had everything under control."

"I know you did, but I had to see for myself. Anyhow, I was ready to jump ship, so to speak."

"Bored, huh?" Tim asked.

Lindsay ignored the mocking smile that seemed itching to break across his thin lips. "A little." She shrugged, unsure of what else to say. She hadn't sorted through all the emotions that were warring inside her as yet, so she couldn't share them with anyone.

"Now that's a problem I could love," Tim said.

Cooper snorted, then glared at his first-born. "That *is* your problem. You don't want to work."

"That's not true," Tim countered mildly.

So mildly that Lindsay picked up on the insincerity behind his tone. It was obvious Cooper had, too, for he snorted again, this time with more disgust.

Tim's face flooded with color, but he didn't say anything.

In order to fill the growing and uncomfortable silence, Lindsay asked, "How long do you have to stay in bed?"

"Through today only," Cooper said fiercely.

Tim merely looked at him. "We'll see."

"No, you're the one who will—"

"Hey, time out!" Lindsay exclaimed. Then, turning back to Tim, she added, "Now that I'm home, I'll see that he behaves."

Cooper's eyes shone with disapproval. "I'm not at all happy you cut short your trip and deserted your friends."

Tim held up his hands. "I'll let you two duke that out. I'm gone."

"Don't go. Not yet, anyway," Lindsay said quickly. "Dolly's making some tea cakes."

Tim halted with a smile. "In that case, I'll meet you on the porch."

Once her brother had left, another silence descended over the room. Finally Cooper broke it. "You're a good daughter, Lindsay."

"I try," she said, not sure where this conversation was leading. His out-of-the-blue statement took her aback. Rarely did Cooper compliment her on anything. Yet there were moments when he was warm and appreciative of her and what she did for him. These moments she treasured.

But by and large, he made more demands than anything and expected them to be carried out. Within the confines of the house and grounds, one soon learned that Cooper ruled and didn't like to be crossed.

"Sometimes you try too hard."

Lindsay almost shivered, thinking how difficult he was to love, and how much he tried to make both Tim and her bend to his strong will.

"How's that?" she asked, though she already knew the answer.

"You know. It's time you married and had children. You're certainly not getting any younger."

How well she knew. At twenty-six, she had never even lived away from home. She had remained here, occupying her own suite. When she wasn't busy raising money and heading her favorite charity, she acted as Cooper's hostess when he entertained, which was often.

To the outside world looking in, she had everything money could buy.

"I want you to stop dallying and set a wedding date."

Lindsay rubbed her forehead. "You know I don't want to marry Peter."

"Why the hell not?"

"You know that, too. I don't love him."

"So what?"

"Daddy!"

"You'll learn to love him. It's that simple."

Lindsay felt as if she were beating her head against a rock. He was one stubbornly opinionated man. "Simple? I don't think so."

Cooper's features turned cold. "I'm counting on this marriage. Please don't disappoint me. Do it."

Two

When Lindsay walked out onto the porch, she paused for a moment, feeling a sudden but added sense of homecoming, thinking that houses without porches were like diamonds without the sparkle. They were missing something truly special.

"Hey, your tea's waiting."

Lindsay forced her limbs to move, reaching for the glass of iced tea her brother held out to her. After nodding her thanks, she gazed at the beauty that surrounded her, drawing the sweet smell of roses into her lungs.

Summer.

This was her favorite time of the year, especially on a day when the sun was about to call it quits.

"You look beat," Tim said, his head cocked to one side, eyeing her carefully.

"I am. Actually, I feel like someone beat me."

Tim almost smiled. "Not someone, but some-*thing*—jet lag."

"That and worry about Daddy."

"You should feel better about him now."

Lindsay made her way to the white wooden railing and leaned against it, feeling the gentle breeze ruffle her hair. "I do, but I'm still concerned about his heart."

Tim sipped his tea, then shrugged. "That'll always be a concern, that's for sure. But at least the wreck didn't seem to put any extra stress on it."

"I hope that continues to hold true," Lindsay said in a slightly unsteady voice.

"We both know there are no guarantees in this world."

Lindsay's own heart skipped a beat. "Are you trying to tell me something?"

"Nope. At least, nothing you don't already know. Accident or no accident, Dad's heart could stop at any time."

Although Lindsay hated to face that brutal fact, she had no choice. Admitting that, however, hadn't been easy. Even though Cooper had had several attacks already, caused by a defect that couldn't be fixed with bypass surgery, she had refused to acknowledge that he wasn't immortal. He'd always been so big, so full of life, so larger than life, that she couldn't imagine him not being *alive*.

"On the bright side of all this," Tim added, "Dad could live to the ripe old age of ninety-five, going full steam ahead."

Lindsay sipped on her tea. "He's definitely in that mode now."

Tim's lips twisted. "What's he on your case about this time?"

"Same old thing, only he came right out and gave me an ultimatum for setting a wedding date."

"Why the hell don't you just tell him you're not going to marry Ballinger, and be done with it?"

Lindsay's eyes flared. "I already have, but he still refuses to take no for an answer."

"Well, I'll admit you have a problem. When the old man digs his heels in, it's his way or the highway."

"Tell me something I don't know," Lindsay said.

Tim merely shrugged.

Lindsay crossed to the antique swing, which was comfortably cushioned in a floral pattern. Once she was seated, she held her silence, setting the swing in soft motion.

"Would you be willing to help me out?" she asked at last, feeling her insides unwind.

"Depends."

"Maybe if you talked to him." She was testing uncharted waters, as she rarely ever asked her brother for anything, especially when it pertained to something personal. She never felt she could count on him.

"Wow, hold on a minute. You'll have to take care of this one on your own. It's your baby, you'll have to burp it. Besides, I've got enough problems of my own."

She still couldn't count on him, she thought, and not without a trace of bitterness. "Problems seem to go hand and hand with this family," she said on an emotional note. "And that shouldn't be. Both of us have the best of everything."

Tim cut her a sharp glance. "Speak for yourself."

Lindsay cringed against the whine underlying his succinct statement. It grated on her nerves.

"Oh, come on, Tim, you should be on top of the world. You have a wonderful wife, a practice that other doctors would die for, since you took over all Daddy's patients. And what about your side business, your chain of pharmacies? My God, you shouldn't have a worry in the world, especially a financial one. Yet—'' Lindsay broke off when she saw the scowl darken his face.

"I always seem to be broke," Tim finished with a sardonic laugh. "Was that what you were going to say?"

"Yes, and I don't understand why, unless you're still playing the stock market and losing."

"You got it."

Lindsay glared at him. "You've got to stop."

"I'm trying, only it's not that simple."

She knew her brother was addicted to playing the market. From the look of despair on his features, she suspected he might even have depleted the trust their mother had left each of them.

"It *is* that simple, brother dear. Just stop playing Russian roulette with your time and money."

Tim clenched his jaw. "Sorry, I forgot I was dealing with Miss Perfect, who never makes any mistakes."

Lindsay flushed, then murmured, "That's a cheap shot."

"Maybe, but it's the truth. If things were simple, you wouldn't still be here under Daddy's roof, at his constant beck and call."

"You don't know that," Lindsay said tersely, her eyes flashing.

"The hell I don't. And what do you have to show for getting up every morning? I don't see you setting the world on fire."

Following that outburst, Lindsay fell silent, her insides churning. He was right, of course. Who was she to be giving advice? To date, she hadn't done anything with her own life that counted for a hill of beans, except her work with the women's shelter. And at times even that failed to use up all her energies.

But she hoped to change all that. In fact, she'd been mulling over an idea for some time now and had worked herself into the excited stage. Even so, she wasn't ready to share her innermost thoughts with anyone, least of all her brother.

"Look, sis—"

"If you're about to apologize, don't. I had it coming. But I wouldn't count me out—not just yet, anyway."

Tim didn't respond. However, a few minutes later, after their glasses of iced tea were empty, he broke the silence. "Do you ever think about Mother?"

That starkly spoken question so surprised Lindsay that, for a moment, she couldn't say anything.

"Hell, you don't have to answer that," Tim said, his features pinched. "Just forget I asked."

"Of course I think about her." Lindsay's chest constricted. "Every day."

"Me, too." His tone was harsh, but with a sad undertone.

Lindsay felt a sting behind her eyelids and blinked. She dared not cry—not now, not when she was already feeling vulnerable from Cooper's accident and his pressuring her to marry a man she didn't love. If the tears ever started, she might not be able to stop them.

"Do you ever ask yourself why she did it?"

"You know I do," Lindsay responded softly, staring into the agony twisting her brother's face, agony that she knew was duplicated on hers.

"Sometimes I hate her," Tim muttered fiercely, "for what she did to us, to our family. Maybe if Garnet was bigger, without the *Peyton Place* mentality, it would've been different."

Lindsay curled her nails into her palms and felt them pierce her skin. But that pain was nothing compared to the pain in her heart. Heart pain—through the years, she had learned it was the worst kind. Once it got its grip on you, it wouldn't let go.

"Sometimes I hate her, too," Lindsay admitted. "And no matter where we lived, it would *not* have been different." Her voice caught. "But she was sick. Believe me, I understand that now."

"I know you do." He paused, then added, "God, if it had been me who had..." His voice trailed off.

"Found her lying in her own blood, dead," Lindsay whispered, barely getting those words out before her own voice faded into nothingness.

Tim blanched, then nodded.

In some respects, Lindsay couldn't believe she was having this conversation with Tim. Always before, he'd refused to talk about their mother's untimely and tragic death from a self-inflicted gunshot wound.

At the time, he had retreated into his own shell of personal pain and fear. She hadn't faulted him then, nor did she now. Besides, she'd been too distraught herself to think about anything other than her own broken heart and shattered dreams.

Even though Cooper was the strong one in the

family, the one who made the major decisions, Lindsay had nonetheless adored her mother, even if it had been from afar. She had learned early on that Emily was different from other mothers.

Emily had had deep bouts of depression, which often sent her away from home for long periods. It hadn't been until Lindsay was older that she realized her mother was in a private sanitarium for treatment, something Cooper was ashamed of and tried to cover up by refusing to acknowledge or discuss his wife's problem.

Only after Lindsay found her mother's blood-splattered body and plunged into that same world of dark depression did Cooper respond.

"Lindsay, are you all right?"

Jerking her thoughts out of the past, Lindsay tried to swallow back the panic that suddenly threatened to overwhelm her. No, she wasn't all right, she wanted to scream. Instead, she made the swing go faster, as if to outrun her mind.

Why now, of all times, did Tim have to bring up their mother's suicide?

"Of course you're not all right," Tim muttered, seemingly more to himself than to her.

Lindsay licked her dry lips. "I'm okay, really. Mother was not something I expected to discuss, that's all."

"Me either," Tim admitted, his weak chin jutting slightly. "I don't know what the hell came over me."

"It's okay. You don't have to feel guilty for talking about her."

"But I do," he said harshly. "It all happened so long ago."

"The summer I graduated from the university and you were in med school," Lindsay acknowledged in a dazed voice. "Even at that, it seems like yesterday." Her voice had suddenly turned hoarse, and she cleared her throat.

"Let's change the subject, okay?" Tim said abruptly. "'To hell with her' is the way I see it. If she didn't want to stay with us, then we're better off without her."

"Tim, please, don't talk like that. What would Daddy think?"

"Who gives a damn? Haven't you ever considered that he just might be partly to blame?"

"Of course I've considered it," she responded, a wealth of sadness in her tone.

"His stable of women has always been the talk of the town." His tone was bitter. "Because of that, I'm sure Mother was the brunt of a lot of jokes."

"Tim, don't do this, to yourself or me. It's not healthy, for more reasons than one."

"You know, life sucks."

Lindsay blew out a heavy breath, realizing the tiny moment of closeness she had felt with Tim earlier had disintegrated. He was once more his brooding, untouchable self, while she was becoming anxious, a feeling that frightened her. She didn't want to talk about Cooper's penchant for women or dissect his role in her mother's death. It wasn't healthy.

"I'd rather not talk about this any more," she said stiffly, voicing her thoughts.

His face darkened. "Ditto."

Lindsay stopped the swing. "I guess I'd best get back and check on Daddy."

"Ah, he's all right. If not, we'd have heard."

Lindsay didn't argue. However, she got out of the swing, walked back to the railing and stared into the distance. What a lovely and tranquil place, she thought, aching for some of that tranquility to filter into her soul.

"Why do you stay?"

Lindsay gave her brother a taxing look, trying to curb her temper. Another unsettling question out of the blue. This was a side of Tim she hadn't seen in a long time. He usually had very little to say to her. "You know why."

"No, I don't. He's perfectly capable of taking care of himself. He's just too selfish and ornery to do so."

"It's not all him." Lindsay's voice suddenly shook. "I've never wanted to be by myself."

"I can understand that."

A short silence followed his bleak words. Lindsay broke it by saying, "My main concern right now is convincing Daddy once and for all that I'm not going to marry Peter."

"Well, good luck. You've got a daunting task ahead."

Another silence ensued as Lindsay's eyes returned to the colorful grounds. It was then that she saw a man sauntering across the nearby lawn as if he owned it. He was a big man, with a loose, long-limbed gait that bespoke of self-assurance, if not a bit of arrogance.

An attractive hunk, she thought wryly, unable to remember the last time she'd been affected by any man. Of course, she wasn't affected by him, she corrected herself quickly, except in a purely objective way. After all, he was obviously an employee, and much too old for her, to boot.

Still, her gaze lingered. He had a strong, rugged profile, and dark hair that curled slightly at his nape. But it wasn't his face that held her attention. It was from the neck down.

He was shirtless, and even from where she stood, she could see the contour of his body. And a fine body it was, too.

For a moment Lindsay forgot all about Cooper, Timothy and—especially—Peter. She was intrigued and wondered who the man was, though she had never before taken an interest in the people who maintained the huge estate.

As if he sensed he was being watched, he swung his head sideways, and their eyes met. She was trapped. Caught staring. Her face flooded with color, especially when he seemed to be surveying her with guarded eyes.

What was he thinking? More to the point, why did she care?

Suddenly, his brows arched in a deliberate and dismissive gesture, then he turned his head.

Lindsay didn't know why, but that look irritated her no end. She had never considered herself a snob, but she felt like putting him in his place, wherever that might be.

She yanked her gaze away from him and back to her brother. "Who's that man?"

Tim's eyebrows shot up. "You mean Mitch Rawlins?"

"I don't know. That's why I'm asking."

"He's our new estate manager."

"Don't you mean head gardener?" Lindsay asked in a catty tone.

Tim gave her a perplexed look, then said with a touch of mockery, "I'd say he's a bit more than that. Why do you want to know?"

"No reason," Lindsay snapped, even as her hungry eyes once again sought the man out.

Three

Mitchum Rawlins, known as Mitch by his friends, continued to stare at the boss's daughter. Or rather, the lady of the manor, he corrected himself with a smirk, long after she had turned her haughty little nose up and away from him.

He wondered if she thought her snubbing him made any difference. His smirk deepened as he rubbed his stubbled chin. Having only been working on the estate as its main caretaker for a month, he'd never had the opportunity to meet Lindsay Newman firsthand. Word had it that she had gone to Europe. He guessed her old man's accident had brought her back home.

While she was in no way hard on the eyes, she caught his attention mainly because everything about her seemed to radiate a restless energy. And usually, where there was energy, there was passion.

Although she appeared on the thin side, she was still well-proportioned. Her small, jutting breasts and narrow waistline bore that out. But it was the strawberry-blond hair swirling around her face that was the eye-catcher.

He would bet anything she had the freckles that usually went along with that coloring. He would also bet she had dark eyes. As for her age, he was less sure about that. He'd put her somewhere in her middle to late twenties.

Finally realizing what he was doing, Mitch let go of a stinging curse, then forced his mind off the spoiled brat who wouldn't have cared if he took another breath.

The last thing he needed was to have anything to do with Dr. Newman's daughter. More to the point, he didn't want anything to do with anyone, especially a woman.

For the first time in years, he was sleeping like a baby. Using his hands, he did an honest day's work for an honest day's pay. Suddenly Mitch peered down at those large, tanned hands, which were both callused and strong, and thought again what a lucky son of a bitch he was.

When his wife, Wendy, left him and his other job became intolerable, he'd walked away in the opposite direction, leaving behind a world filled with responsibilities and sleepless nights.

Regrets?

None whatsoever.

Anything would beat what he'd done and where he'd been. Now he felt free in every sense of the word. He could grow anything, build anything, repair anything. God-given talents—all of them. And he was using them wisely. The only thing that bugged him was an occasional loneliness, a real need to touch and be touched by another human.

But that feeling didn't come often or last long. Nope, he wouldn't change the new direction his life had taken for a minute, nor was he about to let a woman anywhere near him, certainly not an obviously spoiled brat like Lindsay Newman.

Still, he found himself casting another glance in her direction. His stomach tightened. He had never even talked to her, for God's sake. And yet the intensity of the attraction he felt for her was staggering. It was as if his eyes had caught sight of an unattainable "perfect" woman and a lust-adrenaline cocktail had hit him in the gut.

Well, he would just have to get over it. He was not about to self-destruct over another woman, no matter how hot he was for her.

He turned and stomped back inside his living quarters.

But even after he had slammed the door behind him, Mitch kept seeing the lovely lines of her face, something that made him mad enough to bite a tenpenny nail in two.

What was wrong with him? What was there about her that had brought about the impossible? Stirred him up? Maybe he had been alone too long. Maybe it was time to scratch this sudden itch before it got any farther out of control. Maybe he should call up an old girlfriend and enjoy a roll in the hay. Even if the lady of the manor wouldn't be interested, he knew several who would.

Nah.

In the end, it wouldn't be worth it. The price was too high. He would just take a cold shower, drink a cold beer, then crawl into a cold bed.

Alone.

"Still feeling better, Daddy?"

It was the evening after she had returned from her

trip that she decided to pay Cooper an impromptu visit. She hadn't seen him all day, as she'd been busy unpacking, reading through mail and returning phone calls.

Even though she knew he was okay, she couldn't blot out the morbid trick her mind continued to play on her. She envisioned walking into her daddy's suite and finding him on the floor, dead, just like she'd found her mother.

"I'm still fine," he said in a gruff voice. "I wish you wouldn't fuss so."

"I wish you'd do like your cardiologist told you and take it easy," she said. "Which didn't include playing a round of golf."

Cooper's bushy white eyebrows drew together. "I see Dolly's been running her mouth."

"That's right."

"Well, I didn't play," he announced in a petulant tone. "I just rode around with a friend, and I'm none the worse for it. And as you can see, I'm already in bed, though I don't like it, mind you."

Probably because he was without a woman beside him, Lindsay thought, recalling her conversation with her brother. Like Tim, would she ever accept the unvarnished truth that her daddy was a ladies' man, that he had most likely been unfaithful to her mother? She doubted it. After all these years, that fact still rankled. Yet he'd never married again, which had always puzzled her. But then, she had never pretended to understand her daddy, and knew that she never would.

"You look nice, my dear," Cooper said, bridging the short silence.

"Thanks," Lindsay murmured, looking not at him but out the French doors.

"Are you about to have dinner?"

"Shortly."

"With Peter?"

Lindsay smothered a sigh. "No. I'm dining alone, actually."

"You shouldn't be," he snapped. "I'm sure Peter would be more than happy to join you."

Lindsay wanted to lash out and say that Peter was his pet, not hers. But she didn't. Instead, she told him, "I didn't feel like company. I'm still suffering the effects of jet lag."

"I meant what I said last night, Lindsay."

So much for her good intentions. However, she hadn't been called her father's daughter for nothing. She could be—and often was—as stubborn as he was.

"Daddy, I—"

He held up a hand, halting her flow of words. "I know what you're about to say."

"Then let me say it."

Cooper's lips tightened. "I don't want to hear it."

"I know, but—"

He interrupted again. "It's past time you were married."

"That way of thinking is archaic, Daddy. I'm only twenty-six years old, for heaven's sake."

"That's beside the point, and not even the most important issue. No young woman of your prestige and status should be without a husband." He paused, as if to let his words sink in. "I've already pointed that out countless times. How long is it going to take before it soaks in?"

Lindsay flushed and bit down on her lower lip.

"It's just not proper. Your mother would have agreed with me one hundred percent."

Lindsay bristled but continued to hold her tongue, again wise enough to know that now was not the time for a final showdown, not when he was recuperating from a nasty accident. Yet his old-fashioned attitude sent her irritation factor soaring off the charts.

"We'll talk later, Daddy." She made her way toward the door.

"Good night, my dear."

She swung back around and smiled, though not with her eyes. "Good night."

Thirty minutes later, Lindsay was sitting in the parlor, sipping on flavored coffee from the silver pot that Dolly had left on one corner of the table. She had just finished a delicious meal in the small, less formal dining room and was feeling her eyes grow heavier by the minute. Moments after they closed, she heard the doorbell chime.

Groaning inwardly, her lashes fluttered open and she saw Peter standing in the doorway. Oh, brother, she thought, her heart plummeting.

"I hope I'm not intruding."

"Hello, Peter," she said, not bothering to hide her aggravation.

If he picked up on it, he didn't show it. He crossed to the couch and sat down on the opposite end. "Dolly let me in," he said inanely. "She thought you might enjoy some company, said you seemed lonely."

Boy, was Dolly in big trouble. "I'm not lonely. I'm exhausted."

"In that case, I won't stay long."

A silence fell between them.

Peter didn't have to say anything for her to know that he was mentally shifting gears, getting ready for what he hoped was the big and final pitch.

"Lindsay, you already know how I feel about you."

She deliberately set her cup down on the tray and looked at him. "I know that you don't love me."

He was obviously stunned by her bluntness and seemed to scramble for a suitable reply. "You don't know any such thing."

"Look, Peter, this is not a good time—not when I've just arrived back home and not so soon after Daddy's accident." God, did she sound like a broken record or what?

He let out a deep sigh. "All right, Lindsay. But you should know, I'm not going to go away."

She hadn't thought he would, not because he loved her, but because Cooper wanted him in the picture. And for whatever reason, Peter seemed content to be led by the nose.

Unwittingly, the thought crossed her mind that the "gardener" she had seen earlier could never be co-erced into doing anything he didn't want to do. The set of his jaw and his air of self-confidence had said as much. But then, like her brother, Peter was weak in many ways. If she were to marry him, they would live in the big house, in her suite, which was something her daddy also wanted.

Would there ever come a time when pleasing Cooper wasn't important to her? Or would the legacy of her mother's suicide always force her to feel overly dependent on the one parent she had left, even when he didn't always deserve the level of her devotion?

"I don't know about you," Lindsay said suddenly, "but I need some fresh air."

Before Peter could respond, she was up, had the French doors open and was out on the cozy side veranda. Peter followed suit with their cups. It was when she reached for hers that her hand froze.

Him. Again.

"Lindsay, what's wrong?" Peter demanded.

"Er...nothing." She forced a smile, and with fingers that weren't quite steady, she took the cup.

However, her eyes never strayed off Mitch Rawlins, who was standing on the front porch of his cottage, leaning against a post. Even though he was too far away for her to see his eyes, she sensed he was also staring at her.

Lindsay's heart raced, and her palms turned sweaty. Before she could begin to sort through this explosive and unexpected reaction, Mitch pushed his big body away from the post. Yet his gaze seemed to be stuck on her.

She stiffened as a myriad of emotions charged through her. This was the second time she'd seen this man. Both times she'd responded in an animalistic way. Her face flamed. It was purely physical, she told herself, which in itself was crazy.

The feeling would go away, she assured herself, forcing down the desperation closing in on her.

Yet there was something about him, something about his razor-stubbled face and big body, that messed with her hormones. Suddenly she felt torn between her body's betrayal and her mind's determination to keep her distance.

"Damn," she muttered.

Peter gave her a strange look. "Did you say something?"

"Don't pay any attention to me," she said lamely. "I was just thinking out loud."

"Care to share?"

"No," she said bluntly.

She heard his sharp intake of breath and knew that she'd angered him. But when he spoke, his tone was conciliatory.

"Well, it was a good idea to come outside. The evening's lovely."

Lindsay didn't bother to respond. She was too busy watching Mitch turn and saunter back into his house. Only after he disappeared did she release her breath.

Four

"Good morning."

When she heard Mary Jane Morgan's voice on the phone, Lindsay's face brightened. M.J., as she was affectionately called, had been her friend since grade school. A divorcée with no children, she worked as a paralegal for a prestigious law firm.

"Hey, I was thinking about you," Lindsay said, reaching for her coffee cup and taking a healthy sip, hoping the caffeine would nudge her into action. She hadn't slept well; as a result, she felt a tad hungover.

"But not enough to call me, you wretch."

Lindsay laughed. "Hey, give me a break. I just got home."

"Excuses, excuses."

"So when are we going to get together?" Lindsay asked, already feeling much better. M.J. was like a strong tonic. Her jaded sense of humor could cure almost any ills, especially hers.

During the months and years following Lindsay's mother's suicide, she didn't know what she would have done without M.J., who had stuck by her side through the worst of times.

Even though her own life hadn't been littered with roses, Mary Jane never complained. She'd gotten divorced shortly after she married, having learned her husband was gay. That blow had been so severe, it had taken her a long time to get over it. Now, however, she was on the prowl again, a fact she would readily admit. Her honesty about it tickled Lindsay.

"So how's the lord of the manor?"

Only M.J. could refer to Cooper in such a manner and get by with it. But she did it in such an unmalicious way that Lindsay never took umbrage.

"He's still lording over everyone."

M.J. giggled. "Figures. All joking aside, how's he doing?"

"He's good, which is actually a miracle, considering what he's been through."

"Then you really didn't have to cut your trip short—but I'm glad you did. I hate it when you're gone. I don't have anyone to whine to."

"Well, it's good to know I've been missed—for whatever reason," Lindsay said drolly.

"So what's up now that you *are* back? Same old one and two?"

"I hope not."

"Don't knock it, my friend. I could handle being spoiled and rich and a lady of leisure."

"So that's what you really think of me," Lindsay said with forced lightness, trying not to take what her friend said as anything other than a joke. "Some friend you are."

"I'm just green with envy, that's all. But hey, I was only teasing. You know that. You do more for others than anyone I know—or will ever know, for that matter."

"I'd do more if only Daddy was more understanding,'' Lindsay said. He's after me big time to marry Peter.''

M.J. groaned. "I thought you had that all settled before you went to Europe.''

"I thought so, too, but I guess I was mistaken.''

"I hope you're not weakening. Peter's a jerk.''

Lindsay sighed. "I agree one hundred percent. However, Daddy thinks he's the man for me.''

"Screw whether you love him or not, right?''

"Right.''

"If it's grandkids he wants, why doesn't he go knock on Tim's door?''

"Because Tim would tell him to butt out in a heartbeat.''

"So why don't you do the same thing?'' M.J. hesitated. "Don't you think it's past time? You're strong now, Lindsay. You've come a long way, and you don't need Cooper like you once did.''

"I know, M.J. It's just that old habits die hard.''

"What you ought to do is move out of that house, get an apartment.''

Lindsay was silent for a long moment, choosing her words carefully—not that it would do any good. Mary Jane could read her like a book without a cover. "You're right, only I don't have the guts. I'll admit it.''

"At least you're honest.''

"But I do have something in mind.''

"Oh?'' Mary Jane's voice perked up considerably.

"Don't 'oh' me. I'm really serious.''

"Are we talking about a plan, or what?''

"I guess you could call it a plan. Yeah, that'll work.''

Lindsay could picture Mary Jane's petite features scrunched in a frown while the wheels were turning inside her head.

"So?"

"So I'll tell you about it another day, over lunch."

"That's a dirty trick to play on me."

"Well, it'll get you out of that office for a little while, anyway."

"I'm out today."

"Only because it's Saturday," Lindsay pointed out. "And the day's not over yet."

"Boy, have you got my number."

"Just like you've got mine."

M.J. laughed. "So are you going to the shelter?"

"Maybe this afternoon."

"Any news from there?"

"No," Lindsay said. "But then, I haven't called Rita."

Rita Thomas, director of the women's shelter, was another person Lindsay adored and could identify with, the main reason being that they had both suffered great heartaches in their lives.

Even though Lindsay hadn't been associated with the shelter all that long, her newest charity project had quickly turned into one she was quite passionate about.

"Call me when you're ready to share the big secret."

"Actually, my news involves the shelter."

"That's great, especially if it keeps you out of the shrink's office."

"So far, so good," Lindsay said.

"Well, I've certainly seen a difference in you since you took the shelter under your wing."

"We'll see if it pans out."

"My, but you sound mysterious."

"Well, you'll just have to put your curiosity in cold storage for a while longer."

"Whatever. Meanwhile, get rid of that prick Peter."

Lindsay's lips twitched. "Yes, ma'am. Talk to you later."

The instant she placed the receiver back in its cradle, her smile fled. She wished Mary Jane hadn't mentioned Peter again. The thought of him could ruin her day.

She got up and stretched. When Mary Jane called, she had just finished dressing in leggings, a long shirt and her running shoes. Now she was ready to hit the outdoors. Losing sleep had definitely put a damper on her body and her spirits. However, a trek outdoors would remedy that. It would also serve as a morale booster for when she approached Cooper later with her idea—something she didn't have to put off, since he was definitely on the mend.

Still, it wasn't a discussion she was looking forward to.

A few minutes later, Lindsay strolled through the kitchen. "Morning, Dolly."

"Mornin', child. Want some breakfast?"

Lindsay kissed her on the cheek. "Not until after I exercise."

Dolly snorted, her black eyes looking Lindsay up and down. "That's the last thing you should be doing. You need some meat on those scrawny bones."

"Don't start. Exercise keeps me sane."

Dolly merely sniffed this time, but kept her silence.

"So where's Daddy? Has he been down?"

"Hours ago, or so it seems. He's having coffee with some of his men friends."

"That's a good sign."

Dolly positioned her hands on her hips. "You should worry more about yourself than him, you know?"

"I know."

Lindsay smiled, walked out the door, and immediately wavered. For a late June morning it was hot and muggy, a rarity. The eighties was the norm. She shuddered to think what the remainder of the summer would bring. She considered returning to her room and putting on shorts. But she didn't. It wouldn't hurt her to perspire; if nothing else, it would clean out her pores.

Suddenly Mitch Rawlins came to mind, and her good mood instantly disappeared. Still, she couldn't stop herself from wondering if he ever broke a sweat. Somehow, she doubted it. After all, he had a crew to do the manual labor.

That was why, when she rounded the corner of the big house and saw him in the flesh, she pulled up short, barely able to keep her mouth from flying open.

She was shocked enough at having come upon him unexpectedly, but the fact that he wasn't wearing a shirt made matters worse. And droplets of sweat were flying off him as he dug a shovel into the rich earth.

She stood mute and swallowed hard. What to do?

For some inexplicable reason, she wanted to turn and run. Yet she wanted to stay put, too. The latter won out, especially when he stopped what he was doing and faced her.

"Mornin'," he said in a low, mocking tone, though he was looking at her with something akin to a fluid passion that seemed to link them.

"Hi," Lindsay responded in a breathless voice, while her eyes—half wild, half afraid—stared greedily at him.

Was her face red? Probably. She couldn't stop staring, totally captivated by his six-foot-plus frame, her gaze homing in on that bare chest matted with dark crisp hair that curled its way down to his navel, stopping at the waistband of his jeans.

And though she had no intention of taking her gaze any farther, she did, then jerked her eyes upward again, warmth climbing into her cheeks.

Heat boiled inside her suddenly, and her insides felt scalded. Jerking her gaze away from him, she schooled her features to show none of the turmoil raging inside her.

"You're Lindsay Newman," he said in a low, easy-sounding voice.

Lindsay forced her eyes back on him. "And you're Mitch Rawlins."

He gave her another mocking smile at the same time that he took several fingers and wiped a thick layer of sweat off his forehead. Besides having a billboard body, his face was easy on the eyes, though not handsome in the true sense of the word. His features were too strong and his beard too heavy, giving the impression that he needed a shave, which in itself was a bizarre turn-on.

His eyes were a dark blue, complementing his dark hair, which had a gray streak running through it, another turn-on. While his looks had certainly garnered her attention, it was the fact that he was actually working the ground himself that upped her curiosity another notch.

"Is there anything I can do for you?" he asked, interrupting the growing silence.

His words were pointed, which boiled her blood again, but for a different reason. "I can't think of anything," she said, forcing a casualness to her tone that she didn't feel.

"Well, then you won't mind if I get back to work."

His straight-from-the-hip directness drew both her anger and her admiration. "What are you going to plant there?"

He paused, raised his head, and though his lips twitched, she couldn't say he was smiling.

"Do you really care?"

This time that directness hit a raw nerve. Nonetheless, she didn't blink. "Not really."

The corners of his sculptured lips rose in a real smile. "Didn't think so."

Even if she'd wanted to move, she couldn't have. The power of that smile held her feet to the ground. "I guess I'll see you around," she finally managed to say.

He leaned on his shovel. "Probably will."

She watched the sweat trickle down his belly be-

fore she lifted her eyes to his. Though the contact
was brief, it was lethal.

"Have a good day, you hear?"

His drawling words broke the spell and jolted her
into action. She turned and took off, her heart beating
faster than her feet could possibly run.

Five

"Ouch!"

Lindsay figured Cooper and Dolly had heard her muttered groan of pain. She'd been in the small office in her bedroom suite all morning, going over her upcoming charity commitments. But every time she moved, she winced with pain, either silently or out loud.

Her shins were a mess. In fact, she had shin splints worse than she'd ever had them. She had no one to blame but herself for this predicament. Following her less than satisfying encounter with Mitch Rawlins, she had started to jog, thinking it would work off some of her frustration.

The problem was, she got carried away and took her stress management too far. She ended up jogging six miles instead of the three she normally did. Now, two days later, she was still paying for her over-industrious whim. Still, it had made her feel better, even though thoughts of Mitch Rawlins had run alongside her.

What was it going to take to strike him from her mind? Right off, she couldn't think of anything. Disgusted, Lindsay turned back to the computer screen, to the words she'd typed. If she wanted to remove them, all she had to do was hit the delete key.

Voilà! Gone. *Poof.* Like magic. Too bad she couldn't do the same with her erotic thoughts of Mitch Rawlins.

If only Peter attracted her in that way, then maybe there would be hope for them. But there was nothing about him that turned her on. The few times he'd kissed her, she'd felt nothing.

It wasn't that she hadn't tried. She had—admittedly more for her father than for herself, which in itself was wrong. Nonetheless, a future with Peter, for whatever reason, was not in the cards. But that didn't mean she didn't want a man in her life, though the thought of deeply caring about someone else and the responsibility that carried sent her into a panic.

She also panicked when she asked herself a hard question. After the real-life nightmares she'd lived through, could she ever sustain a lasting relationship with a man? What if... No! She wouldn't sabotage herself like that—not when she'd been doing so well lately, especially now that she had a project in the making that she felt passionate about.

Speaking of passion... Her tummy suddenly flip-flopped as once again her mind betrayed her. She wondered if Mitch was married. She hadn't seen a ring, but that didn't mean anything. With luck, he would be attached, which would put the brakes on her thoughts as nothing else could.

On the other hand, if he wasn't attached, then... Stop it! she told herself. So he had a great body? So what? She'd dated others who looked as good. Well, maybe not, but nearly. The one guy she'd been crazy about in college, had even gone to bed with, had had all the right stuff. Or so she'd thought. Obviously there had been something missing, because their relationship hadn't endured.

Maybe it was Mitch's eyes, she mused. They were such an unusual shade of blue, which made them seem mysterious. When he'd stared at her that last time, she had wished she could dive into those eyes and learn all his secrets.

Lindsay shivered, wondering if he thought the same thing about her. Talk about secrets—her heart was crowded with them.

Suddenly tired of this craziness, Lindsay lurched up, only to groan again, having forgotten how sore her body was. Damn, but she was more out of shape than she'd imagined. Maybe she should be the one putting in some quality time on the other end of that shovel. She would bet Mitch could run forever and not know it. He looked in perfect physical condition.

She shook her head, clearing him from her mind. He was the groundskeeper, for heaven's sake. Even if she wanted to have sex with a man, it wouldn't be with him.

She peered at her watch and decided now would be as good a time as any to talk to Cooper—something she'd intended to do two days ago. And though she dreaded it, postponing it wasn't going to make it any easier.

Five minutes later, she knocked on his door. No answer. Frowning, she turned and made her way very gingerly down the stairs. She hoped he wasn't on the golf course, for more reasons than one.

Dolly was polishing the bottom part of the banister. When she saw Lindsay, she stopped and shook her head in disapproval.

"Don't say a word," Lindsay warned.

Dolly rolled her black eyes high and around. "You younguns don't have any sense. None of y'all. Just beat up on your body when there's no call for it."

"I know, Dolly. I'm guilty as charged."

"You need to see a doctor."

Lindsay tried to smile. "What I need is to stop hurting, and no doctor can remedy that."

Dolly merely shook her head, all the while muttering to herself.

"Do you know if Daddy's here?"

"He's on the porch, finishing his lunch."

"Thanks."

Moments later, Lindsay eased onto one of the colorful plush settees that faced Cooper.

"Well, I see you're still crippled," he said, eyeing her up and down.

"Don't you start. Dolly's already put in her two cents' worth."

"And well she should," Cooper responded briskly.

Lindsay took a deep breath, trying to catalog her thoughts. "Do you have a minute to spare? I'd like to talk to you." Before Cooper could say anything, she went on. "And it's not about Peter, either."

"That's all right," Cooper said in a condescending manner. "We'll save him for another time."

Red hot anger surged through Lindsay. She wasn't fooled. She knew what was going on inside his head. Cooper saw her rebellion as a whim. He thought if he was simply indulgent and patted her on the head, she would come around to his way of thinking.

"Go on," he said into the silence, putting down the newspaper. "I'm listening."

Lindsay unclenched her fingers. "I had been thinking about this before your accident, only I hadn't acted on it. Now I want to."

"What are you talking about, Lindsay?"

His impatience was obvious, but she overlooked it and went on. "You know how much I've enjoyed the benefits I've reaped from working with the women's shelter."

"Yes, though I can't for the life of me see why. It would certainly not be my choice for you."

This was going to be harder than she'd figured. His mind was already closed. But she wasn't about to turn back now. Besides, she didn't really need his approval; she just wanted it.

"Anyhow, there are some women at the shelter with children who could and would do better if they had any kind of help at all."

"You mean other than what the shelter provides?"

Although Cooper's tone sounded almost terse, at least he was listening. "That's exactly what I mean. As you know, the shelter's only temporary—a stop-gap measure, if you will."

"So I can assume you're about to suggest something more permanent, right?"

Dismissing his patronizing and less-than-serious attitude, she forged on. "As a matter of fact, I am. I'm envisioning a place where those special families can live, go to school and access child care—all at no cost to them."

Cooper laughed, though without humor. "Surely you aren't serious?"

"I'm as serious as I've ever been about anything."

"Place? What kind of place, for God's sake?"

"A campus of sorts. Different buildings for different needs. Apartment-style complexes, a free-standing day-care center—" Lindsay broke off, her eyebrows coming together in a frown. "At this point, I'm not really sure. It's still sketchy in my mind."

"In my mind, it's preposterous," Cooper sputtered, color surging into his face.

Lindsay knew he was getting angry, but she didn't care—as long as that anger didn't harm him. She'd gone this far, and she wasn't pulling back now, even though it would have been easier just to give in.

"The primary aim of this venture or program or whatever you want to call it would be to get these young parents out of the welfare system and help them become contributing members of society."

"While that all sounds good, I don't see it working."

"Why not?" Lindsay demanded.

"Because it's never worked before."

"No one's ever tried what I'm proposing before."

"My point. That's because it won't work."

Lindsay's eyes sparked. "I disagree. I think it will work and work well."

"So call our congressman and tell him," Cooper said in an offhand manner. "Let him pursue it."

"I don't want to call our congressman," Lindsay said, her voice tight but even. "I want to spearhead it myself."

Cooper lunged to his feet. "That's the craziest notion I've ever heard."

"It may be crazy, but it's not impossible."

"Just say I thought it was a good idea—which I don't—" Cooper added quickly "how the hell do you propose to pull it off?"

"With lots of money and lots of time."

"*Your* money and *your* time, right?"

Lindsay didn't so much as blink under the harsh glare of his criticism and censure. "That and grants. There's all kinds of money out there. You just have to know where to find it, then how to get it."

"And I suppose you do?"

She ignored the mocking edge in his voice and said, "Of course not. I don't have all the answers yet, but it's something I really want to try. Something that will give my life direction."

"That's baloney. Your life has direction. When you and Peter marry—"

"Don't, Daddy. Peter's off-limits."

"As far as I'm concerned, this poppycock idea is what's off-limits."

"I thought you might even be willing to donate some of the money," Lindsay said in a dull tone.

"Like hell!" Cooper raged. "I don't want you that involved with those kinds of people, you hear?"

Lindsay blanched, mortified at his choice of words. "'Those kinds of people'?"

"Yes," he hammered on. "You're a Newman. You're meant for bigger and better things."

"Like what?" she asked fiercely, fighting off her disappointment and forcing back the tears. She'd had such high hopes that for once he would see things her way, support her in just one thing *she* wanted to do. She should have known better, she told herself, bitterness coursing through her like poison.

"Like marrying Peter and making a home for him," Cooper said into the reigning silence, his tone grim.

Lindsay's chin jutted. She was determined not to waver from her game plan. She refused to be lured into another blazing gunfight about Peter. Besides, when Cooper got on his high horse, like now, there was no reasoning with him.

"And acting as my hostess," he went on. "Something that is damn important to me. Which reminds me, now that I'm feeling like my old self again, I want to have a dinner party. Not a large one, but a party, nonetheless." His eyebrows shot up. "Need I say more?"

No, but she was about to. "Why haven't you remarried, Daddy?"

Lindsay knew she'd shocked him again, but that was okay. That question was one she had wanted to ask for a long time but hadn't had the courage to. Now it just slipped out, and somehow it seemed to fit the natural order of things. Cooper loved to entertain, and he loved women. In her mind, the two were closely linked.

"I intend never to remarry," he said coldly.

"Do you think that's what Mother would've wanted?" Lindsay asked, fishing for something that even she couldn't identify. She blamed Tim. He had scraped the scab on an old wound that had never healed. Now it was festering again.

Cooper's features turned more frigid than his

voice. "I'd rather leave your mother out of this conversation, if you don't mind."

"But I do mind," she said, her eyes wide and questioning. "You never want to talk about Mother, what happened to her—or to me, for that matter."

"You're right, I don't. End of discussion." He got up and strode back into the house.

Lindsay withdrew her gaze from his rigid back and stared into the distance. But nothing was visible. Her eyes were too full of tears.

Six

Tim rubbed the back of his neck. He felt awful, like he'd been drinking for days and was being punished with a humdinger of a headache. He wouldn't have minded the pain, if only he could say he'd reaped the benefits. Unfortunately, he hadn't had a stinking drop of alcohol.

Eve. She was to blame. She had caused this roar inside his head, and judging from the way she was glaring at him through her dove-gray eyes, she was just getting started.

"I'm waiting for an explanation, Tim. And not very patiently, either."

"What if I'm not prepared to give you one?"

She set her teeth, making her face appear more pointed than it normally did. She was an attractive woman, though not beautiful in the true sense of the word—not like Lindsay was beautiful. Maybe "pleasing to the eye" was a better way to describe his wife.

"Well, I'm not prepared to accept that." Her tone was filled with sarcasm, something that was rare for Eve.

Under most circumstances, she was the quiet and dutiful wife he'd married while in medical school.

He'd always considered them to have an okay marriage, because she was content to be his wife and nothing more. She had been a career woman once, but when they'd married, she had given it up.

Tall and willowy, she had shoulder-length dark hair that helped hide the fact that her neck was too long and scrawny. Her strong suit was the fact that she loved to entertain and did it well. She had been the perfect wife for him, and he hated like hell for anything to mess with that.

Now, thanks to his fuck-up, their marriage and everything else he held dear was in jeopardy.

Tim felt that roar in his head shift to his stomach, causing it to rebel. For a minute he thought he might actually have to head for the toilet. He took several deep breaths in succession, and it settled.

"You're not leaving this room until you tell me what is going on." Eve paused and seemed to fight back tears. "I've never been so humiliated in my entire life."

He had just come in from the office, later than usual, and he was tired. This had been one day when he'd been forced to work far more hours than he liked. He'd had visions of coming home to a hot shower, followed by a hot dinner—not to a wife with an ax to grind.

"I'll have some money in the account tomorrow," Tim said, though he didn't know where the hell he was going to get it.

"Why wasn't there some in there today?" Eve snapped. "I couldn't believe it when the teller told me our account was overdrawn."

Tim turned his head and rubbed his neck harder.

"Look at me. This is serious, and I have a right to know what's going on."

"It's just a temporary setback," Tim said lamely.

She laughed without humor. "A setback? It that what you call this? That's good, Tim. That's real good."

"I'll take care of it first thing in the morning," he said tersely. "Now, can we please drop the subject?"

Eve walked to the window in the huge living room, decorated to perfection by one of Garnet's leading interior designers. Tim was proud of this house and the status it represented. The thought of losing it made his stomach do another unwanted tap dance.

She swung back around, her eyes troubled. "No. I'm afraid it's not that simple."

"Dammit, Eve, I'm tired."

"And I'm still humiliated."

"You'll get over it." He was getting mad himself, and it showed. He would hate to have to get ugly and put her in her place, but he just might have to.

"Don't you talk to me like that," Eve retorted. "Like I'm some imbecile."

Tim's eyes widened in surprise at the venom he heard in her voice. "Now, see here, Eve, I—"

"What have you done with all our money, Tim? Why is it that a doctor of your caliber and success has a zero bank balance?"

"I've run into a little bad luck in the stock market."

She frowned. "But I thought all our investments were protected."

"They are, at least—" He broke off, exasperation

getting the better of him. "Look, you don't need to worry your pretty head about all this any longer. You just do your thing, and leave the business end to me."

"I know you, Tim, and right now you're walking on eggshells. So just how broke are we?"

His mouth tightened. "I told you, it's nothing I can't take care of. I'm just in a bind right now."

"What about your mother's trust?"

"What about it?" he snapped.

"Get some of it and put it in the account."

He didn't say anything, which was the wrong move. His silence obviously spoke louder than words.

"Oh, my God!" she cried, though her voice was low. "You've depleted that, too, haven't you."

"No, I haven't," he lied.

"I don't believe you, Tim."

"That's too bad," he lashed back. "I'm in charge of this household and the money." His tone dripped with ice. "Now, I suggest you see to dinner."

Eve's eyes brimmed with unshed tears, but she held her ground. "I'll leave it be for now. But I'm warning you, you'd best make things right at the bank. I refuse to be without money, even if it means borrowing from your sister or your daddy."

"That's not going to happen," he snapped again, feeling as though the floor under him had shifted. He was losing ground fast.

"Then take care of the problem," Eve said in an unsteady tone. "I've never been without funds, and I don't intend to start now."

With that, she turned and walked out of the room,

leaving a trail of perfume behind that added to his queasiness. He fell into the nearest chair and stared into space.

What a mess he'd gotten himself into. His gaze fell on the telephone on the nearby table. He headed toward it, but his steps faltered. He had an alternative, but it wasn't one he was overjoyed about.

In fact, he hadn't planned on having to take this route at all. But one bad investment after another had taken its toll, leaving him no choice.

Lindsay was already on to him. Now Eve. He figured it wouldn't be long until Cooper found out. There would be hell to pay then, for sure.

He couldn't risk that.

"What the hell!" he muttered, forcing himself to move to the phone. With a racing heart, he lifted the receiver and punched out a number.

The second he heard the strong voice on the other end of the line, he didn't waste time. "It's Newman. I've changed my mind."

"You won't regret it."

"I'm depending on you to see that I don't."

"Let's meet."

"You say where, and I'll be there."

Long after he'd replaced the receiver, Tim still hadn't moved. He shuddered to think what he'd gotten himself into.

Mitch stretched, then flinched.

"What's wrong, boss? You stove up?"

Mitch pinned one of his hands, Jesse Valdez, with tired eyes. "Yeah, as a matter of fact, I am. Every muscle in this old body is creaking."

"It's your own fault, if you don't mind me sayin' so."

"Damn straight it is, Jesse, but I wanted to do it."

"Was no call for you to." Jesse removed his sweat-stained baseball cap, then shoved a hand through a mop of black hair, all the while never taking his gaze off Mitch. "Me and the others coulda cut up that tree in nothin' flat."

"You're right," Mitch said without further explanation.

Jesse shrugged. "Well, as long as you're not thinking we can't do the job."

"Give it a rest, Jess. You and the boys are doing great. I couldn't be more pleased. But right now, I'm calling it a day and heading to the shower. I suggest you do the same."

"Got no problem with that," Jesse said, grinning.

"Tomorrow's another big day. The material's coming for the new greenhouse. If I'm not mistaken, the dirt's coming, as well."

"We'll be ready."

"See you early thirty, then."

Jesse nodded, then sauntered off. Mitch couldn't help but smile as he watched him, thinking the man was going to lose his breeches any second now, they hung so low on his hips.

Mitch merely shook his head, then turned and scouted the area. After seeing that no tools were left scattered about, he trudged toward his quarters.

Home sweet home.

He smiled, though it reeked with cynicism. He did consider the cottage home, despite the fact that it wasn't much bigger than a popcorn fart, however the hell big that was. That priceless gem had been something his grandmother had said quite often. He'd asked her many times what it meant, but she'd never once told him.

"It means whatever you want it to, sonny boy."

That explanation hadn't made sense then any more than it did now, but it made him think with sad affection of his grandmother, who'd practically raised him.

Cramped or not, the cottage was the perfect home for him, consisting of a combination living room, kitchen and dining area. It even had a fireplace, an amenity that he probably wouldn't use. The rest consisted of a bedroom and adjoining bath. But he didn't demand much for himself. No unnecessary baggage for him.

He'd dropped that three years ago, when he'd simplified his life.

Thirty minutes later, Mitch was out of the shower and had a beer in his hand. Following a long draw on the cold draft, he set it down while he slipped into a pair of worn jeans, then tromped barefoot into the living room.

Once he was seated, Mitch swung his head toward the kitchen. He was hungry as a bitch wolf with nine sucklings. Yet he was too dog-tired to cook himself anything to eat.

This was when he missed his grandmother and his ex-wife, though he hated to admit the latter. Whenever Wendy had been at home for any length of time, she would cook for him.

He would bet she had cooked for her lover, too.

"Aw, shit," he muttered, hating it when he

thought about her, but hating it more when he talked to himself. Not a good sign.

Mitch polished off the rest of the beer, his gaze once again straying toward the refrigerator. Surely he had a TV dinner he could toss into the microwave.

His thoughts shifted to the big house and the feast that the boss and his daughter were most likely sinking their teeth into about now. Instead of tossing that absurd thought aside, Mitch's mind homed in on Lindsay, and lingered there.

She had been the reason he'd used the chain saw all day. He had cut a huge oak that had fallen during a storm into fire logs. His intention had been to work out his sexual frustrations so that he wouldn't think about anything or anybody.

Had it worked? Nope.

He could still remember every word Lindsay had said to him and the way she'd looked at him, her lovely naked eyes a mixture of sadness, curiosity and something else—that same something that he'd felt mirrored in his eyes: instant and liquid desire.

Ah, what a crock. She didn't want him. She already had a stud to service her—the one he'd seen her with on the porch the other evening. Yet she didn't look like anyone was making love to her. No one that lovely ought to be that hauntingly sad.

Maybe that was why he couldn't get her off his mind, why he couldn't stop savoring everything about her, especially the memory of her shiny, styled hair, those sexy freckles that dusted her nose, those pouty, Kewpie doll lips quirked in doubt, and her tight little butt.

When she'd whipped that butt around, he'd

watched her run off, and been reminded of a lithe
and classy Thoroughbred. He had stood there long
after she'd disappeared, feeling like he'd just been
karate-chopped from behind.

And he was still nursing that same painful feeling,
because that last uninhibited gesture had left him
with an unwanted ache in his groin—an ache he
hadn't had in a helluva long time.

As badly as he hated to admit it, that ache hadn't
subsided. In fact, he had a hard-on right now, just
thinking about her. What was the deal? He was no
longer in control of his emotions; that was the deal.

Well, that was just too bad. Lindsay Newman was
a no deposit, no return sort of woman. He'd best keep
that in mind.

Seven

"Gosh, it's good to see you."

Lindsay smiled at her friend Mary Jane. "It's good to see you, too. It seems like ages."

Mary Jane's saucy grin added to the twinkle in her green eyes. "What with you gallivanting around the globe, it's kind of hard to stay in touch."

"Pooh," Lindsay responded good-naturedly, knowing that M.J. wasn't really jealous. Besides, she had the means to travel, only she was afraid to fly. "And I would hardly call a trip to London globe-trotting."

Mary Jane flapped a hand. "Well, whatever."

"So let's grab a seat before they're all gone." Lindsay pointed toward a table in a far corner. "Go for that one."

This Italian restaurant was her favorite, and she ate here often. Today, however, her favorite waitress wasn't here, nor was the manager. Both always gave her preferential treatment.

"Whew, I'm glad to be out of the heat!" Mary Jane exclaimed. "Darn, but it's hot. And muggy."

Lindsay flicked a strand of red-gold hair out of her eyes and stared at M.J. "It's supposed to be, my friend. It's summer."

"Well, you can have summer. Sometimes I wish I lived in the North Pole."

Lindsay frowned. "Uh-oh, things must be bad at work. I hear an underlying whine in your tone. Anything I need to know about?"

"Nah, except I'm overworked and my boss is an asshole."

"Mary Jane!"

She didn't look the least bit contrite. "Well, he is."

Lindsay grinned. "Aren't most men, at some time or other?"

The waitress appeared at the table, and once they had placed their orders and were alone again, Mary Jane shook her bobbed dark blond hair and said, "So tell me what's going on."

"You mean with Peter?" Lindsay asked innocently.

Mary Jane almost spat out the sip of water she had just drunk. "Now, why would I ask you about that prick? You know my opinion of him."

Lindsay's grin widened. "We're awful. You know that, don't you?"

"No, what we are is truthful."

Lindsay merely shook her head.

"So has your idea gelled yet?" Mary Jane asked, switching the subject.

Lindsay kept a straight face. "Idea?"

"You know what I'm talking about—that certain thing you were going to tell me about. Your secret, if you will." Mary Jane snapped her fingers. "Duh. Ring a bell?"

"Of course it does, silly. I was just giving you a hard time."

Although Mary Jane grinned, there was a perplexed look on her face. "My, but you're full of vinegar today. Whatever's going on sure suits you. I haven't seen you this relaxed in a long time."

"I haven't been this excited in a long time."

Before Mary Jane could respond, the waitress brought their food, refilled their water glasses and shuffled to the next table.

"Let's eat first," Lindsay said. "Then we'll talk." She peered at her watch. "Hey, do you have time? It's later than I thought."

"No, I don't have the time." Mary Jane shrugged. "But screw 'em. I'm not going to be in any hurry. I've given that office overtime galore, none of which I've been paid for."

"Atta girl."

Mary Jane sighed. "What's it really like to be a lady of leisure?"

"Hell." Lindsay's tone was flat.

Mary Jane's grin fled, and her eyes lost their twinkle. "Oops, you took that personally, and it wasn't meant that way. I was just teasing."

Lindsay forced herself to lighten up. "I know that. You don't have a malicious bone in your body."

"Oh, I wouldn't say that, but not toward you, anyway." Mary Jane paused. "Am I missing something here? I mean—"

"It's me, M.J. I guess I'm beginning to see a side of me that I don't like."

"Why, that's ridiculous. Good Lord, after what

you've been through, I think you've accomplished a miracle just to get up every morning.''

"Some days I still think I have a long way to go.''

"Don't you dare get down on yourself,'' Mary Jane warned fiercely. "Why, just a minute ago you seemed on top of the world.''

Lindsay's mouth turned down. "Well, that's a bit of an overstatement, but I really do have something on the burner that I'm excited about.''

"So let's hear it.''

Lindsay told her about her plan for battered women and their children.

When she finished, Mary Jane's face was glowing. "I think that's great.'' Mary Jane paused again, her face losing its animation. "Uh, have you told your daddy?''

"Yep.''

"Not good, huh?''

Lindsay gave a sarcastic laugh. "You got it.''

"Now why am I not surprised?''

"I won't bore you or humiliate myself by repeating his reasons for not backing me. But the bottom line is that he had a conniption.''

"I bet a more apt description is that he was frothing at the mouth.''

Lindsay grinned, in spite of the fact that her stomach was clenched in knots. "You're right, he was.''

"So are you going to scrap it?''

Lindsay could hear the disappointment in Mary Jane's tone, which strengthened her resolve not to let her friend down. But most of all, not to let herself down. "No, I'm not.''

"Praise the Lord!'' Mary Jane exclaimed.

"Shush," Lindsay whispered, looking around to see if anyone had heard M.J.

"Ah, you worry too much about what other people think. But you come by that honestly. That's Cooper's *modus operandi.*"

"And Tim's."

"Like father, like son. What can I say?"

"So will you help me?" Lindsay asked. "If this idea comes to fruition, I'm going to need lots of volunteers." Her features sobered. "Actually, I'm going to need a lot of everything."

"What do you mean, *if?*"

Lindsay's eyes clouded. "You know how hard it is for me to buck Daddy."

"Dammit, Lindsay, he's dominated you long enough."

"I know. But I've spent so many years pleasing him that it's hard to stop now."

"But *now* is the time to stop. This idea is great. When you talk about it, your face lights up, which is something I haven't seen since you—" Mary Jane broke off, then added, "Never mind about that."

"I know you're right." Lindsay took a deep breath. "It's just that I wanted Daddy's approval, as well as his help."

"I'll jump aboard, that's for sure. What about Tim? Do you think he'd help?"

"Are you kidding? He's got too many problems of his own to care about anyone else."

Mary Jane's eyes widened, but she didn't say anything.

"For months I've had all these ideas dancing around in my head like sugarplums. Now I'm ready to put them on the computer and get officially organized."

"Do you think Cooper'll try and sabotage the project?"

Lindsay sipped on the cup of fresh coffee the waitress had just poured, all the while staring at Mary Jane over the rim, a pensive look on her face.

"He might."

"Well, you can't let him, you hear?"

"All he wants is for me to marry Peter, live in the big house and have babies."

Mary Jane harrumphed. "God, what a miserable existence."

"I agree."

"If I had to wake up and see Peter's head on the pillow next to mine, I'd puke."

Lindsay grinned. "As always, you're the best tonic I could ever hope to have."

"You go, girl. Don't let Daddy shift your gears. You take this project and run with it."

"Just pray I don't chicken out," Lindsay said, Cooper's scandalized face popping to the forefront of her mind.

"You won't," Mary Jane said with airy confidence. "I'm not going to let you." She peered at her watch. "Oops! Gotta go or I'll be pounding the pavement looking for a new job." She grinned as she gave Lindsay a hug. "I'm counting on you to hang tough."

Later that same afternoon, Lindsay was trying to do just that, only to find her self-confidence in jeopardy, especially after she came home and turned on the computer. To raise money, to round up volunteers—to co-ordinate a project of such magnitude—suddenly seemed overwhelming.

Nonetheless, she had no intention of throwing in the towel until she had at least tried. Her game plan was to officially start the ball rolling in the morning. First she would talk to two very influential people whom she not only considered friends but who had the financial means to help fund the project. Next on her agenda was to approach the local junior college, which she hoped would become part of the triad that included the women's shelter and her proposed facility.

Her palms turned sweaty as her faltering self-confidence soared into full-blown panic. What if she couldn't do it? What if she failed?

Simple. Daddy would win.

Everything inside Lindsay cringed at such a thought. She pushed her chair back from the computer screen and rubbed her eyes. It was at times like this, when she was tired and discouraged, that she tended to think about her mother—missing her, reflecting on what her life might have been had Emily Newman lived.

More than that, Lindsay wondered if her own troubled past would always overshadow and undermine her future. Was she emotionally able to tackle such a task? Would she crash and burn again?

Like mother, like daughter?

Suddenly her eyes drifted toward her mother's cedar chest, positioned at the foot of her bed. Every so often she opened it and fingered Emily's personal items. The only item she hadn't touched was the stack of letters from her mother's best friend, who was also deceased.

Someday she planned to read them, hoping to better understand the woman she had called Mother.

Feeling her dissatisfaction and restlessness reach a dangerous level, Lindsay jumped up, changed into her workout clothes and bounded downstairs.

"I'm going to run," she told Dolly, who was in the kitchen making a peach cobbler.

Dolly sniffed. "When you finish, I expect you back for a bowl of cobbler and ice cream."

"I just might do that."

"Huh!" Dolly snorted. "You best stop telling stories, child. The Lord's gonna get you for sure."

Lindsay's only response was to plant a kiss on Dolly's chubby cheek.

"It's still too hot for you to be out there."

"Love you," Lindsay called over her shoulder.

Dolly's satisfied grunt followed her out the door, where she instantly froze. Dear Lord, not again. Mitch Rawlins, along with his crew, was working the huge flower beds next to the porch.

When he saw her, his eyes locked on her, and for a long moment, blue met brown. Lindsay swallowed, but it was hard. The saliva inside her mouth seemed to have dried up, leaving it feeling like she'd been munching on cotton.

"Afternoon," he said in his low, gravelly drawl. "We're gonna have to stop meeting like this, you know."

Lindsay stood transfixed, unable to take her eyes off his sweat-glistened chest. "Uh, right," she finally managed to get out, mortified by her obvious confusion.

But he shouldn't be so enticing, sweat and all. Every time she saw him, her body responded, becoming more pliant with a need that was threatening to careen out of control. On top of that, she felt torn by her mind's resolve not to get involved at any cost.

"Going for another run?"

"It's good for the old mind," she said inanely.

He almost grinned. "Don't you think it's a bit hot?"

"You sound like Dolly."

He frowned.

"Our housekeeper."

"Oh, yeah."

Their eyes met again for another long awkward moment in the ensuing silence. "Do you ever exercise?"

"All day, every day."

She flushed. "I don't mean that. I mean jog, like me."

"Nope."

"You ought to try it some time."

She had no idea what made those idiotic words pop out of her mouth. But when she was around him, she seemed to become someone else, someone totally out of character.

"Is that an invitation?"

Her heart drummed in her ears while she licked her lower lip. She saw his gaze settle there and linger. "What if it is?" she finally said, her voice coming out on a husky note.

Suddenly his features changed, turning hard, almost brutal.

"Count me out. As you can see, I don't have the time or inclination to entertain a bored rich girl who has nothing worthwhile to do."

Lindsay sucked in her breath against his frontal attack and held it, her mind reeling. Just who did he think he was?

"You go to hell," she said through clenched teeth, then swung her back to him and, as before, took off running.

Still, no matter how fast her legs moved, she couldn't outrun the tears that rolled down her face. She wished she could say it was sweat, but she couldn't.

First Mary Jane, now Mitch. Within the same day, two people had made comments about her easy, stress-free life. Mary Jane knew better, of course.

Damn him. Damn her for caring what he thought, how he perceived her. And damn her more for finding him attractive.

But what cut even deeper was how her apparent idleness appeared to other people outside her rich circle of friends.

Well, that was about to change. Lindsay straightened her shoulders. She wouldn't fail this time.

She *wouldn't*.

Eight

"Sara, what are you doing here?"

"Oh, for heaven's sake, Peter," she responded in a bored tone, "give it a rest. You can get your shorts in a wad quicker than anyone I know."

Peter's mouth formed a cruel line as he grabbed his current mistress by the arm and all but shoved her into a deserted corner of the bank. Once there, he loomed over her and spat, "You listen to me, you little bitch. You'll do what I tell you."

Sara Risinger jerked her arm free, then stuck out her lower lip. "Ah, honey, don't be like that. It's just that I wanted to see you, and I needed some cash."

"People in hell need ice water, too, and they don't get it."

Her overly made-up face turned ugly. "Now, you see here, I—"

"No, *you* see here," Peter interrupted. "I'm calling the shots. When I want to see you, I'll come to you."

"You're a real bastard, Peter."

He felt himself shaking on the inside and sweating on the outside. He glanced around to see if anyone was aware of them. He didn't want to be seen with this woman who could give the best blow jobs he'd ever had but who looked like an honest-to-God streetwalker one day and a businesswoman the next.

Today she looked like the streetwalker.

He had met her at a party, and when she'd immediately pushed him into the nearest room and unzipped his pants, he'd known he had to have her for his latest plaything, at least until he got tired or married, whichever came first.

Thinking of getting married heightened Peter's anger and made him sweat that much more. He turned and scrutinized the lobby. If Cooper were to come in and see him with this woman, the old man would croak on the spot. Then where would that leave him?

Out on his ass.

Well, he wasn't going to allow that to happen. Nothing was going to stop him from marrying Lindsay Newman—certainly not any stupid moves on his own part.

"Am I going to see you tonight?" Sara cooed, her clear blue eyes steady on him.

"Depends," he said absently.

"On what?" she pressed.

"None of your business."

She gave him a coy smile. "Aw, we both know that's not true. Why, it'd be a shame for your good family name to get ruined."

She might be overly made-up and overdressed, but she was no dummy, nor was she shy, Peter reminded himself. And she wasn't afraid of him, either, which was something he didn't understand.

"Are you threatening me?"

"Of course not, darling. There you go again, getting yourself all worked up for nothing."

Peter shoved his hand into a pocket and pulled out several bills. With flashing eyes, he slapped them in her hand. "You got what you came for. Now get out of here."

Despite his obvious revulsion, she leaned over and pecked him on the cheek.

He jerked back. "You know better than that."

She grinned. "Ta-ta, darling."

From that moment on, the rest of the day was downhill. Shortly after Sara's stunt, he was called into the president's office, where he was chewed out because of a bad loan he'd made.

Later, his mother, Harriet, called and wanted him to run some unnecessary errands for her. If only he still had money, he wouldn't have to be indebted to anyone.

Part of the problem was that at one time he *had* had money. His entire family had had money—until his father squandered it. Once the attorney had delivered the bad news to him and his mother, he had never been the same. His *life* had never been the same. Even though his old man was long dead, he still damned him to hell.

Only after he met Lindsay and, subsequently, her father did he start to climb out of the toilet. Even so, it took a while before he realized the doctor had something else on his mind—finding a suitable husband for his daughter.

When Cooper had first mentioned that to him, Peter had almost laughed in his face. "I mean no disrespect, sir, but people don't arrange marriages anymore, not even in the South."

"That's not at all what I had in mind, young

man." Cooper's tone was cold and condescending. "If you're interested in my daughter, then it's up to you to make her fall in love with you."

Love? Hell, he hadn't cared about that. But if that was what it would take to feather his own nest, then so be it.

"Why is that so important to you, sir?"

"I think it's time she settled down and had a family of her own."

"Don't you think she's capable of handling that on her own?"

"No, I don't," Cooper replied, his tone remaining cold.

"So what's in it for me?" Peter asked bluntly, thinking, what did he have to lose? Besides, from where he stood, he seemed to be in the driver's seat. This man wanted something from him. And nothing came free—at least, not as far as he was concerned. He might as well get that straight right up front.

"Let's just say I'll make it more than worth your while."

"Can you be more specific?"

Cooper's face turned unnaturally red. "Even though you're from good stock, you lack manners, boy."

Peter didn't so much as flinch. "What I lack, sir, is cash."

"Once you're married to my daughter, your money woes will be past history. Is that plain enough?"

"Absolutely."

Immediately after that chat with Cooper, he had upped his pursuit of Lindsay. To date, however, he'd made little headway. The road had been much rockier than he'd anticipated.

Lindsay had a hard shell around her that he hadn't been able to crack. And he was getting disgusted. But Cooper wanted them married. His mother wanted them married.

Somehow he had to convince Lindsay that *she* wanted to be married. To him.

That thought was still uppermost in his mind when he left the bank and stopped by the Newman mansion. He was getting out of his vehicle, parked behind Lindsay's in the circular drive, when she bounded out the front door.

He watched as a look of displeasure changed her features. Though anger surged through him, Peter managed to hang on to his control. "Hey, where are you going in such a hurry?"

"To the shelter."

"Is there a problem?"

"Not an urgent one, no."

It was her aloof and somewhat patronizing attitude that irked him, made him want to shake her. "Then don't go. I'd like to take you to dinner."

"Sorry, I can't."

"Can't—or won't?"

Her lips twisted. "Look, Peter, don't start, okay?"

"Fine. Another time."

Lindsay gave him a weak smile before getting into her car and driving off. He turned and rang the doorbell. Moments later, Dolly showed him into the parlor, where Cooper was indulging in a before-dinner drink.

"Ah, Peter, it's good to see you. Come on in and have a seat."

"Thanks," Peter said, forcing his voice back into its normal range. He was still smarting from the cold shoulder that Lindsay had given him.

"Care for a drink?" Cooper asked. "You look like you could use it."

"In the worst way."

"Feel free to help yourself."

Peter nodded, then made his way to the small bar, where he poured himself a stiff drink. He took a healthy swig of it before he sat across from Cooper, who was watching him with raised eyebrows and a displeased expression on his face.

"What's wrong?"

"This hasn't been one of my best days."

"We all have them," Cooper responded in an impatient and dismissive tone.

Peter knew where Lindsay got her holier-than-thou attitude, but that didn't make dealing with it any easier. And if the truth were known, he knew he was guilty of the same behavior, though the loss of money and status had tempered him.

"What's the deal with Lindsay?" he asked.

Cooper's body stiffened, but he didn't sidestep the question. "I wish the hell I knew."

"She acts as if I'm contagious, or something worse."

"Then it's up to you to change that."

Peter almost strangled on his sip of vodka. "What do you think I've been doing? Hell, Cooper, I don't even think she likes me."

"She doesn't know what she likes right now."

Cooper scowled. "She's on this bloody crusade to save all the battered women and their children in Garnet."

"Great."

"Only I'm not standing for it, and I told her so."

"Do you think she'll mind you?" Peter knew he was being glib, if not disrespectful, but he didn't care. He was about at his wits' end, trying to woo Lindsay. But he couldn't afford to give up. He didn't have that luxury.

"In the end, she'll come around," Cooper said. "She'll do like she's told."

"I'm counting on that."

"But you have to do your part, you know. Make her want you."

"I'm aware of that," Peter snapped, "but for some reason, Lindsay remains immune to my charm."

"I may be partly responsible for that. I've given her a grace period."

"Meaning?"

"Meaning I've backed off from demanding she set a wedding date."

Peter gave him an incredulous look. "Do you think that's wise?"

"Yes," Cooper said in a self-assured tone. "I know how to work my daughter."

Peter shrugged.

"But in the end, I'll have my way. She *will* marry you."

"Works for me," Peter quipped, then finished off his drink. "I can't wait to be a kept man."

* * *

Mitch squeezed the phone receiver so tightly that he felt the pressure on his knuckles. If he weren't careful, he would break them. And for what—because his ex-wife had called him?

Hell, he didn't need this aggravation, but short of hanging up on her, he didn't have much choice. All the more reason why he should not have answered his phone.

Why had he?

"So what's up, Wendy?" He tried to hold his irritation to a minimum, but wasn't sure he'd pulled it off.

"Nothing, really."

He blew out a harsh breath, then forced himself to ask, "So how've you been?"

"Not so good, Mitch."

He wasn't about to ask her to elaborate. Experience had taught him that. If he dared show any sympathy whatsoever, she took advantage.

"I still miss you lots."

"Your ploy won't work, Wendy. For your own sake, you've got to stop fanning the embers. They're stone cold."

"I refuse to believe that," she wailed.

"Where's your husband, Wendy?" he asked in a tired voice. "You *are* still married, aren't you?"

"Yes, but—"

"Then I don't think it's a good idea for you to call me."

She hiccuped.

"Ah, I get it. You're drinking."

"I see you haven't changed," she said, her voice now tainted with unsuppressed venom.

"Look, I'm going to hang up before we both say things we'll be sorry for. Take care of yourself."

Once he was off the phone, Mitch felt as if he'd been beaten with a wet rope. Did one's ex ever completely disappear? He was beginning to think not, though he hadn't heard from Wendy in quite some time, not since she'd remarried. Apparently that marriage had also gone sour. He hated that, but it had nothing to do with him.

Women. His best recourse was to avoid them, period. Except, maybe, for Lindsay Newman.

An expletive colored the air as Mitch made his way to the sink, where he placed his empty glass. He had to forget her. But how could he, when she kept popping up at the most unexpected times?

What was going on? Were those encounters an accident? Or were they accidentally on purpose? He didn't have a clue, nor did he want one. Nor did he want to think about her with another man. He would guess she probably had to beat men off with a stick.

Another expletive zinged the air. Maybe if he hadn't taken a lunch break, he wouldn't have had time to think. But today the rain had been impossible, so he'd given the hands a break.

No excuse.

Thoughts of her were forbidden. While she made a great package, a package he wouldn't mind unwrapping were the circumstances different, nothing was going to happen. The reason was obvious: the circumstances *weren't* different. So he might as well keep a tight rein on his libido and try his best to ignore her.

Yeah, right, like he could ignore a throbbing tooth-ache.

"Hey, boss, you in there?"

Mitch gave a start at the unexpected voice. Pulling his jeans up a bit higher, he strode to the front door. Jesse stood on the porch, hat in hand.

"We got trouble," he said.

"How so?"

"A tree's done gone and fallen across Ms. New-man's balcony, but she wasn't hurt."

Mitch rolled his eyes back in his head. Super. Just what he *didn't* need.

Nine

"I cannot believe this," Lindsay moaned, her chocolate eyes meeting those of the housekeeper.

Dolly was the first to roll hers heavenward. "Don't you worry none. Mr. Mitch will take care of this mess."

At the mention of Mitch's name, Lindsay's heart suddenly turned over. What would her heart do when he actually got here? No matter—she was glad he was on his way.

Lindsay's gaze roamed the room. Dolly had called this a mess. Well, that was a gross understatement. The tree, sprawled across the balcony just shy of the French doors leading into her room, was a disaster.

For the past two days it had done nothing but rain—the hard, earth-soaking kind. Still, Lindsay had had no idea that the weather could topple a big oak.

"It could've been worse, child."

"You're so right, Dolly. It could've crashed into my room or hit my computer." Lindsay shuddered to think about that, because she'd put in so many hours at that screen, working on her project. Of course, she had a backup diskette, but it was beside the computer, which meant it could easily have been destroyed, too.

"It could've hit you," Dolly pointed out. "I'm not worried about some ol' machine."

"I am," Lindsay muttered.

"Do you need me to stay here?" Dolly asked.

"Absolutely not. You go ahead and do whatever you have to do."

Dolly nodded. "I'll tell Mr. Cooper to come up when he gets home."

"Oh, I'm sure you won't have to. There'll be more commotion around here than if the alarm had gone off."

Dolly merely shook her head. "I'll check on you later."

"Thanks, love," Lindsay said, watching the housekeeper waddle out the door.

Once she was alone, Lindsay plopped down on the edge of the bed, wondering how long it would take to clean up all the debris and repair the balcony. Several days, she suspected, since the damage also affected the rooms directly under hers.

At least something positive had come out of the day. She had made contact with her two wealthy, charity-minded friends, Ash Fisher, an oilman with mega bucks, and Peggy Potter, a socialite with the same big bucks. After pitching her project to them, they were both very interested and wanted to be kept informed as she went forward.

While neither had actually committed funds, Lindsay knew their money would be forthcoming if she could pull the details all together. She had held her breath, waiting for at least one of them to ask about Cooper's role in her undertaking. To her relief, that particular question had not been asked.

She doubted her daddy had given their conversation any further thought once he had gone on record with his disapproval. He undoubtedly figured she would drop the idea like a hot potato.

Wrong. Now that she had someone else interested, she was determined to steamroll ahead. Most likely, there would be a price to pay for her flagrant show of independence, but she would gladly pay it.

If only she could get Cooper to the shelter... Lindsay smiled a bitter smile. That was never going to happen. But if he were ever to weaken and walk through the doors, he would understand where her passion stemmed from.

Today would have been a perfect example of how critical the circumstances were. After she had left her friends, she had gone to the shelter and spent the remainder of the morning there, meeting with the director, Rita Thomas.

If ever there was a saint, it was Rita. Lindsay admired her more each time she met with her. She was doing an outstanding job with the women and the budget. But sometimes the load seemed too heavy to bear.

Still, Rita never complained. She was undoubtedly one of the sweetest and warmest women Lindsay had ever known. Though she was only in her early forties, she had lived a lifetime, having barely escaped with her life from an abusive husband. But since his death several years ago, Rita had gotten herself back together and made her life count for something.

Lindsay often thought the reason they had hit it off so well was that they had both suffered terribly, though in totally different ways and for totally different reasons. But it didn't matter. They had each weathered some severe storms and had come out the stronger—or at least Rita had.

Lindsay wasn't so sure about herself. It seemed she still had a lot to learn and a long way to go. However, she never failed to draw strength from Rita, and today had been no exception.

"So what's up?" Rita had asked, once she had poured them a cup of coffee and sat back down at the two-seater table in the small kitchen.

Lindsay studied her friend, thinking something was different about her. Yet she couldn't pinpoint what it was.

"It's my hair," Rita admitted in a shy, hesitant tone. "I cut it."

"Right!" Lindsay exclaimed. "And it looks great, too."

A blush crept into Rita's leather-textured cheeks, giving her a glow that had heretofore been missing. "Thanks. It's so much easier to take care of now. It doesn't take me nearly as much time."

"And time is something you don't have enough of."

Rita's face sobered once more. "You can say that again. We have so many women to place with nowhere to place them, that it's completely overwhelming."

"I know."

They were quiet for a minute, each sipping on her coffee.

Rita was the first to break the silence. "So, again, what's up?"

"How do you know anything's up?" Lindsay tried

to contain her excitement and keep a straight face, but she knew her eyes had given her away. They always did.

"Your eyes."

"I knew it." Lindsay grinned. "But you're right, I do have something up my sleeve."

"Let's hear it. I need some good news."

"Well, here goes."

By the time Lindsay finished outlining her plan, tears were running down Rita's face.

"Oh, Lindsay!" she cried. "I don't know what to say."

"Don't say anything yet. It's not a done deal by any stretch of the imagination. We have to raise the money."

"Do you think that's possible?" Rita's voice was filled with awe.

"I'm going to give it my best shot."

"Then I know it will come about."

"Meanwhile, I certainly need your input. When you get some spare time—ha, that's a joke—jot your thoughts, needs, ideas and goals down on paper."

"Consider it done."

They both swallowed another sip of coffee as they got up. Then Lindsay gave Rita a hug. "I'll call you later."

"I'll walk you to the door. Come on."

They heard the sobbing almost immediately, coming from the front room of the facility. Lindsay and Rita looked at each other, their eyes clouding over, then headed toward the pitiful sound.

Lindsay was the first through the door, her heart in her throat. "Oh, my God, Annie."

The woman who stood in front of her had been helped by the shelter, but had recently gone back to her husband, convinced he'd turned over a new leaf. When Lindsay had learned that, she'd been upset, thinking Annie and her precious five-year-old daughter Bridget would be perfect candidates for her proposed facility.

And she hadn't thought for one minute that Annie's husband had changed one iota. Unfortunately, her fears had been right on target.

Now Annie was hurt, battered and bruised. And bloody. Bright red blood was splattered all over the front of her blouse. Suddenly Lindsay felt the room spin as her mind roared back to another time, another place—to her mother's blood-soaked body.

"Are you all right, Lindsay?"

Rita's soothing voice at her shoulder suddenly righted the world. That was when she noticed that the blood had resulted from a split lip, not anything life-threatening. "I'm fine," she whispered, then went to Annie and wrapped her arms around her.

"Oh, Miss Newman," Annie gulped, "I'm so sorry."

"Shh, it's going to be all right," Lindsay said, fighting back her own tears. "You need to get to the hospital."

Annie left Lindsay's arms and went to Rita, who had taken charge. Lindsay dropped to her knees in front of the child, who looked like she'd seen a ghost.

"Are you all right, sweetie?"

The little girl's chin quivered, and tears spilled from her wide green eyes. "My daddy hurted my mommy."

"Did he hurt you, too?" Lindsay's hands were gently running up and down the tiny, malnourished body, searching for possible injuries.

"No." Bridget sniffed. "Mommy hid me."

"Good for Mommy."

Lindsay held the child close for a long moment, feeling her small body tremble. Once she pulled back, she brushed the straggly strands of hair out of Bridget's eyes.

"Is my mommy going to get well?"

"Of course," Lindsay assured her in a choked voice. "Don't you worry about that for one minute."

"Can I go with her?"

"No, darling, not right now." Lindsay peered up at Rita, who was hovering above her after seeing that Annie was taken to the emergency room. "You can see her later. Okay?"

Bridget nodded, though her lower lip couldn't seem to stop quivering.

"Go with Miss Rita, and I'll see you soon." Lindsay brushed the tears off the child's thin face.

"You promise?"

"I promise and cross my heart."

Bridget gave her a wet kiss on the cheek before reaching up to Rita. Lindsay didn't know how long she stood there, her throat all lumped up, before she could find the wherewithal to turn, walk out the door and make her way home.

Now, as she jerked herself back to the moment at hand, she frowned. Where was Mitch? That thought hadn't done more than hit her when she heard a tap on the door.

Mitch? No, that wouldn't be him. There was no

reason for him to come inside. Most likely it was her daddy, or Dolly. She got up, hurried across the room and jerked open the door, only to have the bottom drop out of her stomach.

Mitch stood facing her.

She tried to ignore the excitement that leapt through her veins. He smelled faintly of mint and sweat, and needed a shave.

"Are you all right?" he asked, not bothering to mask the concern in those incredible eyes of his.

"I'm fine," she said, feeling dizzy.

"May I come in?"

She licked her dry lips. "Uh, sure."

Still, he didn't cross the threshold. Instead their gazes met and held. He absolutely looked good enough to eat, she thought, color seeping into her face. She feared he could read her mind.

Mitch cleared his throat, breaking the thick silence. "It'll only take a second to assess the damage."

"No problem," she said, stepping aside and letting him pass.

She watched, admiring his tight tush as he strode to the French doors. What was happening to her? Every time he spoke, every time he moved, it cut through her physically, sending strange and unwanted images to her brain.

She shivered.

"Hey, you sure you're all right?"

Lindsay shook her head and forced a smile. "I'm fine, really. But I have to say, this was a close call."

"That's for sure. It's a miracle no one was hurt."

"Isn't it, though?" she said, finding it hard to be-

lieve they were indulging in small talk while a tor-
turous tension filled the air.

His eyes surveyed the room, then landed back on
her. "Nice."

For some crazy reason, color invaded her cheeks
again. She wasn't sure whether he was talking about
the room, or her. If his eyes and thickly spoken word
were any indication, she would bet the latter.

Was he coming on to her?

"Look, I'd like to apologize for acting like an ass
the other day," he said in a slightly disjointed voice.

Her heartbeat soared off the charts. "It's okay."

"No, it isn't." He paused. "So is my apology accepted?"

"Only if you'll have dinner with me."

Lindsay's eyes immediately widened in horror.
Good Lord, where had that come from? It was as if
her own subconscious had blindsided her.

"Look, forget I asked that," she said in a hurried
and mortified tone. "You left no doubt the other day
how you felt about—"

"Sure. Why not?"

His low, briskly spoken words stopped her cold.
"What did you say?"

"I said, sure, why not." His tone was mocking
now, though a real smile softened his lips.

Lindsay sucked in her breath and held it.

"But right now, it's first things first," Mitch
added. "I need to get downstairs and get the men to
work."

With that, he turned and walked out.

Lindsay covered her scalding cheeks with her
palms. What had she done? She had given in to her

desire. Even now, he was standing in the front of her mind, making her want him. Panicked, she rubbed her arms, feeling as if all her nerves were riding on top of her skin.

If only he hadn't apologized, then maybe she would have kept her mouth shut. If only she hadn't seen Annie all bruised and bloody, dredging up horrifying and unwanted memories.

If only he hadn't accepted her invitation.

She placed her hands on her head to try to stop her mind from playing this foolish game.

What was done was done.

Lindsay sank onto the side of the bed, feeling like someone had uncorked a valve inside her and let all the air out of her body. She fell back, limp as a rag doll, and stared at the ceiling.

Ten

Lindsay clutched the basket tighter in her hand, but she kept on walking. She was on an emotional roller-coaster ride, a ride that she didn't want to end.

The roller coaster had started the instant Mitch had appeared at her door, and the bumpy ride had intensified after she'd gone downstairs and watched the crew remove the tree from her balcony.

Afterward, Mitch had grabbed the chain saw and started to work. She had stood spellbound by the display of straining muscles and a lock of hair that settled on his forehead.

God, but he'd looked rugged and manly. And dangerous.

She didn't know why that word had charged to the forefront of her mind, but it had. She'd been tempted to blurt out that she had changed her mind, that he was off the hook for dinner.

Only she hadn't.

Instead, she had stood motionless, watching him work with the energy of a well-oiled machine, crazy to know what there was about this man that made her heart pound and her palms sweat. No other man had ever appealed to her in such a stark sexual way, or so hard and so fast.

As a result, her emotions had been fragile. Everything inside her was raw. She hadn't wanted to be alone.

And despite the surly edge he often wore like a proud shield, she sensed an underlying core of strength, and not just in brawn, either—a strength that she had obviously needed and been drawn to.

She wondered what his motive for accepting had been.

She was the boss's daughter, for heaven's sake, she reminded herself. Under the circumstances, what else could he have said? No? Her gut instinct reassured her that Mitch wasn't anyone's yes man, that he did his own thing, according to his own rules.

In the end, however, her conscience had won, and she'd given him a way out. When he'd finished with the tree and she had thanked him and the men, she said in a low tone, "Look, are you sure..." Her voice trailed off at the same time that her face began to feel scorched, and not from the sun, either.

"Are you getting cold feet, Miss Newman?"

His eyes were warmly mocking, causing her heart to pound that much faster. But she didn't flinch. "Not in the least."

"Me, either."

Her tongue circled her bottom lip. "So—"

"So I'll meet you at my place," he said in a gravelly voice, his gaze locked on her coral-colored mouth.

Her eyes widened in alarm.

"I didn't figure you'd want to be seen in public with me."

Her face burned hotter. "I—I hadn't really thought

about it." And she hadn't. She'd just flown by the seat of her pants. Now she was having to face the consequences.

"Didn't figure you had," he replied in a throaty drawl.

"What are you suggesting?"

"That I fix dinner for you."

"You cook?" she asked inanely.

His mouth twitched. "Yeah, I cook."

"Well, you shouldn't have to. I invited you, so I'll bring dinner."

His eyes settled back on her face. "Are you sure?"

"I'm sure."

He hunched his shoulders. "Suit yourself."

She had. She'd gone to Dolly and asked her to pack a picnic basket full of goodies. Although Dolly had looked at her strangely, she hadn't asked why, much to Lindsay's relief.

Now, as twilight was fast approaching and his cottage came into sight, Lindsay swallowed against the knot of panic in the back of her throat. Pausing, she inhaled a deep breath, though it did little to calm her. The air was too thick and heavy as it passed through her lungs.

Forbidden.

What she was doing was forbidden. To say that her daddy wouldn't approve was an understatement. He would be livid if he knew where she was and what she was up to. But he didn't, thank goodness. He had gone out for the evening to a dinner party with his latest woman friend.

If Dolly did by chance see her, she wouldn't say anything.

Still, Lindsay found herself casting a furtive glance around. Nothing. The grounds were quiet, except for the sounds of the night critters. Yet they offered comfort for her troubled mind and soul.

"Lindsay."

The deep pull of Mitch's voice suddenly unlocked her legs, and she walked toward the porch, toward him. He was dressed in a white T-shirt and low-slung jeans. His hair appeared damp, as if he'd just gotten out of the shower.

She had chosen similar attire, wearing an aqua-colored T-shirt, cutoffs and sandals. She felt his eyes sweep over her and perhaps linger a tad on the thrust of her firm breasts.

Forcing herself not to blush under his scrutiny, she surrendered the basket to his outstretched hand, careful not to touch him.

"Come in." His tone was on the brusque side.

"Thanks," she muttered, stepping around him, only to stop just inside the door.

"What's wrong? Having second thoughts?"

He was so close behind her that she felt his breath graze her cheekbone at the same time that the subtle, clean smell of his body washed over her.

Lindsay rebelled against the panic and forced herself to move forward. He went around her and strode to the dining table nestled in one corner of the cozy living area, where he set down the basket.

Then he turned and frowned at her. "What the hell's in there?"

She forced a smile. "Food."

His eyebrows shot up. "A helluva lot of it, I'd say."

"Well, you *have* been felling trees."

He chuckled. "You got that right."

Without warning, an awkward silence descended over the room as it dawned on her what had happened. She had fallen for him like a ton of bricks. No rhyme or reason. No logical explanation.

"Look——" she began, trying to hide her burgeoning panic.

"Sit down, Lindsay. You're safe."

She swallowed. "I never thought I wasn't."

"Yeah, right." He paused. "Keep in mind that you're not Little Red Riding Hood and I'm not the Big Bad Wolf."

In spite of herself, Lindsay smiled. "Is that supposed to make me feel better?"

"Yep. So why don't you sit down and relax?"

"Uh, right."

He gave her another mocking smile before he turned and walked into the kitchen. Once she was seated, Lindsay perused her surroundings and found that his living quarters offered no clue as to who this man was, or what made him tick.

Nothing personal adorned the furniture or walls. He lived there, yet he didn't *really* live there. She wondered why he chose to exist in such a stark environment. Maybe he had no intention of remaining long.

After all, she knew nothing about him, she reminded herself. She suspected Cooper did—at least enough to have hired him.

"I can see the wheels of your mind turning,"

Mitch said, making his way back into the room with a glass of wine in one hand and a beer in the other. "I hope you like white wine."

"Actually, it's my favorite."

"I'm sure it's not what you're accustomed to, but it'll have to do."

"Meaning?"

He shrugged as he sat down on the other end of the sofa. "Meaning it's a cheapo."

"In spite of what you think, I do enjoy things that *aren't* expensive." His assumption that she didn't irritated her more than she cared to admit.

He took a swig of his beer. When his head came back down, his gaze landed on her. "So what about your boyfriend? I bet he wouldn't approve of you being here."

His unexpected question caught her totally off guard, and for a moment she couldn't respond. "I don't know who you're talking about."

"Sure you do. I saw you with him the other evening."

"He's not my 'boyfriend,' as you so bluntly put it." Her tone dripped with unsuppressed sarcasm. "He's just a friend, though I have to admit, my daddy would like him to be more."

A smirk crossed his face. "Ah, so Daddy's picked out the man for his little girl to marry."

"Which isn't going to happen," she said crossly.

"Are you sure about that? Cooper's a lot like me. He's a sore loser."

"We'll see," she said, red-faced. Peter was the last person she wanted to discuss. "What about you?"

"What about me?"

"Is there a woman in your life?"

"Nope."

"Care to add to that?"

"Nope."

Lindsay's lips tightened on the rim of the glass. She took a larger sip than she should have. The wine burned far beyond her throat as she watched him stretch his legs in front of him as if he hadn't a care in the world.

She knew better, or at least she hoped she did. She wanted his stomach to be coiled as tightly as hers was.

Mitch stood suddenly, seeming to tower over her. "I'll get you some more wine."

Why not? she thought. She needed something to temper her jangled nerves. "I'd love some."

Once he'd returned and refilled her glass, he eyed her carefully. Rather than look at him, she lowered her gaze and took a more than generous sip of the wine.

"Are you hungry?"

His question forced her head up. "Not really."

His trademark smile rearranged his lips. "Let's eat, anyway."

"Maybe that's not a bad idea," she said, beginning to feel a bit woozy, though she made it to the table just fine.

She had her hand on the cloth covering the food when the phone rang.

Mitch, who was already at the table, stiffened, but he didn't move.

"Aren't you going to answer it?" she asked, staring at him, at the muscle twitching in his jaw.

"Excuse me," he all but snapped, then strode into the bedroom, which was directly off the living area.

Although he closed the door behind him, she could still hear his voice. Whoever was on the other end of the line wasn't making Mitch happy. Quickly, she set about unpacking the food, glad to have something to occupy her mind and hands.

However, nothing she did kept Mitch's harsh, angry voice at bay. She couldn't hear the exact words, but the gist of the conversation was not friendly. That much was obvious. She wondered who it was. Most likely a woman, she thought with a stab of unwanted jealousy.

"Sorry about that," he said, finally returning to the room, his tone and facial expression as bland as a piece of dry toast.

"No apology necessary." Lindsay cocked her head to one side. "Is everything okay?"

"Ginger peachy," he said, his features closed.

Lindsay smothered a sigh. Who was this man who guarded his privacy like a cache of gold? Furthermore, what was wrong with her that she cared? Suddenly, none of this made a bit of sense, nor could she begin to justify it.

"Are you ready to chow down?" he asked into the silence, his body close to hers as he pulled out a chair for her.

The chair was a welcome relief, because her knees were wobbling, much to her chagrin. Then she brightened. Maybe it was the wine and not his closeness that was causing her unsteadiness.

Fat chance—as in *no* chance.

Once he was seated across from her, they filled their plates with fried chicken, potato salad and other goodies that Dolly had prepared. But Lindsay couldn't eat. The first bite she took stuck in her throat. It took another large drink of wine to wash it down.

She felt his eyes on her. What was he thinking? Perhaps that she was a lush, which could not have been farther from the truth. While she enjoyed a glass of wine with dinner and an occasional one with Mary Jane, she certainly didn't make a habit of drinking it daily or in large quantities, like now.

"I wish you wouldn't look at me like that."

"Like how?" he murmured huskily, shoving his paper plate aside.

Lindsay could feel her heart beating inside her head. "You know."

Another muscle twitched in his jaw. "Like I'm about to turn into the Big Bad Wolf and eat you up?"

Eleven

Lindsay opened her mouth, but nothing came out. Finally she snapped it shut and averted her gaze.

"Hey, I was just kidding," he said huskily. "That's not going to happen."

Lindsay's breath rushed in and out of her lungs. The truth was, she wanted it to happen. She wanted him to turn into the Big Bad Wolf and devour her. My God, but this was all so crazy, so out of character. Yet it seemed as if everything she did was intentionally to provoke him, to stir up a matching hunger in him.

"Lindsay."

She moistened her lips, then took another large sip of wine. Was she getting tipsy? She hoped so. On the other hand, she had no choice but to hang on to a semblance of control. She felt so split inside.

"You'd better take it easy on that stuff," Mitch warned, staring at her out of those eyes that she still wanted to jump into.

"Not to worry. I'm all right. Actually, I'm feeling better than I've felt in a long time."

His lips quirked. "That's obvious."

"I'm not drunk, you know."

The quirk deepened. "That's debatable."

Deciding to test her ability to walk, Lindsay got up from the table and made her way back into the living area. Though her head felt twice its normal size, she had her sea legs and could definitely function.

However, the sofa looked awfully good when she eased onto it. Mitch was behind her, and once she was down, he followed suit, sitting close but not touching.

"Okay?" he asked, his tone indulgent, his eyes delving.

He might as well have touched her, she thought. When he looked at her like that, her nerves went haywire. "Uh, I'm...great."

He merely shook his head, though a smile toyed with his lips. "So what's this all about?"

"I don't know what you mean."

"Okay. I'll make it plainer. Why did you want to have dinner with me?"

Before she could answer, he reached across her lap and captured a hand, then concentrated on the inside of her wrist, massaging it with his thumb.

The room was warm. Too warm. Hot. On fire. Or was it her skin that was on fire? "Would you believe me if I said I didn't know?"

With his free hand, Mitch rubbed his chin, which wasn't quite smooth, then sighed deeply. "Yeah, I'd believe you."

"Good, because that's the truth."

Suddenly Mitch's mouth compressed, and he dropped her hand. "So I can safely say I was right— that this invitation was a lark, something someone who is bored and aimless would do?"

Lindsay's breath caught, his sudden mood swing from sexy to critical taking her aback. But only for a moment. She rebounded, anger replacing her hurt feelings. "I'm not bored, nor am I aimless."

"Oh? Exactly what do you do besides cater to your daddy?"

Her eyes flashed. "Who told you that?"

"No one in particular." He shrugged. "And every one in general."

"Gossip," she said flatly.

He shrugged again. "Partly. Only I don't pay much attention to that. I can pretty well figure what's going on for myself."

"Well, you're wrong about me." Her chin tipped with defiance as she took another sip of wine. "I do work."

"Really."

Lindsay quelled the urge to slap that condescending look off his face. It had been a mistake to come here. "Not officially, maybe, like you. But I work, nonetheless, mainly with charities."

"Can't fault you for that."

Although his tone had lightened considerably and no longer sounded judgmental, she suspected he wasn't all that impressed. And suddenly it was important to her that he be impressed, that he think more of her than that.

"Actually, I'm hard at it on a project to aid my pet charity, the women's shelter."

Mitch turned pensive. "You know, that's something I've never understood—how a man could strike a woman."

"Me, either," Lindsay said with a shiver. She took

another sip of wine to warm her now cold insides.
"But it happens every second."

"So is your project for public knowledge?"

Her spirits rose. "You want to hear about it?"

"Yeah, I do."

She told him in detail and watched his features
carefully for his reaction—good, bad or indifferent.

"That's a huge undertaking but a mighty noble
one." He paused. "Somehow, I think you can pull
it off."

"Thanks," she said, realizing again how much she
wanted his approval.

"If there's anything I can do, let me know."

She gave him an incredulous look. "Are you serious?"

"Yeah, as a matter of fact, I am."

He stared at her, then shifted his body. Her gaze
was irresistibly drawn to the power in his long legs
as he stretched them out in front of him.

Feeling a flush ascend over her face, Lindsay
turned away before her eyes ventured lower, to the
bulge between his thighs.

"What about you?" she asked breathlessly.
"What do you do besides back-breaking labor?"

"You don't want to know."

Lindsay raised her eyebrows. "Yes, I do, or I
wouldn't have asked."

He smiled, though it didn't reach his eyes. "Not
much, actually."

"No hobbies?"

He seemed to hedge. "Nope."

"Oh, come on. Surely there's something you like
to do besides work."

"There is. Work."

The corners of her mouth turned down. "Cute."

He stared at her for another long moment through eyes that were completely unreadable, then he stood. "I shouldn't offer you any more wine, but—"

"Thanks. I'll have some."

He chuckled. "Hope you know what you're doing."

She didn't, of course. But he didn't need to know that. Besides, she wanted to know more about this man, who was much too private to suit her.

"So what about your family?"

He tensed. "What about them?"

"Well, do you have one?" she pressed.

He blew out a breath, then took a swig of beer. "Yes and no."

"That makes perfect sense."

Mitch sat back down, his features brooding. She waited in suspense, fearing he would tell her to mind her own business and get the hell out of his house. In fact, she couldn't have been more surprised when he didn't.

"I'm an only child of parents who divorced when I was eleven."

"That's too bad."

"It was a nasty divorce, and I was caught in the middle. Neither one cared, but they chewed over me anyway, like a dog chews on a bone."

"How awful."

"My mother wanted me for the child support," he continued in a bitter tone, "while my dad just wanted to get back at her."

"Meanwhile, who took care of you?" Lindsay

asked in a small voice, thinking they had a lot in common, after all—souls filled with pain.

"My grandmother, God rest her soul."

"So you were special to each other."

"You could say that." Mitch had a faraway look in his eye and a matching tone in his voice. "She encouraged me to go for broke, to be anything I wanted to be."

"Do you think she'd be proud of you now?"

He gave her a knowing smile. "Obviously *you* don't think she would."

Lindsay flushed. "I didn't say that."

"But you thought it."

Her flush deepened, and he chuckled. "Hey, it's okay. You're right. She would've been happier if I had used my law degree."

Lindsay's mouth dropped. "You have a law degree?"

"That I do, though I've never used it."

When he lapsed into silence, Lindsay prodded in a dazed tone, "Anything else you'd care to add to that?"

"Not a thing."

His eyes roamed over her, which caused her heart to turn a somersault. There was a lot more than she'd realized to this complex man. However, he wasn't about to share anything else. His posture and his harsh tone said as much.

"What about you, Lindsay Newman? What makes you tick?"

"Do you really care?"

His expression softened for a moment. "For some reason, I do."

She couldn't remove her gaze. It was as if he had mesmerized her with his now-soothing tone and those smoldering eyes.

"It's not a pretty story."

"I'm pretty tough."

She almost smiled. "The summer I graduated from the university, I walked into my mother's bedroom and—" Lindsay broke off, unable to go on. Would the pain of that day always haunt her?

"Go on," he encouraged in that same soothing tone, as if he sensed something terrible had happened.

"I found her dead. She had taken a gun, put it in her mouth and pulled the trigger."

"Good Lord," Mitch whispered.

Lindsay closed her eyes. When she opened them again, his face swam in front of her. She blinked several times in order to bring him back into focus.

"Why did she do it?"

"We don't know. She didn't leave a note. I have my suspicions, but…" Lindsay's voice faded on a pitiful note.

"You don't have to say anything else."

Lindsay went on as if he hadn't spoken. "She was depressed all the time, and ended up spending most of my brother's and my childhood in a private sanitarium."

"How damn unfair."

"It gets worse. After finding her like that, I went through hell." Despite the numbing effect of the alcohol, every breath she took was labored.

"No doubt."

"I sank into a depression myself, so severe that I

was also put in a hospital. Not once, but several times.''

''There's no shame in that, Lindsay,'' he said gently.

''I'm...working on that.''

''I hope so.''

''Mother's suicide wasn't easy on any of us,'' she added, her tone remaining listless. ''But like I said, I was the one who crashed. When I was finally released for what I hoped was the final time, Daddy had his first major heart attack.''

''Jesus.''

''That's why I've never left him, why I've never gotten a 'real' job. I felt so strongly that my place was with him, that I should be here for him if he should need me. After all, I'd lost one parent and couldn't bear the thought of losing another.''

''That makes sense,'' Mitch said, before reaching over and taking the glass out of her trembling hand.

''But it hasn't been easy,'' she went on, as if the dam had burst inside her and she couldn't stop talking.

And while she was mortified by her own actions, there was something about Mitch's ability to listen— and not in a judgmental way, either—that loosened her tongue. And the wine, of course. She couldn't forget that.

''Daddy's hard to live with. He wants his own way about everything. And he still sees me as a child who should obey him unconditionally.''

''He's just jerking your chain, that's all.''

''Absolutely,'' she admitted. ''And I've let him get away with it.''

"Is he supporting you on the project?"

"Are you kidding? He's against it."

Mitch snorted. "Now why doesn't that surprise me?" He paused and seemed to grope for his next words. "How does he feel about your having been in an institution?"

"Embarrassed, humiliated." Lindsay paused, feeling a sudden sting behind her eyelids. Please, dear Lord, don't let me cry—not in front of him. "He felt the same about my mother."

"Maybe he blames himself."

"Maybe he does," she said on a sigh.

Mitch stood abruptly and peered down at her. "You okay?" His voice was low and thick.

She couldn't respond. Her heart was unraveling.

For another moment, he regarded her from beneath lowered lids. "Look, I'll be right back. I need another beer."

As he left the room, she followed him with eyes as empty as the pit of her stomach.

Twelve

Mitch gripped the edge of the counter with such force that he heard his knuckles pop. He didn't care. What he really wanted to do was jerk the entire counter away from the wall.

He was just that angry. In fact, he didn't know when he'd been so furious with himself. First off, he shouldn't have agreed to have dinner with her. That was the first big mistake. Second, he should have taken her somewhere, so they wouldn't be alone. Third, he never should have let her drink to the extent that it loosened her tongue.

He didn't want to know about her past. He didn't want to feel sorry for her, not in the least. To add insult to injury, he wanted to kick his own rear for not keeping *his* mouth shut about himself. She'd asked about his family, and, hell, he'd told her.

Mitch's grip on the counter tightened. Why did she have to smell so damn good, like she'd just bathed in a tub of sweet-smelling flowers? And why did she always have to *look* so good? No doubt she made a dynamite package with her red-gold hair, ivory skin dusted with freckles, and eyes so brown they looked like chocolate.

And her body. He couldn't forget that. It was the

best part of the package. He liked his women tall and thin and small-breasted. She was all that and more, especially her breasts. They were perfect.

No bra.

Even now, in his mind's eye, he could see the pout of her nipples visible under her T-shirt. He groaned, raising an unsteady hand to his forehead, now damp with perspiration.

But the perfection didn't stop there. She was feisty, with a barely subdued wildness about her, making her that much more attractive. *And forbidden.* Mostly that, he reminded himself, pushing himself savagely away from the counter and crossing to the refrigerator, where he latched on to a beer. Once the top was off, he tossed his head back and drank half of it at one time.

But it didn't help. The booze had no effect on his fractured mind. If he drank a whole six-pack, then maybe he would get some relief. But that wasn't going to happen. He didn't dare do anything *that* stupid. When he went back into that room, he needed to be in full control of his libido and his emotions.

Scowling, Mitch walked back to the sink and stared outside. He should go back to her. But then, there was no problem with his being missed. He would bet anything she was sound asleep, which could be another problem. He would have to touch her to wake her up.

He muttered an expletive. If her old man knew where she was, he would have apoplexy, and he would blame Mitch for sure. Lindsay had no business messing around with him. Even if he weren't an employee, he shouldn't have anything to do with her.

He was too old for her, in years *and* in experience. As far as the world was concerned, he'd lived a lifetime compared to her. Besides, he was empty on the inside. He had nothing left to offer any woman, much less one as full of piss and vinegar as she was.

That phrase suddenly brought a shadow of a smile to Mitch's lips. It was something his grandmother used to say all the time and make no apologies for. But then, she was a salty and sassy old woman, much like Lindsay would be if she lived that long.

He had to stop thinking about her in such a personal way. More than that, he had to get her out of his place now, before he did something he would regret for a long time to come.

He didn't want to lose his job. He liked working here. Even though he figured Cooper Newman could be a real bastard if the occasion called for it, so far, he'd had no trouble getting along with the doctor. He had hoped to remain here as long as he wanted. When he got bored, he would move on. That was the way he liked it—no ties that bound, no one to worry about but himself.

Until he'd seen Lindsay, that is.

He wanted her. No use denying that any longer. But he wanted a lot of things he couldn't have. Lindsay was just another in a long list.

Home.

That was where she belonged, and that was where she would go. Two seconds later, Mitch strode back into the living room, only to pull up short. He had been wrong. She wasn't asleep. She was standing by the window with her back to him, the glow from the lamp washing over her.

Mitch swallowed hard and stood transfixed, the desire to run his hands over those curves so strong that it made him ache low in his stomach.

Cursing silently, he took a step forward. When he did, she swung around, and their eyes met.

Tears. They were the first thing to register on his fogged mind. Some were still pooled in her eyes, while others were dried on her face. Without warning, he was mesmerized by her haunting vulnerability, and knew instinctively that underneath her outgoing facade was a deeply troubled and lonely young woman—the most dangerous kind, he reminded himself.

"I wish you wouldn't cry," he said in an anguished voice.

Her chin quivered. "I wish I wouldn't, either."

"You can't live in the past."

"That's easy for you to say."

"We all have our demons, Lindsay," he said gently. "Some worse than others. Yours happen to have been one of those worst-case scenarios."

She drew a trembling breath. "Pieces of me are missing," she said in a strained whisper, tears shimmering in her eyes. "Do you think I'll ever find them?"

He forced himself to keep his distance, but it was tearing chunks out of him. "Of course you will. You're young and strong."

"Do you feel sorry for me?"

His throat tightened, and it took a full minute before he could speak again. "Why would you think that?"

"Because I've been institutionalized," she said,

her voice almost lost under the pain. "There's a stigma—"

"Screw the stigma and those who think it." A scowl twisted his features.

Lindsay smiled through her tears. "That'll work."

"Look—"

Lindsay lifted her hand and stopped him. "Hey, it's okay. I'm okay, really. I had too much to drink, and when I do, I talk too much."

"Maybe you needed to talk. Did you ever think about that?"

Another fleeting smile touched her lips at the same time that he crossed the room, stopping within touching distance of her. He didn't touch her, though. He didn't dare. Yet his wanting her was like a magnet, drawing him toward her, in spite of his efforts to the contrary.

It was all he could do not to grab her, haul her into his arms and kiss her until she begged him to stop. Only he wouldn't have stopped. Tasting her would have sent him over the edge.

"Uh, thanks for listening," she whispered, then licked the tears off her upper lip with a tiny flick of her tongue.

He groaned inwardly, feeling the constraints of his zipper. "I'm not usually that good a listener," he said in a voice he didn't recognize as his own.

"You're wrong. You're a great listener."

"You should go, you know," he said roughly, that edge getting closer.

"I know."

Silence.

Mitch swallowed again and watched as more tears

gathered in her eyes. Clenching his fists to his sides, he said, "Hey, stop it. I can't let you go home like this."

"I'm a mess, aren't I?"

"What you are is beautiful," he murmured thickly.

Her eyes widened on him, and she swayed forward, as if her lovely legs were no longer capable of sustaining her.

"Whoa," Mitch said, reaching out to steady her.

"I'm sorry." Her voice sounded strangled, as though she had something caught in her throat.

"Stop saying you're sorry."

"I'm sorry I keep being sorry."

A smile suddenly relaxed his stiff mouth. "You don't have a damn thing to be sorry about."

She fooled with her lower lip again and just looked up at him.

He sucked in a breath, then waited a beat, fighting for control. That was when he realized he still had his hands on her. He dropped them suddenly and stepped back.

"Mitch."

It wasn't the fact that she spoke his name that sent a renewed shot of heat to his groin, but rather the way she said it—husky and desperate.

And she was still looking at him out of those big, sad eyes.

"Lindsay, you have to go." He heard the desperation in his own voice but was powerless to do anything about it.

"Hold me, please."

He closed his eyes against the onslaught of raw desire that almost buckled his knees.

That was when she dove into his arms.

"Lindsay!" His words came out a muted cry, even as his arms folded around her, drawing her close to his chest. He didn't know whose heart was beating the loudest or the fastest, but he didn't give a damn.

He was touching her, holding her, though he knew it couldn't last. This was not good. He had to let her go before he couldn't.

"Lindsay," he breathed into her hair. "We can't—"

She lifted her head then and stopped his words with her soft, moist lips. For a moment he froze, certain his chest wasn't large enough to hold both her and his pent-up breath.

But when she moaned and sank her lips deeper into his, he no longer cared. He stopped thinking about anything other than satisfying his own craving for her.

Answering her moan, he greedily parted her teeth so that he had access to her tongue, unwilling to deprive himself of one morsel of her sweet nectar. It was only after his hand seemed to move under her shirt of its own volition and surround a breast that the alarm bell banged him upside the head.

Shaken to the core by his actions and her response, Mitch jerked his mouth off hers and stepped back.

"No, Mitch." Her cry came out a harsh whisper.

"Yes, Lindsay," he responded in agony, though he didn't leave her completely. His hands remained around her forearms to make sure that she was steady and functioning on her own.

When he felt that she was, he dropped his arms, stepped out of touching distance and watched as she circled her arms across her chest.

"Why, Mitch?"

He shoved all five fingers of one hand through his hair. "Because I was about to forget who you are."

"The boss's daughter, right?" she responded with sharp bitterness. "And I'm not worth losing your job over?"

"You got it." His tone was purposely cruel and harsh.

She lifted her chin, though she couldn't disguise the pain in her eyes. "You've made your point. I won't bother you again."

"Will you be all right getting home?"

"Goodbye, Mitch."

She slammed the door behind her so hard it sounded like a gunshot. He flinched, sick inside about everything.

"What's going on, friend?"

Lindsay pursed her mouth as she stared at Mary Jane across the table. They had met for lunch at their favorite hangout and had just finished their food, topping it off with a frozen cappuccino, which satisfied their sweet tooth as well as the need for a caffeine boost.

"What makes you think anything's going on?" Lindsay responded with forced lightness.

"Don't pull that crap on me. I know you like the back of my hand. Besides, you look like you've been ridden hard and put up wet."

"Thanks, M.J.," Lindsay snapped, then stuck out her tongue.

They both laughed, which relieved some of the tension inside Lindsay. She almost relaxed, though not quite. Mary Jane was right; she was a mess both inside and out.

No wonder, considering how she had behaved.

But the instant she'd seen him on the porch, seen his irregular features, his damp salt-and-pepper hair, his gorgeous physique, then smelled his clean, earthy scent, she had ceased to be responsible.

And later, when his lips had devoured hers at the same time that he slipped a hand under her shirt and fingered her nipple until it swelled in his palm, she'd thought she might not survive the onslaught of emotion that charged through her, making her feel weak and wet in just the right places.

"Stop stalling," Mary Jane said, breaking the silence. "Go ahead and spill your guts. You'll feel much better afterwards. Guaranteed."

Lindsay rolled her eyes. "You have such an unladylike way of putting things."

"No point in pussyfooting around."

Lindsay sighed, pushing her cup away. The sweetness was adding to the upheaval in her stomach. "I met a man."

Mary Jane's mouth dropped open. "For real?"

"For real."

"Well, that's great. Why are you so down in the mouth about it?"

"Because of who he is."

Mary Jane flapped a hand. "Hell, as long as it's not tight-ass Peter, it doesn't matter."

Lindsay laughed, but with zero humor. "That's where you're wrong."

"Ah, now I am intrigued."

Lindsay didn't know quite how to begin, so she just jumped in with both feet. "It's Mitch Rawlins, our estate manager."

This time Mary Jane's mouth not only dropped open, but stayed that way.

"Close your mouth," Lindsay demanded through clenched teeth.

"Are you talking about the gardener, for chrissake?"

Lindsay heaved a sigh. "Funny you should ask that. I'm guilty of asking Tim the same thing."

"Are we right?"

"No. He's much more than that."

Mary Jane grimaced. "I don't get it. Surely you're putting me on."

"No, I'm not."

Mary Jane gave her an incredulous look. "Have you seen him alone?"

"Yes."

"Lordy, I can just see Cooper now."

Lindsay felt color seep into her face. "I'd rather he didn't know, if you don't mind."

"Oh, I can't imagine why." Mary Jane's sarcasm was up front. "Nothing's happened, right? I mean—"

"He...kissed me. Or rather, I kissed him."

"Have you lost your ever-loving mind?"

"I think I must have."

Mary Jane shook her head. "When you could have

any man you want, what could you possibly see in someone like him?''

"Have you ever seen him?''

"Not that I recall.''

"Oh, you'd recall,'' Lindsay said with punch.

"That nice, huh?''

"Most definitely.''

"So tell me, why is it you'll go after a man who's no good for you with such aggressiveness, but you won't stand up to your daddy?''

"It's simple. Mitch is dispensable, and Daddy isn't.''

"That's crazy.''

"And I *have* bucked Daddy. I'm still going forward with my project.''

"We'll see about that.''

Lindsay let that slide, unwilling to argue about her relationship with Cooper. Besides, her daddy was not who was on her mind at the moment.

"So what's so special about this Mitch Rawlins?''

Lindsay's eyes sparked. "For one thing, he makes me feel alive again, something I haven't felt since Mother...died.''

"There's nothing wrong with that.''

"And there's something about him that intrigues me—'' Lindsay broke off suddenly, remembering the way his eyes had spoken to her with a combination of irritation, sympathy and passion.

"Care to share what you're thinking?'' Mary Jane asked with another dose of sarcasm.

"Look, you can stop worrying. Nothing's going to happen. I have no intention of seeing him again.''

"You're lying through your teeth, Lindsay Newman."

Lindsay flushed. "I am not."

"Well, you'd better mean that. As the old saying goes, you play with fire, you're going to get burned."

Lindsay couldn't have agreed more. Only problem was, she not only wanted to play, she *wanted* to get burned.

Thirteen

"I thought you told me your finances were going to improve."

Tim drove an unsteady hand through his hair, then rubbed his out-of-shape mustache, something he always did when he was nervous. And he was nervous. His guts were in such a knot, he doubted they would ever straighten out.

"They *are* going to improve," Tim stressed to his accountant, Larry Fuller, who was staring back at him over the rims of the thin, wireless glasses that matched his thin, wireless face.

A smile almost broke through Tim's tension at that comparison; he'd never paid much attention to his accountant's appearance before. But no smile was forthcoming; smiles of late were all dried up.

"When?" Larry demanded, mincing no words.

Tim lurched out of the chair, then stood, his breath coming in short spurts. "Soon."

"Well, it had better be, or you just might be looking at bankruptcy."

What little color Tim had left in his face disappeared. He stared at Larry with his mouth hanging open.

"You needn't look at me like that," Larry

snapped. "I'm not the bugbear here. It's you, with your crazy notion that you can outsmart the stock market."

Bankruptcy!

Tim's stomach was roiling. God, if that were to happen, Cooper would kill him—even if Eve didn't. But he wouldn't panic. Help was on the way. He had to hold on to that thought and pray that his plan wouldn't fall through.

However, that good thought was short-lived. He'd gotten himself in such a deep hole financially that he was going to need a long-handled shovel to dig himself out.

Larry broke the silence. "You act like you're shocked."

Tim fell back down in the chair, feeling as if he'd been sucker punched. "It doesn't matter how I feel. Bankruptcy is not an option."

"Well, I'm doing all I can on this end. But there are just so many miracles I can perform without getting my ass in the proverbial sling with Uncle Sam."

"I understand."

Larry leaned forward in his chair. "Do you, Tim? Do you really understand that the only thing between you and bankruptcy court is a mighty thin thread?"

Tim's stomach tightened. "You just do what it takes to juggle the books a while longer."

"Tim—"

"Don't let me down, Larry," Tim pleaded. "You've stuck with me this far. Hang on."

Larry's pale eyes narrowed. "All right, good buddy. I'll continue to do what I can. But no fooling, something has to give—and soon, too."

"Thanks. I owe you."

Larry smirked. "Owe me? That's an understatement. If I pull this off, your ass belongs to me."

Tim stood and reached a hand out. "You're too goddamn honest to own anyone's ass."

Larry's smirk improved. "Go on, get out of here. I've got paying clients to deal with."

Tim had gotten out, and now, two hours later, he was waiting for a man he'd never met—a man he'd talked to only on the phone. Nonetheless, he was the most important man in Tim's life at the moment.

In fact, he could very well turn out to be his savior.

Tim stared at his watch, then looked around the gourmet coffee shop that was a beehive of activity. Perfect. No one would notice them. Even if they did, it wouldn't matter.

His contact had insisted they meet away from Garnet for obvious reasons. Tim had been all for that. He definitely didn't want to be seen with the man, though nothing illegal was going on—or so he'd been told.

Still, in his high-profile business, he couldn't afford to take unnecessary chances.

Tim squirmed in his seat as he took another sip of his tepid coffee, while keeping his eyes glued on the door. A fine sheen of sweat tickled his mustache. Mr. Clayton Freeman, whoever the hell he was, was late.

If only he could have gone to his dad or sister and borrowed a truckload of money, he wouldn't be here, sweating like a stuck pig. They both had the cash, but they weren't about to share it with him.

Then there was Eve. If he wasn't careful, she would leave him over this, which would raise a big stink. Cooper wouldn't like *that,* either. The social gossip columnists would have a field day, splattering the details of a nasty divorce all over the papers.

That thought almost made him choke on his drink. It was while he was wiping his mouth that his contact walked in. He had described himself as tall and gangly, with dirty blond hair and a space between his front teeth.

Tim couldn't vouch for the space, but the other part fit him to a tee. Once pleasantries had been exchanged and Freeman was seated in front of him, Tim noticed the space. Yep, this was the right guy.

"So are you still committed to this venture?" Freeman asked in an low, easygoing voice.

"If it's something I can live with."

"Oh, you can live with it, all right."

Tim placed his elbows on the table and leaned closer. "You can guarantee me the goods?"

"Absolutely."

"So how's all this going to work?" Tim's eyes were cuttingly sharp. "I need to make as much money as I can as quickly as I can."

Freeman tongued the gap between his teeth.

Tim glanced away. What a nasty habit. Hopefully this was the last time he would have to come in contact with this guy.

"Making money is what this is all about."

"So what do I have to do?" Tim asked.

"Give me a list of all your pharmacies and their locations."

"That's no problem. I have that with me." Tim handed him a sealed envelope. "Anything else?"

"Not at the moment." Freeman scooted the chair back and stood.

"Hey," Tim said anxiously, "where're you off to in such a hurry? I have some more questions. I want to know exactly what I'll be getting and when."

Freeman's features turned cold. "All in due time, Doctor."

"And you can assure me that this is all above-board, that the product's the real thing?"

Freeman smiled. "Of course. Don't give it another thought. This is going to be the easiest money you've ever made."

Tim hoped so. God, he hoped so.

"Good morning, Daddy."

Cooper acknowledged Lindsay's greeting with an absent smile before leaning his head back and draining his coffee cup.

"Are you headed to the golf course?" she asked, her eyes giving him the once-over. It seemed as if he'd never been in an accident, much less an almost fatal one. He seemed one hundred percent his old self.

"That's right. But I'm going to stop by the office first."

"Ah, checking on Tim, huh?" Lindsay's tone was teasing.

Cooper didn't respond in kind. "Unfortunately, yes."

"Oh, Daddy, you ought to leave him alone, let him do his own thing."

Cooper snorted, then wiped his mouth with his

napkin before tossing it down beside his plate. "Just like you're doing *your* own thing, right?"

Lindsay blanched, but her tone was innocent. "What's that supposed to mean?"

"That doesn't deserve an answer, because you know what it means."

Lindsay curbed her anger. She didn't want to begin this hot but clear day arguing with her daddy. But if he had his way, that was how it was going to be.

She had come to the sunroom with its array of green and flowering plants and colorful furniture to get inspired. While the computer was a valued tool, she oftentimes did her best work away from it.

She hadn't expected to find her daddy already there.

"I suppose you're talking about my project," she said at last.

"What else?" Cooper's tone was clipped, and his mouth was set. "How could I not? After all, you asked two of my oldest and dearest friends for money."

Lindsay didn't flinch under his harsh words and scrutiny, but she wanted to. It was still so hard for her to buck Cooper, to go against what he wanted for her. But if she didn't, she would shrivel up and die inside. It had come to that.

"I didn't mention money," she said quietly.

"But you will."

"For now I'm only asking for their time."

"Time and money." Cooper gave a heavy shrug. "One always follows the other."

Lindsay forced a smile at Dolly, who walked in

and refilled Cooper's empty cup. When they were alone again, she asked, "How did you know I'd been in contact with Ash and Peggy?"

"They attended the same dinner party I did last evening."

Lindsay smothered a sigh. That was what she'd anticipated would happen, but she had kept her fingers crossed that if it did, they would influence him to join the cause. Such was apparently not the case.

"I know you don't approve—"

"You're damn right I don't."

Lindsay's lips snapped shut, and she looked beyond him through the expanse of glass. A squirrel was sitting on a flimsy limb, its paws gripping a nut of some kind, while its little mouth was busy munching. For a moment the sight of the animal held her spellbound.

So much for the simple side of life, she thought, a sinking feeling settling in the pit of her stomach. Her daddy had just given her self-confidence another whack.

It had been three days since her mind-boggling encounter with Mitch and her subsequent lunch with Mary Jane. During that time, she had tried to keep herself busy, to keep from thinking about Mitch and how much she would love a repeat performance of that evening.

She had worked like a Trojan on the project itself, trying to iron out the details. While she had accomplished a great deal, she still had a lot of loose ends to tie up. Hence this morning's brainstorming session.

"I'm still convinced this crazy idea of yours will never get off the ground."

Her daddy's harsh statement forced her back to the moment. "It will if you don't sabotage it."

Cooper's mouth thinned. "I won't have to. In the end, I'm convinced you'll come around to my way of thinking and let it go."

If he wanted to think that, then so be it. At least it got her off the hot seat. She stood, then leaned over and kissed him on the cheek. "I'll see you later."

"No, you won't. I'm leaving town after my golf game."

"Oh?"

"Patty and I are driving up to her horse farm for the night."

Patty was his latest woman friend. She seemed really nice—one of the few older women he took out. "Be careful, and have a good time."

"What are you going to do?"

Lindsay shook her head. "Don't ask. You don't want to know."

Without waiting for a response, she turned and made her way back upstairs to her room, where she remained until late afternoon firming up plans for an upcoming banquet. She had suggested this fund-raising event to her friends, who in turn had suggested they use the banquet to organize a golf tournament, also for the purpose of raising money.

Lindsay had been ecstatic and couldn't wait to get started.

She also spoke with the president of the board of

the local junior college, who agreed to meet with her the following week.

All in all, it was a productive day.

So why, later, did she feel so restless, so in need of human contact? She knew the answer to that. It wasn't in her best interest to be alone. Her psychiatrist, Dr. Milbrook, had stressed that over and over. It allowed her too much time to think about things she had no business thinking about.

Mitch Rawlins was certainly one of those forbidden things. She felt a tightening down low—the same feeling she had experienced when he'd kissed her.

She closed her eyes, imagining him in her mind, imagined him touching her in all the right places. Her breathing quickened, and she placed a trembling hand to her damp forehead.

Lindsay lurched out of the chair, fighting off a suffocating feeling in her chest. What she needed was some fresh air to clear thoughts of that reckless evening from her mind. She had been cooped up too long.

With that, she fled her room, not realizing she was holding her breath until she reached the outdoors. Her eyes scanned the premises as she started to walk. All seemed clear. The workers had apparently shut down for the day, which meant Mitch was probably in his cabin.

Dare she?

Her heart upped its beat even as she told herself *no,* that what she was thinking was ludicrous and *not* going to happen.

Still, she found herself heading in that direction, as if her legs and feet had a will of their own. She refused to delve into the sane part of her brain that might know why she was pulling a stunt like this.

By the time she reached his cabin, her breath was burning her lungs. "Don't do this," she whispered, hearing the desperation underlying her own words. "Please, don't do this."

Her footsteps didn't falter until she stepped up onto the porch, where her conscience once again pricked her. However, curiosity mixed with desire won. She peered in a window. Instantly her feet froze to the spot, and she stared, her mouth gaping.

He was walking across the living room, as naked as the day he was born.

Fourteen

Lindsay couldn't move. She could only stand there and continue to stare with her heart beating in her throat. Even when he moved, she remained motionless, watching as he strode to the refrigerator, grabbed a beer and popped it open.

He tossed his head back and took several healthy gulps. Lindsay's eyes soaked in every angle and curve of his hard, tanned body, targeting the washboard-flat stomach that tapered to his manhood.

Perspiration. It was oozing through every pore on her skin. Though the air was hot and humid, her condition had nothing to do with the weather.

Lust.

That was what she was experiencing—pure, raw lust, as she watched him take another swig of the beer, then swipe his mouth with the back of his hand. She felt herself dissolve under the heat of that lust, melting as though she were made of wax and had been set on fire.

As if he sensed something was not quite right, Mitch turned and peered through the window. She saw rather than heard him catch his breath. An incredulous expression crossed his features at the same time that the flesh between his legs burgeoned. She tried desperately to avert her gaze, but her efforts proved futile.

Mitch dropped the beer and strode toward her. Suddenly he seemed more like a stranger than ever— a *dangerous* stranger.

Rather than turn and bolt the way she should have, Lindsay stood her ground, though her mind screamed at her to move. But again her body failed to cooperate. It was as if it had control of her, instead of the other way around.

Lindsay's breath rushed in and out of her lungs at such a rapid rate that she feared she might black out. She dug her fingernails deep into her palms and watched him charge out the front door into the inky blackness, one expletive after another spilling from his lips.

"Mitch...I'm sorry," Lindsay whispered, dry-mouthed.

He stopped in front of her, within touching distance, his eyes piercing and his breathing hard— harder than hers.

"What the hell do you think you're doing?" he muttered harshly, continuing to bear down on her.

She peered up at him out of shocked, rounded eyes. But when she opened her mouth, nothing came out.

"Dammit, Lindsay," he said in a strangled voice.

Then, without warning, Mitch grabbed her by the arm and pushed her toward the door. Once they were inside, in the middle of the room, the lamp cast an eerie glow around them. Lindsay's teeth began chattering as the repercussions of what she'd done and where she was hit her.

And he was still naked.

She closed her eyes for a second and took a deep, shuddering breath. That didn't help. All she did was pull the clean scent of him into her lungs, feel herself drowning in it. Dear Lord, had she indeed lost her mind?

"Lindsay, look at me."

He sounded thick-tongued, as if he'd been drinking too much. She knew better, especially when she stared into those killer blue eyes. They were as clear and heart-stopping as ever. But he wasn't nearly as in control as he appeared. His voice had given him away.

"I'm looking," she whispered, another shudder going through her.

"This is insane," he rasped.

"I...know."

"You also know what's about to happen, don't you?"

Heat boiled anew inside her, but when she swallowed, it felt as if she had nails in her throat. "Yes."

She barely got that tiny word out of her mouth before he had her backed against the wall, his lips grinding into hers. There was no pain, only pleasure, as those lips probed, delved, sucked until she thought the top of her head would come off.

Lindsay had never before been kissed like this— not with such all-devouring intensity. And while it should have frightened her, it didn't. She gave him carte blanche, returning his passion with a fire all her own.

When he pulled his head back, his eyes were blazing. But he didn't say anything. Instead, he scooped her up in his arms and carried her into his bedroom, where another lamp burned in the far corner.

She whimpered as he laid her on the bed, then leaned over and sank his lips on hers again with that same hungry intensity. She curled her arms around his neck at the same time that he ran a hand under her shirt and rubbed her breasts.

"Mitch," she moaned against his lips.

"Does that feel good?" he asked thickly.

"Oh, yes."

It was too late to pull back now. Lindsay had asked for what she was about to get. Minutes ago, she could have sneaked back into the night without his knowing she'd been there. Yet she hadn't. As she'd thought that day with Mary Jane, she *wanted* to get burned.

Why?

The answer was a no-brainer. She wanted him. She had wanted him from the first time she saw him, and she was no longer going to deny that, even to herself. She just hadn't realized just how severe the craving was until now. Until she had seen him naked. Now she *had* to have him, as if he'd become an addiction.

Yet she knew what they were doing was wrong, being done for all the wrong reasons. And while the sane side of her demanded she call a halt to this madness, she couldn't.

Without taking his heated gaze off her, Mitch suddenly ripped the buttons off her camp shirt, then tugged at the snap on her cutoffs. With her panties entwined around his strong fingers, he jerked them off her.

Wordlessly, his mouth fused with hers again. Her

arms circled his broad shoulders; she wanted him as close as possible, ached to feel all of him.

As if he had read her mind or was rabid for the same thing, he pressed against her until they were heart to heart, belly to belly.

"Please," she said achingly.

"Please what?"

His voice was even thicker now, like rich cream that couldn't seem to shake loose from its container.

She couldn't answer. His mouth was on her breast, sucking on the nipple, while his hand kneaded the other breast.

When his lips deserted that nipple, she made a strange little sound, wanting him to continue his sweet assault. He did, taking his mouth lower.

While she clung to him, he licked a fiery trail between her breasts, down her slender belly, and stopping at her navel.

"Oh, Mitch," she panted, his tongue spearing that tiny hole time and time again, while the palm of his callused hand moved to the apex of her thighs, where it simply rested.

But not for long. Soon he began to rub ever so softly, up and down and around, causing that ever-building heat to spark all through her body.

"Mitch, please."

This time she was begging, begging him to put out the fire that was scorching her insides. He didn't relent. He seemed to take pleasure in driving her mad, and himself, as well.

She could feel him. He was so hot and hard, as if he could explode at any second. She wanted him to—but inside her. She wanted him to fill that void that his lips and hands had created.

Yet he seemed determined to punish her, but ever so sweetly, with those lips and hands, continuing to touch, to kiss, to nibble, showing her absolutely no mercy.

Then he touched her there.

Her hips bucked, and her eyes widened on him. He peered at her, and their gazes locked. Finally he broke the contact, lowering his head and dipping his tongue into the dewy center of her.

"Oh…"

Lindsay dug her fingers into his hair, clutching him in a death grip, reveling in the feel of him as he took her to dizzying heights, heights she'd never reached before.

Then he was above her, spreading her thighs. She arched her body, and when she did, he thrust into her, robbing her of her breath.

He was so big, so hard, so filling, that she was powerless against his strength. But she need not have worried. He was gentle, moving ever so tenderly. At first, that was, until the length of him was high inside her. Then he upped his pace and his strokes to the savage level, taking her on the ride of her life.

Their ahs and oohs rended the air simultaneously.

For the longest time afterward, neither said a word. He moved off her but didn't let her go, turning her so that their sweat-drenched bodies faced each other.

"Mitch…"

He touched her lips with a finger. "Don't say anything."

"I guess there's really nothing to say."

"Not now." He kissed her on a breast that was still as firm as an unripened peach. "Our bodies just said it all."

Lindsay sighed as his arms closed tightly around her, holding her as if he would never let her go.

And the problem was, she didn't want him to.

Lindsay couldn't say how long she slept.

She didn't bother looking for a clock when she disengaged herself from Mitch's arms. He moaned, and for a second she feared she'd awakened him. But she hadn't, thank goodness.

As silently and as cautiously as possible, she eased out of bed, slipped into her clothes and tiptoed to the door, then out.

By the time she reached her own bedroom a few minutes later, she was completely out of breath, having run all the way home.

Immediately, she shed her clothes and stepped into the shower, where the tears flowed along with the water.

She had done it.

She'd had sex with Mitch. Fear welled up inside her as she turned off the faucet and reached for a towel. Once her body was dry, she padded back into her room, climbed into bed and curled into a fetal position.

In retrospect, she had definitely gotten what she'd asked for. And more. Much more. Having Mitch inside her had been everything she had ever hoped for. Yet she knew there would be no repeat performance.

Even if their worlds weren't on a collision course, there was Cooper, whose image loomed large in her mind. Her father would go berserk if he ever found out that she'd had sex with an employee.

Cooper would terminate Mitch on the spot.

She couldn't allow that to happen. What had happened had been her fault. She'd come on to him, and he'd given her exactly what she'd asked for.

If she had it to do all over again, would she do the same thing?

Yes.

In spite of the chill of the air conditioner, Lindsay felt her body rekindle its fire for him. Even now, she ached for the feel of his hands and mouth on her. So how could she stay away from him?

She couldn't—not when he made her feel as she'd never felt before—desirable and *whole*. Oh, Mitch, she wept silently.

Come morning, Lindsay still hadn't closed her eyes.

Fifteen

Mitch climbed off the ladder, sweat saturating his entire body. Once he was on the ground, he reached for the handkerchief in his back pocket and wiped his face, just so that he could see.

"Hey, boss, why didn't you let me do that?"

Mitch waved a careless hand at Jesse. "Mainly because you were doing something else."

"The other coulda waited."

"Don't worry about it." Mitch raised his eyes to the roof of the greenhouse. "Those sheets of roofing won't blow off again. I can guarantee you that."

"Man, the wind sure has been something lately, especially for this time of year."

"I don't like it, either—not when we're trying to finish a project." Mitch dusted off his jeans with his right hand, then turned and gave the greenhouse a closer look. "Won't be long now till it's done."

Jesse grinned. "I think we done a good job, too, don't you?"

Mitch grinned back. "The best."

"Has the doc seen it yet?"

"Not that I know of, though I'm about to get him down here. I want to make sure it's on the money."

Jesse scratched his head, frowning against the brutal sunlight. "Well, it oughta hold all the plants he wants from now till kingdom come."

"That's a given," Mitch said, half-smiling.

"So what do you want me to do now?" Jesse asked. "Me and the boys finished trimming and weeding around the south pond."

"Bring 'em back here, and we'll get started on the inside."

"Gotcha."

Mitch watched Jesse amble off before facing the ladder once again and frowning. He hated like hell to climb back up on that metal roof. But since it had already given them trouble, Mitch felt the need to make one more inspection.

He also needed all the backbreaking labor he could stand—the harder, the better. That way, when he fell into bed at night, he wouldn't think. He would be too weary in both mind and body.

Fearing where his thoughts were leading, he cursed, then got back on the ladder. By the time he'd checked everything out, the hands were back.

"Yo, boss," Jesse said. "Give us our orders."

Mitch did.

Hours later, Jesse pulled off his wet hat and squinted his dark eyes on Mitch. "Man, this was a killer day."

"Is that a nice way of saying I'm a slave driver?" Jesse grinned. "Yup."

"Consider it a job well done. Go on home now, and get some grub and some sleep. I'll see you tomorrow."

A short time later, Mitch was in his cabin, having had his shower and his supper. With a second beer in hand, he made his way into the living room and practically fell onto the sofa.

What a day. He didn't know when he'd been so bloody tired. But that was a good thing. Maybe he would sleep, instead of lying in bed, staring at the ceiling, watching Lindsay's face dance across it.

He hated the sudden leap in his pulse.

But he had only to *think* her name, and every nerve in his body responded. His eyes dipped south. Bingo. His dick bulged against his jeans, as hard as a baseball bat, making him bloody uncomfortable.

He wished... Hell, it was too late to wish. He'd already wished himself into a pickle of a mess. More to the point, he had probably wished his ass right out of a job.

Mitch closed his eyes, then opened them, wishing that making love to her had been merely an erotic dream. There he was, wishing again. But it was no damn dream, and that kind of game-playing was wearing thin. He'd always been one to face the stark realities of life head-on, then deal with them.

Now, however, that philosophy didn't seem to be working.

Lindsay and his hot desire for her had blindsided him. Fool that he was, he hadn't seen it coming until it was too late and he was in too deep.

After going to great lengths to simplify his life, he had once again complicated it. What he should do was pack his bags, get the hell off this property, *out of Mississippi,* and never look back.

Who was he kidding?

He wasn't about to do that. Lindsay had managed to find a crack in his carefully erected barrier and slip through it. He hated to admit it, but he was smitten.

He groaned, thinking of how she'd looked when he'd caught her watching him through the window—frightened, yet unrepentant. And when he'd practically dragged her into the house and backed her pliable body against the wall, she still hadn't quailed under the sucking-down heat that he'd pressed against her.

So where did that leave him, for chrissake?

In a world of hurt.

He reached for his beer and drank, then slammed it back down on the table. Right now, he would give almost anything for another shot at her in the sack.

She'd been so hot. So willing.

But no way could he lure her back into his bed. He couldn't afford to get any more involved, not with the likes of her. As he'd already pointed out to her, she was just a spoiled little rich girl out for kicks because she had too much time on her hands.

Suddenly his conscience pricked him. He recalled the conversation he'd had with her the evening she'd brought the picnic basket. He had learned there was another side to Lindsay Newman, a side with a soul—damaged, maybe, but a soul nonetheless.

Still, that didn't mean she should be exonerated for showing up at his place. She had asked for that romp in the sack. But if she was out for any more kicks, she would have to look elsewhere.

Yet he had to admit that keeping his hands off her was going to be tough. Making love with her had been the best—the best ever. She had radiated guilt-free sex, and he'd taken the bait.

A chill darted through Mitch. Nothing was ever free. He'd learned that the hard way. He hadn't used any protection—that was how hot and fast the heat had flared between them. He cradled his head in his hands, praying there would be no repercussions from that stupid move.

Nah. He was worrying needlessly. He would bet she was on the pill. After all, she had What's-His-Face drooling over her. Mitch jerked his head up, jealousy cutting through him like a whipend. The thought of that sap touching her the way *he'd* touched her made him crazy.

Then, realizing what he was thinking, Mitch released a string of expletives. He guessed that was why he didn't hear the knock on the door until it became a bang.

His stomach dropped to his toes. Lindsay? With a gait that was jerky, he went to the door and opened it.

"Hello, Mitch."

He cringed inwardly as he stared into the eyes of his ex-wife. What next? There was just so much a man could take in one day. But she was here, on his porch, and he would have to deal with her.

"Surprised to see me?" Sarcasm lowered her usually high voice.

"You know the answer to that, Wendy," he responded in a tired but resigned tone.

She tilted her head. "Are you going to ask me in?"

He moved aside. Once she swept past him, he closed the door and leaned against it. Instead of saying anything, he simply looked at her, feeling all the old guilt from the past resurface—something else he didn't want to feel.

If only he had loved her enough, maybe both their lives would have turned out differently. They would probably have a brick home in the suburbs with two children, etc., etc. Only he hadn't loved her enough. He had often wondered if he'd ever loved her at all.

She wasn't a bad-looking woman. At one time she'd been lovely, with dark hair and eyes and a well-proportioned body. No longer. Too much booze, too many cigarettes, too many men—all had made an overweight old woman out of her, even though she was two years younger than he was.

Right now he felt nothing but pity for her, and he hated that, for both of them.

"I guess you're wondering why I'm here?"

Mitch folded his arms across his bare chest. "You could say that."

For a moment he tracked her eyes as they slid up and down his body. He couldn't be sure, but he thought he saw a flare of desire. He hoped not. If that was why she was here, then she was sure as hell out of luck.

"How about something to drink?"

"Beer's all I have."

She frowned. "Forget it, then."

"How did you find me?" Mitch raised his hand, then shoved himself away from the door. "Forget I asked that. I know."

"I'm sorry you're not glad to see me." She tilted her head a bit more. "I was hoping…"

"What, Wendy?"

She picked up on the flatness in his tone and

flushed. "That maybe we…maybe you…" Her voice faded, and she glanced away.

"That's not ever going to happen. You know that. It's been over between us for a long time. Besides, you're still married, right?"

She nodded.

"Then what is this all about?"

"I'm leaving him, Mitch."

"So leave him."

"It's not that simple. He's cut me off."

"Ah, so you don't have any money."

"I didn't say that."

"Wendy, you've got to get some help, get control of yourself and your life."

She gave an unladylike snort. "Like you've done, I presume?"

"That's right," he said, fighting down a surging anger.

Wendy bowed her shoulders, then said in a forlorn voice, "If only you hadn't fallen out of love with me."

"If only you hadn't slept with my best friend."

She flinched visibly. "You'll never forgive me for that, will you?"

"Oh, I forgave you, but I also stopped loving you. Maybe I never loved you, at least not enough to try and repair the damage."

"I guess that about says it all."

"You knew that when you came here."

"Are you happy, Mitch?"

"Who knows? I'm not sure I even know what that word means." He paused. "Look, has husband number three hurt you? Physically, I mean?"

"No. He's just spending his money on his other women." She gave him a bitter smile. "I'm sure you're thinking I'm getting exactly what I deserve— that it's payback time."

"Actually, I wasn't thinking anything at all. If it's money you need, I can help you out there."

"Are you serious?"

"Yeah, but there is a string attached—don't come back here anymore."

Her face drained of color. "You were the best thing that ever happened to me, Mitch. But I was lonely. Your work came first and—"

"Stop it, Wendy. Don't try and flog a dead horse. We gave him a decent burial. Let him rest in peace."

Having said that, Mitch crossed to the bedroom, picked up his wallet and returned with a wad of bills in his hand. "Maybe this will get you by for a while."

"I may not be able to pay—"

He cut her off again. "Don't worry about it. I don't want the money back."

Before she could say anything, Mitch strode to the door, opened it and gestured for her to go ahead. She walked out on the porch, and he followed her.

Silence filled the air as he stared at her for a long moment, suddenly feeling free of his ex-wife for the first time since he'd met her. No more guilt and no more regrets. Life was too short.

"Take care, Wendy. I wish you the best."

She stood on her tiptoes and kissed him on the cheek. "Thanks, Mitch. In spite of yourself, you're a decent man."

Long after she was gone, Mitch remained on the

porch, his eyes on the big house—on one room in particular.

Blood.

It was everywhere. On her hands, on her face, on her clothes, on her body.

"Get it off me!" she screamed.

No one heard her. Or if they did, they ignored her. Why were they treating her like this? Couldn't they see she was covered in all that red, sticky stuff? Couldn't they see that? They weren't blind, were they?

And the smell! God, it was driving her mad. She couldn't stand it on her another second. She stared at herself in the mirror, then began tearing at her clothes. Once she was naked, she stared at herself again. But it was still on her hands, on her body. Oh, God! It was never going away.

She sank to the floor and screamed.

And screamed. And screamed some more.

Lindsay sat straight up in the bed, her breathing coming so fast she couldn't control it, nor could she control her thundering heart. She thought it was going to pound through her chest wall.

Calm down, she told herself, her eyes darting around the room. You're not in that horrible place. You're home. Although her heart settled somewhat, the feeling of fear and hopelessness remained with her. Still, she lay back down, but she knew she wouldn't stay there. Once she had that dream, sleep turned elusive.

Turning her head, Lindsay peered at the clock. The

hands were on eleven. Usually it was way past midnight before she even attempted to go to bed, but tonight had been an exception. She hadn't felt good, and she'd had a long day, so she had indulged herself.

A lot of good it had done her.

Disgusted, she tossed the sheet back and sat on the side of the bed, where she rubbed her throbbing temples. Would she ever get over her mother's suicide? Would she ever get over finding her bloody body?

The blood was the worst part. Her fixation on that and her inability to cope with it had been the catalyst that had sent her to the private hospital to start with.

Shuddering, she wiped the tears off her face.

Now, years later, she was still having that dream. And she always awakened with the same fear haunting her.

Suicide.

Was it hereditary?

She knew such a thought was ludicrous. But the fear associated with her mother's fate was so deep that she felt it was permanently tattooed on her soul.

Don't panic, she told herself, continuing to suck air into her lungs. She was going to be fine. She wasn't going to sink back into that black hole. She no longer felt that she didn't belong anywhere or to anyone, or that she was inadequate. No more doubts.

Liar.

When she had this nightmare, it usually followed something traumatic... *Mitch.* That evening spent in his arms had turned her world upside down.

Suddenly she scrambled off the bed, opened the doors to the balcony and walked outside. Even though the air was hot and humid, it felt good to her battered body.

But if she had it to do all over again, she would do the same thing. She couldn't stop thinking about him, couldn't stop thinking about how he made her feel. Was that why she'd walked onto the balcony? Had she hoped to get a glimpse of him?

Suddenly Lady Luck smiled on her. As if on cue, Mitch walked out on the porch. Only he wasn't alone. A woman was with him.

The fire that had flared inside her was instantly snuffed out. Lindsay clutched at her stomach, feeling sick with jealousy.

Was Mitch having an affair with someone else?

Sixteen

"Was that Peter?"

Lindsay cast troubled eyes on her daddy as she sat back down on one end of the plush sofa. "Yes, it was," she admitted in a hesitant tone.

She had just returned from a meeting with a group of volunteers who had agreed to finalize the banquet plans and the subsequent golf tournament. When she walked in, Cooper had been in the sunroom; she had joined him there.

Shortly after Dolly had brought her a glass of flavored iced tea, the phone had rung. It had been Peter.

Cooper's green eyes pinned hers. "He asked you to dinner, didn't he?"

"That he did."

"Forgive me for sounding like a broken record, but are you going?"

"No."

"So what's your excuse this time?"

"The same as before. I don't want to."

Cooper's lips thinned. "I won't tolerate you being rude to him."

"That wasn't my intention," she said mildly, not in the mood to start World War III with him this evening. She had too many other things on her mind.

"Well, from what I heard, it came across that way."

"Daddy, I don't want to discuss Peter."

He snorted. "You never do."

Switching the subject, Lindsay said, "You're not supposed to have that drink."

"Don't you start."

"Turnabout's fair play, you know," she said, her tone mildly teasing, trying to lighten the atmosphere.

Cooper flapped a hand at her. "We're talking about apples and oranges here."

"No matter. Your doctor wouldn't be happy if he saw you with that glass in your hand."

"Hell, it's just wine. And I'm a heart doctor, too, remember—the best. The fact that I'm no longer practicing doesn't mean I don't know what the hell's going on."

"I didn't mean to imply that, and you know it. It's just that I'm concerned about you."

"I don't need your concern. I need your cooperation."

"Daddy—"

"You might be able to run from Peter, but not from me. I'm not giving up on the two of you marrying."

Lindsay didn't say anything. What was there to say that hadn't already been said a dozen times over? Sooner or later, her father would be forced to face reality. She would just bide her time until that happened.

Meanwhile, she had to make sure he never found out about her liaison with Mitch. Lindsay's blood suddenly ran cold, then hot, through her veins. God, but she was playing a dangerous game.

"If you don't marry soon, I'm going to be too old to enjoy my grandchildren."

"I don't buy that for a second."

Cooper's lips stretched even thinner. It was in that moment that Lindsay realized he was indeed looking older, even though he wasn't *old.* Her heart faltered. She couldn't lose him. As it was, she had already lost too much; her recent nightmare had been a grim reminder of that.

She shook her head to clear it at the same time that Dolly made her appearance. "Will both of you be having dinner?"

"Yes," Lindsay said. "Or, at least, I will."

Cooper nodded, as well.

When they were by themselves again, Lindsay asked, "What do you hear from Tim these days?"

Cooper's face darkened. "I'm not happy with him, either."

Oh, brother, she'd set him off again. "He's never going to run the office exactly like you did, Daddy."

"That's not what I'm talking about, though he sure as hell needs to be more hands-on there than he is."

"He's still learning," Lindsay said lamely.

Cooper cut her a look. "That's why he needs to stay in the office more."

Lindsay could have said Amen to that, given Tim's addiction to the stock market, but she didn't. Instead, she diverted the conversation so as not to send Cooper off on another tangent.

"We need to have him and Eve to dinner soon, Daddy—a family gathering."

"Maybe," Cooper said absently, then raised his eyebrows at Dolly, who once more entered the room. "Is dinner ready?"

"Yes, sir, but that's not why I'm here." Dolly's eyes sought out Lindsay. "There's a call for you. It's a woman—says she knows you from the shelter." Dolly paused, her features withering into a frown. "I tried to put her off. That's when she went plumb hysterical on me."

"What the hell is going on?" Cooper bellowed, his gaze menacing.

Lindsay rose quickly. "I'll take it in the library."

"Now, see here, Lindsay!" Cooper exclaimed. "I won't have those people calling here. You know how I feel about that place."

Lindsay had every intention of holding her tongue, of not letting him goad her into a response of any kind. But his attitude, along with his words, rankled to such a degree that she said in a calm but cool tone, "This doesn't concern you, Daddy."

"The hell it doesn't. What concerns you, concerns me." He faced Dolly. "Tell whoever it is that Lindsay's not available."

"No, Dolly. I'll take the call."

"Lindsay—"

Lindsay walked out, leaving Cooper sputtering. By the time she reached the library and lifted the receiver, she was shaking all over.

A few minutes later she said into the receiver, "Stop crying, Beverly, and listen to me. I'll meet you at the police station. Have your friend take you there. Now.''

With that, Lindsay hung up, then dashed out of the room, almost straight into Cooper, who was standing just outside the library.

"Were you eavesdropping?" Lindsay demanded, fury waging another battle inside her and winning.

He ignored her question and asked one of his own. "Surely to God, you're not going to meet that woman?"

"I have to, Daddy," she said, swallowing her fury and opting for another, more conciliatory tactic. "Her husband's—"

"I don't give a damn about her or her husband. I don't want you involved."

Lindsay stood her ground, but her tone was soft. "I *am* involved, of my own free will. Now I have to go." Before he could rebut, she leaned over and kissed him on the cheek. "Enjoy dinner. Don't wait for me."

An expletive zinged through the air, and though she flinched inwardly, she dashed upstairs, grabbed her purse, then tore out of the house.

She had parked her car around back but not in the garage. Once inside her vehicle, she shoved the key in the ignition and turned it.

Nothing.

She turned the key again and again. Still dead as a doornail. Splendid. Apparently she needed a new battery. Her sports Lexus was over three years old, and still had the original one. Of all times for the stupid thing to go on the blink—

"Need some help?"

Mitch.

Lindsay's heart did a tap dance inside her chest, even as her head swung around to him. She hadn't seen him since their romp in his bed. And though she knew a meeting was inevitable, she hadn't planned on seeing him now—not when she was off balance and fractured. She had wanted to be in total control of herself and her nerves.

And she hadn't gotten over the cold fact that he'd been with another woman so soon after her. That was a blow she hadn't yet come to terms with.

"It sounds like the battery," he said in his low, easy drawl.

Lindsay wet her dry lips, a gesture he seemed to pick up on before his eyes darted back up to meet hers. Even though it was near dusk, there was still enough light for her to see him clearly. He didn't bother to hide the desire that smoldered in his eyes.

"Want me to take a look?"

"Actually, I'm in a hurry." Lindsay had a death grip on the steering wheel while her mind raced. His presence robbed her of all rational thought. She didn't need this. She didn't need *him*. "I…have to be someplace. Now."

"I'll take you."

Lindsay's heart did another tap dance. "Look, I don't think…" Her words faded into nothingness, along with her rejection of his offer.

What choice did she have? She could take her daddy's car, only she didn't have the keys, which meant she'd have to go back inside and face him.

Forget that.

"Are you sure?" she asked, refusing to meet his eyes again.

"Come on." He jerked open the door. "My car's around the side here."

Once she was settled in the front seat of his sports utility vehicle, he headed it toward the front gate. "Where to?"

"The police station."

His eyebrows shot up. "Are you serious?"

"Yes."

She felt his gaze linger. "You're not in trouble?"

"Of course not," she said, a trifle breathlessly.

"So who is?"

"It's a long story," she said, staring straight ahead.

"Is there a short version?"

Under any other circumstances, Lindsay might have smiled, but at the moment, no smiles were available. Just overtaxed nerves. She was conscious of everything about him, from his muscled body to the dark stubble on his jaw and chin, to the clean smell of him, as if he'd just gotten out of the shower—which was a good guess, since his hair was still damp.

She had to quell the urge to reach out and touch it to see for herself.

"Lindsay, what's going on?"

The husky note in his voice drew her back around. "It's a woman from the shelter. Beverly's her name. Her husband threatened her and her baby with a butcher knife."

"Sweet Jesus."

"A neighbor agreed to take her to the police station but can't stay there with her."

"Do these women make a habit of calling you?"

"No, but some of my pets there do have my number."

"Do you think that's smart?"

"Probably not, but then, I don't always do what's smart."

He blew out a breath as the air inside seemed to thicken in the silence that followed, as both of them homed in on the far-from-smart thing they had done.

However, when Mitch spoke, his tone was even. "How does your old man feel about this?"

A bitter laugh erupted. "He's livid and doesn't understand." She paused and glanced at Mitch's profile. "I'm guessing you don't, either. Not that it matters."

His jaw tightened visibly, but he had no comeback.

A short time later, Mitch steered the Explorer into the parking lot in front of the station.

"I won't be long," she said, grabbing for the door handle.

"Whoa. I'm coming with you."

"I—"

"That's nonnegotiable."

She shrugged. "Suit yourself."

"I intend to," he countered tersely.

It didn't take Lindsay long to spot Beverly hovering in one of the tiny cubicles, being questioned by an officer. When the woman saw Lindsay, she lurched to her feet. That was when Lindsay stopped, the color draining from her cheeks. A large bandage covered one entire side of the young woman's cheek.

"Oh, Lindsay!" the petite bleach-blonde cried when Lindsay made her way inside the room. "I'm so sorry. I know I promised you I wouldn't go back, but—"

"Shh," Lindsay said in a soothing tone. "Right now, we have to deal with what's happened. Did he hurt the baby?"

She stared at Lindsay through makeup-smeared eyes. "No. I managed to get her away before he could."

"You have to file a complaint this time, Beverly." Lindsay spoke to her as if they were the only two in the room, though she knew both men were taking in every word.

Beverly hung her head. "I know, but—"

"There are no 'buts' any longer," Lindsay said, this time in a no-nonsense tone.

"Okay."

The officer shoved the paperwork across the desk, peered at Lindsay through stern eyes, then at Mitch, who was leaning against the doorjamb. "It's all ready for her to sign."

"Do it, Beverly," Lindsay encouraged. "Not for me, but for you and Shirley."

Beverly leaned over, grabbed a pen and scribbled her name.

Lindsay watched with a soar of relief. "Now we'll get you to a safe house."

The officer stood. "And we'll pick him up."

"Thank you, Officer," Lindsay said. Then, turning

first to Mitch, who nodded, then to Beverly, she added, "Come on, let's get out of here."

An hour later, when Lindsay and Mitch arrived back at the mansion and Mitch killed the engine, darkness was as thick around them as the humidity.

Lindsay wondered whose heart was beating louder, his or hers. But then the harsh chirp of the crickets helped take her mind off them and the cloying confines of the car.

"You're something else, you know that?" Mitch said at last.

For a moment she glowed in his praise. Yet she refused to acknowledge it. "Not really."

"Yeah, really. And you should take the credit."

Lindsay didn't respond, beginning to feel the aftermath of the ordeal set in. When they had taken Beverly to the safe house, the woman had begun to sob uncontrollably, and the bandage on her face had come off in the deluge of tears.

Lindsay had instantly recoiled from the slash on Beverly's cheek. Mitch, on the other hand, had stood silent, though she swore she could feel the heat of his fury.

Now she just felt sad, angry and helpless.

"Look, I should go," she finally said, not looking at Mitch. She felt herself starting to unravel inside, both from his presence and from what she'd just been through.

"Lindsay, we have to talk."

Suddenly her teeth began to chatter, and she couldn't seem to stop them.

"Hey, don't do that."

Before she could react to his huskily spoken

words, he reached for her and pulled her against his hard chest.

"Please," she whispered, peering up at him.

Big mistake.

The moonlight allowed her to see his tormented features before they were blacked out by his head coming down and lips meeting hers. For a moment she clung to him, finding solace in his hot, open-mouth kisses, which made her weak with longing.

It was when his hand found her burgeoning breast and closed around it that she came to her senses and jerked out of his arms. He stared at her with his chest heaving.

"Who was she?" Lindsay asked in a dull tone.

Mitch blinked. "She who?"

"You know," she snapped, trying to rein in her scattered emotions. "That woman who was at your place the other night."

She didn't have any right to ask that. Yes, she did. After all, she had shared his bed. That alone gave her the right, didn't it? No. She had wanted him, and she'd gotten him. That was that.

"How did you know?"

"I saw her."

Mitch bunched his jaw. "She's not important, but if you must know, she's my ex-wife."

"My, how nice that she still comes to visit," Lindsay spat, before opening the door and jumping out.

"Lindsay, come back here!"

She kept on going.

Seventeen

His relationship with Cooper hadn't changed.

Yet Mitch went out of his way to avoid any direct contact with the man except when they met to do what Cooper called "estate planning." What it amounted to was discussing what Mitch and the crew had done, what they were doing, and what they were going to do.

Today was one of those planning session days. And Mitch was not in the mood. But at least he wouldn't have to concern himself with bumping into Lindsay. She had left earlier. He had been on the porch when she'd driven away.

Ah, Lindsay.

It had been two weeks since he'd seen her. Two weeks. He knew exactly. They had been two of the longest weeks of his life, too. He didn't want to think about her. Yet she was all he thought about.

Even now, at three o'clock in the afternoon, when he was winding his way through the grounds, heading for his meeting, Lindsay was with him.

Messing around with her that night in the car had renewed the ache, not only in his loins but inside *him*. He didn't want to feel this way, as if his gut were tied in a permanent knot.

Had he fallen in love?

That thought stopped him in his tracks. No! He'd been bitten by that bug once, and that was enough. Besides, what had happened between him and Lindsay was based on lust. It had started with that, and that was the way it would end—if it hadn't already.

Mitch winced at the thought. Deep in his gut, he didn't want their affair to be over. He hadn't had his fill of her yet. But would he ever? He doubted it. Sweat popped out on his face.

For him, Lindsay had become lethal, as lethal as cocaine. He had never used any drugs, but if getting high on a controlled substance was anything like being inside Lindsay's moist, heated center, then no wonder people got hooked. He was in danger of overdosing.

Mitch winced again, realizing that was exactly what he wanted to have happen. And that was why he was beating up on himself until he was black and blue inside.

He had to make a decision, and soon. He couldn't have his cake and eat it, too. But that was exactly what he wanted. He wanted to make love to her *and* keep his job.

Meanwhile, he had to try to find a livable midpoint. He had to stop constantly thinking about her, wanting her. She was messing with his mind to such an extent that he walked around in heat.

This afternoon was no exception.

His thoughts had played havoc with his body. Ah, to hell with it, he told himself. To hell with *her*. She wasn't worth getting himself in such a stew over, nor was she worth getting fired over. And if her old man ever found out, Mitch would definitely be out on his ass.

Cooper wouldn't find out.

Having come to that conclusion, Mitch felt better, and even managed to put some spring in his step as he neared the back door of the house. And what a house it was, too. Nestled among thirty acres of prime land, it was country living at its finest, only it wasn't in the country. The Newman place was just minutes from a major interstate.

The entire parcel was mind-boggling. That had been his first reaction when he'd interviewed for the job. The Tara-style house was awesome in its grandeur, and reeked of both old and new money.

Still, he wouldn't want to live behind those walls. Having money and prestige carried a high price tag— one he wasn't willing to pay. Nope. He liked being his own man, doing his own thing.

Shoving his thoughts aside, Mitch knocked on the door.

Dolly opened it, a wide grin on her face. "It's about time you got yourself back here," she said, her eyes flashing.

Dolly liked him. She had from day one on the job. The feeling was mutual. "Ah, so you've been missing me, huh?"

"I didn't say that."

Mitch chuckled. "Yeah, you did."

Her features puckered, but that glint remained in her eyes. "Are you here to see Mr. Cooper?"

"Yep."

"I'll have some hot tea cakes for you when you get through."

"A woman after my own heart." Mitch's grin widened. "How 'bout us running off and getting married?"

Dolly tipped her chin. "Not today. I'm too busy."

Mitch laughed as he turned and made his way toward the study. He knocked, then waited for the summons.

Thirty minutes later, Mitch was still there, facing his boss across his desk, sipping on a cup of chicory coffee that Dolly had brought them.

Cooper appeared the picture of health and in total control of himself and everything around him. Except me, Mitch thought. He didn't owe the doctor anything but an honest day's work for an honest day's pay.

"So are we together on everything that affects the grounds?" Cooper asked.

"One hundred percent."

"I'll try and get out to the greenhouse first thing in the morning."

Mitch nodded. "Good. If there are no changes, then we can get that wrapped up." He drained his cup and sat it back on the silver tray. "If there's nothing else…"

"There is."

Mitch cocked an eyebrow. "I'm listening."

"How are your carpentry skills?"

Mitch frowned. "The greenhouse should speak for that. After all, I designed it, and I've hammered my fair share of the nails."

"That's nothing compared to what I have in mind."

For some reason Mitch couldn't pinpoint, he felt

uneasy. So instead of commenting, he remained silent and waited for Cooper to tell him what was on his mind.

"I would like to remodel a portion of the south side of the house, making it into an apartment. Think that can be done?"

"Off the top of my head, I can't say. I'd have to take a look."

"You do that, then we'll talk some more."

Mitch got to his feet, wondering what that was all about.

As if Cooper could read Mitch's mind, he added, "In anticipation of my daughter's marriage, I want the apartment to be ready."

Mitch managed not to flinch outwardly, but inside, that knot in his stomach coiled tighter.

Lindsay getting married? Since the fuck when?

"Is that about to happen?" Somehow he managed to ask the question, though he sounded hoarse, as if he'd suddenly developed a sore throat.

"Yes. Hopefully in the near future."

"I see."

"Oh, by the way, have I told you how pleased I am with your work?"

Apparently this man was as complex as his daughter—maybe more so, if that was possible. "That's good to know," Mitch said, forcing his mind back on track.

"Therefore I'm giving you a healthy raise."

Mitch tried to look grateful, when, in fact, he was green with jealousy inside. Over his dead body would Lindsay marry someone else. "Uh, thanks. Thanks a lot."

"You're welcome. I'll see you in the morning."

Mitch nodded, then strode out of the room, closing the door behind him. But that was as far as he got. Since no one was around, he stopped for the sole purpose of regrouping.

It was while he was jerking himself back together that he heard the voice. It was coming from the library that was around the corner from the study, though still within hearing distance.

The voice was that of a man, and though he couldn't be sure without checking, Mitch thought it sounded like Tim Newman. Ordinarily, he wouldn't have given the fact that son was visiting father and using the phone a second thought, except for what he heard.

As if his feet were on a mission all their own, Mitch stepped closer to the door of the library, which was ajar. He peered inside and saw that it was indeed Tim whose back was to the door. Mitch remained in the shadows and unabashedly listened to the one-sided conversation.

"We had a deal."

Silence.

"The shipment should've already been here," Tim said in a hissing tone. "Mexico's not that far away."

Another silence.

"Well, if you don't get your ass in gear and deliver, I'll find me another supplier."

With that, Tim slammed down the receiver.

Mitch frowned. Sonny boy was sweating bullets over something—something that had an illegal ring to it.

Mitch turned quickly and made his way toward the

kitchen, the smell of fresh-made cookies drawing him.

However, it wasn't eating cookies that was on his mind, but that disturbing conversation. *Mexico. Shipments.* Prescriptions. Money. None of that was to his liking, especially when it was obvious that Dr. Tim Newman had some kind of scheme going.

So what if he did? That wasn't Mitch's concern. He didn't give a damn what the young Dr. Newman was up to. He no longer had to be; that was the beauty of it.

"I have you a tin of cookies ready."

Dolly's voice pulled him up short and forced him to refocus. He grinned, grabbed the tin, planted a kiss on her cheek, then winked. "Let me know when you're ready to run away."

"You best go on and get outta here, Mr. Mitch, before you get into trouble."

Truer words were never spoken, Mitch thought as he made his way back to his quarters. The whole family was bad news.

If he were smart, he would indeed run from this place, as fast and as far as he could go.

Eighteen

Lindsay stared at the cloud-free azure sky. In fact, as far as the eye could see, there was not one blemish on that blue expanse. Such perfection. And on the earth, too, she reminded herself, watching the water wind its way through the creek, listening to its sound, a cadence that would normally have made her want to tap her foot.

But Lindsay wasn't in the mood for tapping her feet. She was in one of her funks. Earlier she'd had Hector saddle her horse Belle, and she had ridden here, to her favorite hideaway on the estate—the place where she'd come after she'd found her mother.

Even though a lot of the memories associated with this secluded area were bad, there were also many good ones. Today the good outweighed the bad. From where she sat at the foot of a huge oak tree draped with moss, Lindsay glanced over at Belle, who was shaking her mane, trying to get rid of a bothersome fly.

"Hang in there, girl," she said with a forlorn smile.

Belle turned and stared at her with those big, dark

eyes, then nodded her head, as if she knew exactly what Lindsay had said.

Lindsay's lips flexed into a real smile, but it was short-lived. A shuddering sigh followed. She was depressed, and that was what frightened her. She'd been so frightened that she'd visited her psychiatrist, Dr. Milbrook. Usually those visits refreshed her mentally, steering her back on track.

Only not today.

She was at fault, not him. He had tried to get her to open up, to tell him what was on her mind, but she couldn't let it go, couldn't uncork her anxieties.

"Lindsay, talk to me."

She had stared at the middle-aged man with his thinning blond hair, rimless glasses and gentle voice, who had been so kind and patient with her through the tough years, and suddenly realized she didn't know what to say to him.

"I'm waiting," he pressed, still in his gentle tone.

"Somehow I can't seem to find the words," she admitted, clearly frustrated.

"Then let me help you." He paused. "Isn't that why you're here?"

"Yes, but—" Lindsay broke off, casting him a guilty look.

Dr. Milbrook sighed. "You know, Lindsay, it's all right if you don't want to confide in me. I understand. But please, don't gnaw on what's bothering you too long before you spit it out."

"I hate being depressed," Lindsay said bleakly. "When it happens, I'm afraid of…"

"Afraid of what?"

He knew, of course. But part of her therapy was telling him, purging her mind and body of those fears. "Of ending up like Mother."

"You know that's not going to happen."

"Do I?"

"Yes. *You're* not going to let yourself. You're strong and healthy now, Lindsay. You have to believe in that and in yourself."

"I had one of those nightmares." She shivered. "Blood was everywhere again."

"Would it help to talk about it?"

"No, because nothing's changed."

"What triggered it?"

Lindsay sighed inwardly. She couldn't hide anything from him. But then, she guessed that was good. "I...I definitely can't talk about that right now."

"All right, Lindsay. When you can, I'll listen. Meanwhile, if you get overwhelmed, you can always go back on your medication."

Lindsay gave her head a savage shake. "No. I don't want to do that."

"I don't want you to, either. So keep reminding yourself that you're in complete charge of your life for the first time in years. Then rejoice in that assurance."

Now, as Lindsay recalled that conversation and continued to perspire in what was left of the late-afternoon sunlight, she wished his words were true. But they weren't. She didn't feel in charge of anything, especially her emotions.

Since she had met Mitch and made love to him, she'd been a mess. She wished she could have told

Dr. Milbrook about him, but she couldn't. And the frustrating part was that she didn't know why.

"Oh, Belle, what am I going to do?"

The mare swished her tail, then nodded her head.

Lindsay smiled. "I know. Neither of us has the answer."

She closed her eyes for a long moment, then opened them, peered at her watch and gave a start. Daddy's dinner party—it was tonight. Ugh. She had forgotten about that, since it was such a small gathering, and she hadn't had much to do except take care of the menu and flowers.

And show up, which was the part she didn't like. Still, she knew she had no choice. Forcing herself upright, Lindsay walked to Belle, grabbed the saddle horn and stepped in the stirrup, only to have the entire rigging slide sideways, taking her with it.

"Ouch!" she yelped as her backside landed on the ground.

"Need any help?"

Mitch?

Scrambling to her feet, Lindsay whirled and faced the direction of the voice, her fingers clenched in a tight ball. Sure enough, her mind hadn't been playing tricks on her. Mitch was in front of her, in the flesh, sitting tall in the saddle.

She despised the way her heart kicked at the mere sight of him. But then, it wasn't just her heart that was affected. Her knees were weak, her hands were clammy, and adrenaline was charging through her.

"What's the deal?" she asked, squinting up at

him. "You seem to know whenever I'm in trouble, and show up."

He dismounted, then strode toward her, a grin on his lips. Or was it a smirk?

"The other night I just happened along," he said in that drawling voice that was so very *his,* and so very sexy, too.

"And today?"

"I deliberately followed you."

She turned away from the glint in his eyes. Nonetheless, she couldn't move. She felt paralyzed as he strode toward her with his easy gait. He had on a pair of jeans and a yellow short-sleeve shirt, both equally worn. Through the thin material, she could see his muscles, almost feel their strength.

There was something so natural, so *sensual,* about him that it made her want to throw caution to the wind and leap into his arms. That was when it hit her. She wanted to have sex with him again with an intensity that shook her to the foundation of her being.

But that was wrong, for the right reason. This "thing" between them was just that—sex. She didn't want someone to screw; she wanted someone to love.

"I'm...okay," she said in a halting voice. "I don't need any help."

He glanced at the saddle, which was still askew, then back at her, one eyebrow raised. "I reckon Belle might think differently."

A smile broke through, answering his. "You reckon?"

He laughed out loud, then stared at her long

enough to send her heat level to scalding before he crossed to the animal and repaired the damage.

"Who saddled her?" he asked, easing his head and body back around.

"Hector."

"You best tell him about this."

"Uh…I will."

"So this is your getaway," he said in a husky tone, though there was a teasing edge to it.

"How did you know?"

He shrugged, but his eyes darkened. "What are you getting away from?"

"You."

She hadn't meant to say that. The tiny word had simply slipped through her lips as if it had to be said.

"Why?" he almost choked, moving to stand in front of her, shielding her eyes from the remaining sunlight.

"Mitch…"

"Mitch…what?" he whispered, reaching and pushing an errant strand of her hair behind one ear, then cradling the back of her neck with his big, callused hand.

She wet her lips. "We can't keep on like this."

"Can you stop?"

"No."

"Neither can I."

"But it's a road going nowhere," she whispered, gazing up at him, knowing that her tormented feelings were there, mirrored in her eyes for him to see.

"I know," he muttered in an agonized voice. "But

you're making me crazy. I can't stop thinking about you. I can't stop wanting you.''

''Oh, Mitch,'' she said hoarsely.

He sank his lips onto hers, hot, hard and deep, while grasping her shoulders and urging her down until their knees were nestled in the velvet-soft grass.

At the contact, Lindsay pulled back and stared into his deeply glazed eyes. ''This—''

Groaning, he covered her mouth again, his kiss hotter and wetter than before. Before she realized what was happening, they were lying on the grass, side by side.

With unwavering eyes, he shoved her T-shirt up and unclasped her bra. A sob tore at her throat as her breasts spilled into his face.

Groaning again, he moved his mouth to each of her nipples in turn, while his hands removed her jeans. Once that was done, he unzipped his, then lifted her top leg over his hip.

''Oh, yes,'' she panted, digging her nails into his shoulders. He slid his hand between her legs, easing a finger inside her. She bucked, clinging to him that much more tightly.

''I wanted to make sure you were ready,'' he rasped.

Before she could so much as whimper a reply, he thrust inside her, where he pounded with the force of a gentle jackhammer.

It was over just as quickly as it had begun. Wrung out from hard, sharp orgasms, they clung to one other for a long time, their clammy bodies stuck together.

Finally Mitch pushed her slightly away from him

and righted her clothes. Then they got to their feet. Lindsay watched him re-zip his fly, then lifted her eyes to his.

"I'm addicted to you, Lindsay Newman," he said in an unnatural voice.

"I'm on the same drug," she admitted, her voice duplicating his.

"I hope I didn't hurt you."

She colored. "You didn't."

"Your breast might be burned." He rubbed his scratchy jaw and chin. "I need a shave."

Her color deepened. "I'll—they'll be fine."

"How 'bout you?"

"Don't ask me that now, please."

"I promise you the next time will be slow and easy."

Her insides turned over. "Are you sure there will be a next time?"

"Won't there?"

She opened her mouth but nothing came out, so she slammed it shut.

"Oh, Lindsay, Lindsay." He pulled her against his chest and held her.

For a moment she was content to remain there, listening to their hearts beating as one, obliterating the sound of the babbling creek.

Finally she shifted out of those strong arms, but she met his gaze. "Daddy must never find out about us."

Mitch's jaw tightened. "For my sake—or yours?"

"For both our sakes."

"Whatever. It's your call."

She turned, walked to her horse, then climbed into the saddle.

"I want to see you again," he said, peering up at her. "And soon, too."

She looked down at him, then nudged Belle in the side and rode off, her heart beating faster than the horse's hooves.

Nineteen

As usual, Mary Jane was running behind schedule.

Lindsay glanced at her watch, then back at the children playing in the park across the street. Their laughter filled the air, along with the chirping of birds in a nearby tree and the gentle sighing of the summer breeze.

It was too lovely a day to waste sitting in the car, Lindsay told herself, suddenly giving in to a spontaneous thought. Why not get out and wait for Mary Jane on the park bench that seemed to beckon her?

Moments later that gentle breeze was caressing her cheeks, which lacked color despite the humidity and heat. Although she tried to concentrate on watching the children ride the merry-go-round—their laughter louder than ever—she couldn't.

Her stomach was a mass of nerves. But she wouldn't panic. Yet when she thought of Mitch's reaction... Stop it! Don't go there. Not yet, anyway. Not until she knew for sure.

Lindsay peered at her watch again, her stomach continuing to rebel, to let her know that it was there. Her daddy thought she was going to see her shrink.

Cooper had confronted her first thing that morning

at the breakfast table. "Something's wrong with you, Lindsay, and I want to know what it is."

"I'm all right, Daddy," she said hesitantly.

"Ever since that party, two weeks ago now, you've been walking around like you're in a daze."

"Have I?"

Cooper's mouth hardened. "You know you have. I presume you're still seeing Harvey."

"Of course I am."

"Well, apparently you're not seeing him enough. I suggest you go today."

"Daddy—"

"Don't 'Daddy' me. I know what's best for you."

"I'm just working really hard." That was an inflammatory thing to have said; she knew that the second after she'd uttered the words.

"On that goddamn project that's a one-way street going nowhere."

Lindsay chewed her lower lip. "It's important to me. I wish you'd be more understanding."

"And I wish you'd just marry Peter and settle down. If you had a husband and children to attend to, you wouldn't—"

Lindsay stood abruptly, her breakfast practically untouched. "Don't start, Daddy."

"I've already started."

Lindsay gave him a perplexed look. It wasn't so much what he said but how he said it that gave her pause. "Started what?"

"Or at least I'm headed in that direction," Cooper added, seemingly more to himself than to her.

"What are you talking about?" She didn't bother to mask her impatience.

"The south wing. I'm going to have it remodeled, made into separate living quarters." He paused, pinning her with a direct look.

Warning bells went off inside Lindsay's head. She wanted to give in to the weakness in her legs; she feared they wouldn't support her much longer. But she wanted to escape more, unable to bear being in the same room with Cooper at that precise moment.

"If it's for Peter and me, you're wasting your time."

Cooper's eyes hardened to match his mouth. "I don't see it that way. I talked with Mitch—"

"Mitch!"

She cried his name before she thought.

Cooper raised his eyebrows, then said in a gruff voice, "Yes, Mitch. Mitch Rawlins. He's our estate manager, in case you didn't know."

Lindsay had to turn away. She didn't dare chance his reading the thoughts that were raging inside her. Her eyes were often a dead giveaway.

"When...when did you talk to him about this?"

Cooper shrugged. "The day of the party. But what difference does it make?"

"Did you tell him why?"

"What if I did?" Cooper's expression was so intense that his wiry eyebrows protruded over his eyes like tiny mustaches. "Who the hell cares what he thinks?"

Me.

"He's an employee, for God's sake. He's here to do what he's told, and that's all."

"Look, Daddy, I have to run. I have an appointment."

"But you haven't finished your breakfast."

"I know. See you later."

"Go see Harvey," he said to her back. "I'll be waiting for a report."

He would still be waiting this time tomorrow, and the next day, Lindsay told herself, pulling her mind off that conversation and back to her present dilemma. Where was her friend? It wasn't that she was going to be late for the appointment. She wasn't; she had plenty of time. She was just anxious to talk to Mary Jane.

"Hey, did you give up on me?"

Lindsay swung around. "Where did you come from? I've been watching for you."

"I'm parked a few cars down from you. I just happened to glance in the direction of the park and saw you."

"Thanks for coming." Lindsay watched as Mary Jane plopped down beside her on the bench. "Did you have any trouble getting off?"

"Nah. Like I told you before, those yahoos better not say too much to me, as much free overtime as I give them."

Lindsay squeezed Mary Jane's hand, and her lower lip trembled.

Mary Jane's forehead wrinkled with concern. "Hey, what's up? You okay?"

"No, I don't think I am."

"Are you sick? I mean—" Mary Jane broke off. "After all, we're forty minutes outside of town, at a doctor's office. Hell, you're scaring me."

"I'm not sick, or at least not in the way you

mean.'' Lindsay paused, then stared into space. ''I think I'm pregnant.''

There, she'd said it—the word she hadn't been able to say even to herself.

Mary Jane gasped. ''Good Lord, Lindsay! Surely you're jerking my chain.''

''You know better than that,'' Lindsay muttered.

Mary Jane had a worried look on her face. ''Peter?''

''No.''

''No?''

Silence beat around them.

''Then who?'' Mary Jane sputtered, her eyes wide and questioning. ''Tell me it's not *him*. Tell me it's not that Mitch character.''

''I can't tell you that. If I'm pregnant, then it's his.''

''Oh, Lordy, Lindsay, I can't believe this.''

''Me, either.''

''What on earth were you thinking about?''

Lindsay's lips quirked. ''That's my problem. When I'm around him, I don't think. At least, not straight.''

''Whoa, this is some more heavy stuff,'' Mary Jane said in a stricken voice.

''Tell me about it.''

Suddenly Mary Jane brightened. ''Maybe you're not pregnant. Maybe your system's just upset.''

''Maybe the home test I took was defective, too,'' Lindsay countered in a flat tone.

''You tested yourself?''

''Yes.''

''Oh, my.''

Lindsay heaved a deep sigh. "I can't even think about it without—"

"Then don't," Mary Jane interrupted, slinging an arm around Lindsay's shoulders. "Don't do this to yourself—not until you know for sure. So let's go get the final verdict, then we'll talk some more."

Lindsay rose and eyed the building across the street. It housed doctors, lawyers and sundry other professionals. She had chosen this particular doctor after having overheard a friend talk about him and how good he was. An added bonus was that he was out of Garnet proper. Hopefully he was far *enough* away, but she doubted it.

Doctors in a surrounding area tended to know each other and stick together like glue. Still, she could hope. And really, when it came down to it, she shouldn't have to worry, because of patient-doctor confidentiality.

"Keep your chin up, you hear?" Mary Jane demanded once they had reached the waiting room and Lindsay's name was called. "I'll keep my fingers crossed."

Lindsay nodded her thanks, her throat too full to respond verbally.

An hour later, Lindsay was looking at Mary Jane across the table in a coffee shop. Both were silent as they sipped on their drinks. Actually, Lindsay was too sick to say anything. It was an effort to get the hot liquid down.

"So you're going to have a baby, kiddo," Mary Jane said, blowing out her breath.

"It seems that way," Lindsay responded in a dazed voice.

"Hey, you gotta buck up. It's not the end of the world, you know."

"That's easy for you to say."

Lindsay felt numb. Dr. Abe Mason had been one of the nicest, kindest doctors she'd ever been to. Still, she'd only gone through the motions of first the conference, then the examination.

"You were on target, Ms. Newman," he'd said. "You're definitely pregnant."

You're definitely pregnant. You're definitely pregnant. You're definitely pregnant. Those words kept playing over and over in her mind, until she thought she might actually lose what little mind she had left.

"Come on, stop beating yourself black and blue."

"If you were in my place, what would you do?"

"Beat myself black and blue," Mary Jane admitted without hesitation. Then she smiled fleetingly. "Just kidding."

"No, you weren't."

"Look, Lindsay, you have choices. I won't pretend to know exactly what's churning inside you right now, but—"

"It's fear, M.J.," Lindsay cut in. "Bone-chilling fear."

"Under the circumstances, you wouldn't be human if you weren't afraid." Mary Jane paused. "Look, tell me to go butt a stump if I'm getting too far out of line here, but when did you and Mitch's relationship heat up to such a degree?"

"Almost from day one."

"You mean you actually—" Mary Jane, who was

never at a loss for words, seemed shocked; her sentence ended in a sputter.

Lindsay didn't pretend to misunderstand her, though she was red-faced when she said in a hushed tone, "Of course not, silly. However, it wasn't long afterward."

"Jeez, he must have something *really* special to have sucked you in so deeply and so quickly."

"I told you he was special, and in so many ways, too."

"For heaven's sake, Lindsay, he's just a gardener."

"And what's wrong with that?" Lindsay's tone had a sudden bite to it.

"Hell's bells, you know the answer to that. Cooper's going to shit a brick when he finds out."

Lindsay shivered visibly. "I can't even think about that."

A short silence followed her words, during which she tried to drink more of her coffee. She couldn't. Even the smell turned her stomach.

"So are you going to tell him?"

"I don't know." Lindsay's voice faltered. "I haven't thought that far ahead."

"Which means you don't know what you're going to do about the baby, right?" Mary Jane asked.

Lindsay's lower lip trembled again. "I can't begin to think straight. I'm still in shock."

"If you were going to mess around, why didn't you use something?"

Mary Jane's blunt question took Lindsay aback for a second. "I don't have an excuse. It just happened so fast."

"I bet anything Mitch thought you were on the pill—that you and Peter were getting it on."

"Well, we weren't."

"Ever? You mean you haven't slept with Peter?"

"No, I have not."

"Well, that shows you have *some* sense, anyway."

Lindsay gave her an exasperated look.

"What about Mitch? When are you going to tell him?"

"I don't know, especially after the stunt Daddy pulled." Lindsay explained about the remodeling project.

"What a mess. No telling what Mitch is thinking."

"I can't bear to think about that," Lindsay said in a small, trembling voice.

Mary Jane reached out and touched her arm. "Look at me. It's going to be all right. Like I said earlier, you have choices. And you know what they are. And you have time to make them. So stop beating up on yourself."

"Aren't you going to ask if I love him?"

"Do you?"

"I don't know," Lindsay wailed. "What I do know is that I can't stay away from him."

Mary Jane shrugged. "Then don't."

"Thanks, but that's not what I needed to hear."

"Yes, it is. That's exactly what you *wanted* to hear, anyway. I've never seen you like this, Lindsay. Never seen you throw caution to the wind and go with your feelings, at least not since your breakdown. And it's not a bad thing."

"Yes, it is, Mary Jane. But I've gotten myself into this mess, and only I can get myself out."

"Well, I'm not going anywhere. Remember that. Whatever you decide, I'll support you."

Lindsay stood. "I'm going to hold you to that."

When she walked into the mansion a little while later, Cooper was still there. Lindsay's steps faltered, as did her heart. He was on the porch, drinking a glass of iced tea. She had assumed—or rather, hoped—he would be playing golf with some of his cronies.

"So did you see Milbrook?" he asked without preamble.

She ignored his question. "I figured you'd be on the course. Are you feeling okay?"

"I'm fine. I wish you'd stop fretting about me. Anyhow, I had lunch with your brother. That's why I didn't play."

"Is Tim okay?"

"He's fine," Cooper said with impatience. "So back to my question. Did you see Harvey?"

"No."

"Dammit, Lindsay. You're depressed again. Even if you can't see it, I can."

"What I am, Daddy, is pregnant."

Sudden silence drummed around them. Then Cooper said in a strained voice, "What the hell kind of sick game are you playing?"

"It's no game," Lindsay replied, her own voice strained to the hilt. "It's the unvarnished truth."

"I wanted you to have a baby. But not before you got married."

"I know you're upset."

"Upset!" He laughed a harsh laugh. "That's just the tip of the iceberg. This is not the way the Newmans do things."

"I don't suppose it is," Lindsay said softly, sinking down into the nearest chair, her stomach as trembly as her limbs.

"I'm assuming the baby is Peter's. And while I'm by no means happy that you didn't wait, at least you won't have an excuse for not marrying him now."

"Daddy—"

He kept on as if she hadn't spoken. "I'll get Mitch going on plans for the south wing, while you, young lady, take care of wedding plans. No one will have to know that—"

"There's not going to be a wedding, Daddy."

He whipped his head around, his nostrils flaring. "Excuse me?"

The only reason she repeated what she'd said was to buy more time. She knew that he'd heard her. "Nothing has changed on that score. I'm not going to marry Peter."

"But that makes no sense."

"Yes it does—because the baby isn't his."

She might as well have dropped a grenade in the room and been done with it. Cooper's jaw dropped. "Not his. Then who—" He stopped as if he'd run out of both words and the energy to say them.

Sudden concern shot through Lindsay. Had she put undue strain on his heart by blurting out her news? Perhaps. But no matter when or how she'd told him, he would have reacted in the same irrational manner.

Still, she could have soft-pedaled it more, but she was mentally hemorrhaging herself.

"I'm not going to tell you who the father is."

Lindsay watched color inch its way into his face until it was bloodred. He was enraged, she knew. Another surge of fear went though her while she stilled herself against what she figured would be his next attack—a demand that she have an abortion.

"Fine. Don't tell me. I really don't want to know, and it really doesn't matter."

Lindsay was stunned. "I'm grateful and relieved you feel that way," she finally managed to say.

Cooper held up his hand. "Regardless of who the father is, Peter will marry you, anyway."

Twenty

He would quit.

Mitch scowled into an early morning sky that only hinted that dawn was soon to follow. He had already consumed several cups of coffee, more than his usual. If he didn't watch it, he would be wilder than a buck.

His scowl deepened. Hell, who was he trying to kid? He was already wild—wild about Lindsay Newman. He finished the remainder of the strong liquid, then slammed the cup down on the table nearest him.

Somehow he had to get his act together. But unless he hauled ass out of Garnet, he didn't foresee that happening. With each passing day, his black mood worsened. That wasn't going to improve anytime time soon, either—not with Lindsay hot and heavy on his mind.

It would be a cold day in hell, though, before he lifted a hand to build a cozy nest for her and another man to live in. His gut roiled. No way. He should just leave.

He couldn't. Lindsay might as well have him chained by the ankles.

Even so, he clung desperately to the hope that what he felt for her was lust and not love.

He didn't want to love her. Just the thought was painful. Yet he would like nothing better than to awaken every morning with her by his side, with him embedded inside her, hearing her panting moans as she came.

He thought about her every waking minute of the day, like some pimple-faced high school chump pining over the head cheerleader. But he was no high school chump; he was a grown man, for chrissake!

Still, he was addicted to her and couldn't stand the thought of leaving her or having someone else touch her. He groaned, feeling the pinch of his zipper.

So what was the solution?

As long as she was willing to meet him whenever and wherever, he wasn't going to rock the boat. If her old man ever found out—hell, Mitch wasn't going to think about that, either. He would wait and cross that bridge when and if he had to.

Meanwhile, he would continue to do what he'd always done, and that was work like a field hand and mind his own business.

Mitch frowned, his thoughts suddenly jumping back to the phone conversation he'd overheard between Tim and some unknown person. Despite his efforts not to let it bother him, it did. But he hadn't changed his intentions. He refused to get involved.

What would meddling accomplish, anyway? Nothing good, that was for sure. It was a given that Lindsay wouldn't side with him. Tim was her brother, and while she might admit his faults, she would never believe he was involved in anything shady or illegal.

And maybe he wasn't, Mitch reminded himself

grimly. So back off, his gut instinct told him. Back off and concentrate on Lindsay. She alone was more than enough for any man to handle.

With that in mind, Mitch stamped out into the breaking dawn.

"And how are you this evening, Peter?"

Peter shrugged. "I could be better."

Cooper pointed to the most comfortable chair in the library. "I think your luck's about to change. But first, have a seat, and I'll fix you a drink."

"Bourbon and Coke."

"I remember," Cooper said, crossing to a small bar in the corner of the room.

A few minutes later, both men had drinks in hand and were facing each other. "Thanks for having me to dinner," Peter said, then downed one third of his drink in one swallow.

Cooper's facial expression registered his disapproval, as did his words. "Hey, son, take it easy. At this rate, you'll be loaded before dinner."

"Sorry," Peter muttered, setting down his glass. "It's just that I'm frustrated as hell. Lately, I can't even seem to get on the playing field with Lindsay, much less to first base."

"There's a reason for that." Cooper kept his voice as level as possible, realizing he was about to step on ice-covered ground. He had to tread with extreme care.

"I'm assuming you're going to tell me what that reason is." Peter's expression was as sullen as his tone.

"All in good time," Cooper said. "You must

learn to be patient, my friend. Good things come to those who wait."

If anything, Peter looked more sullen, but he didn't argue. Cooper knew he should stop delaying what had to be said, but this was such a touchy situation.

"Where's Lindsay?" Peter asked into the short silence.

"She'll be down shortly."

Peter reached for his glass and took another healthy swallow. "She does know I'm dining with y'all, right?"

"She's looking forward to it," Cooper lied smoothly.

Peter didn't respond, though Cooper wasn't sure if Peter believed him or not. But it didn't matter. Since push had come to shove, he *would* have his way where both Lindsay and Peter were concerned.

"I'm about to have the south wing remodeled."

Peter's brows shot up. "Is that what you were going to tell me?"

"It's related."

"How does that affect me? If you'll pardon my bluntness, I don't give a damn about anything that doesn't."

"I have no problem with that. After all, we have a deal."

"A deal that your daughter's attitude is putting in serious jeopardy."

"Again, patience."

Peter smirked openly. "Right."

"The south wing is where you and Lindsay will live after you're married."

Peter's face brightened. "So you've finally talked some sense into her."

"Well," Cooper hedged, "not exactly."

Peter's expression turned petulant again.

"Can you handle the fact that she's pregnant?"

Peter's mouth flopped open. *"What?"*

Good thing the man didn't have dentures, Cooper thought inanely, or they would have fallen out. "You heard me."

Peter shook his head, looking like he'd been sucker punched.

"It's going to be all right," Cooper said with conviction. "All is not lost."

"Surely you don't expect—"

"I sure as hell do," Cooper lashed back in a deadly but controlled tone.

"A bastard baby was not part of the deal," Peter retorted, the color gradually returning to his face.

"You keep your cool, and we'll both get what we want."

Peter shrugged. "As long as *I* get what I want, then what the hell? I'm easy."

Lindsay could have cheerfully throttled her daddy.

He had pulled another of his stunts and asked Peter to dinner. She could have pitched a hissy fit and refused to join them, but she chose not to, though she knew exactly what Cooper was up to.

He remained diligent in his efforts to pawn her off on Peter, more so now than ever.

She hadn't seen much of him following the conversation during which she'd blurted out that she was pregnant. She knew he hadn't kept silent and left her alone out of respect for her. This latest antic proved that. It also proved she couldn't trust him.

God, but he was one hardheaded man.

It had been a week since she'd found out about the baby. The better part of that week she'd been on the settee in her room battling extreme nausea. While being pregnant accounted for most of her illness, it hadn't accounted for all of it.

She hadn't been able to stop thinking about Mitch and the fact that she was carrying his child.

A baby.

Growing inside her.

The doctor said so, though she saw no visible proof. Countless times, she had peered at her stomach in the mirror, touched it, massaged it, trying to convince *herself*.

A miracle? Or a curse?

She had wept when she'd asked those questions— questions to which she had no answers. In order to hold on to her sanity, she had forced her mind onto her women's project by making phone calls, drawing up plans, whatever she could think to do.

And now, the one evening when she felt like having a decent meal, her daddy sprang Peter on her and ruined it.

"How 'bout a stroll in the garden?" Peter asked, once dinner was over and coffee had been served.

Lindsay shook her head. "I don't think—"

"I think that's a great idea," Cooper chimed in, his tone robust and cheerful. "I'll be in the parlor. You can join me there later."

Why not? Lindsay thought. This was an opportunity for her to get rid of Peter once and for all, despite Cooper's continuing efforts to the contrary.

"I'm ready when you are," Lindsay said, maintaining her aloof politeness.

They walked in silence through the breezy night air until they reached the arbor. "You want to sit down?" Peter asked.

"No, I'd rather walk through the garden."

"Fine."

They hadn't gone far when she saw *him.* Mitch was on his porch, his foot propped on the railing, a can of beer in his hand.

She came to an abrupt halt, feeling her heart plummet to her toes.

"What's wrong?" Peter demanded, cutting her a sharp look.

"Uh, nothing." Lindsay forced herself to keep on walking. She knew Mitch had spotted them, as well. Something had to give or she was going to disintegrate on the spot.

"Look, Lindsay, I know this is awkward, especially under the circumstances."

"What circumstances?" she asked, that aloofness still present.

"Cooper told me you're pregnant."

Fury mixed with pain boiled up inside her and threatened to erupt. How could Cooper betray her like this? "Don't worry, Peter, you're off the hook, despite Daddy and whatever he might've told you."

Even though she couldn't see him all that clearly, she knew his face was suffused with color.

"What if I don't want to be off the hook?"

Lindsay threw him a startled look. "You can't be serious."

"Oh, don't misunderstand. I'm not happy that you're pregnant." He laughed bitterly. "Actually, that's a gross understatement. Still, I'm willing to marry you."

"Thanks, but no thanks," she said, further enraged.

"Why not?" he snapped.

"That question doesn't even deserve an answer," she snapped back. "I've never wanted to marry you, Peter, and you know that."

"I sure as hell didn't know that. I just thought you were playing hard to get."

"Well then, you're a bigger fool than I thought."

His features twisted. "Who's the father? Who've you been screwing behind my back?"

Lindsay stopped and faced him, her eyes sparking. "That's none of your business."

"It damn sure is my business. Your daddy made it so."

"What does that remark mean?"

"You'll have to ask Daddy," Peter said, his tone rich in sarcasm.

"Go to hell!"

She turned to walk off, only to have him clamp down on her shoulder and swing her back around. "Now, you see here, you little bitch!"

"Get your hands off me!" Lindsay cried, struggling out of his grip.

"I suggest you do what the lady said."

At the sound of Mitch's rough but steady voice, Lindsay went weak with relief. Not that she thought

Peter would ever harm her, but, Mitch's presence spared her further indignity.

"Who the hell are you?" Peter demanded, glaring at Mitch.

"Someone who's about to teach you a lesson."

"In another lifetime, maybe," Peter sneered.

Mitch's features didn't change one iota, yet Lindsay knew Peter had said the wrong thing. She stepped forward, glancing back and forth between the two men. "Mitch—"

Before Lindsay could finish her sentence, Peter spat, "Hey, bubba, go fuck yourself!"

"I don't think so," Mitch said, his right hand shooting out and delivering a right upper-cut to Peter's jaw, coldcocking him.

Peter hit the ground with a *thud*.

Lindsay stood rooted to the spot and stared at Mitch, too stunned to move.

Twenty-One

Peter scrambled to his feet, one hand on the spot that Mitch had crunched with his fist. "Why, you bastard! I'll have your ass for this."

"Peter, please, leave it be," Lindsay pleaded, her voice terse but shaky as her eyes darted back toward the house. Common sense told her that Cooper couldn't see or hear what was going on. Still, she couldn't stop herself from imagining the worst-case scenario.

The moon lit Peter's stark features, allowing her to see the glare that shone out of his eyes. "Now why would I leave it be?" he demanded. "What's this brute to you?"

"Peter, just go home," Lindsay continued to plead.

"You'd best do what the lady says, Ballinger."

Peter transferred his hostile glare back to Mitch. "I don't know who the fuck you are, or how you fit into anything, but you'll be sorry you ever laid a hand on me."

Mitch took two quick strides, putting him once again in front of Peter, who instinctively backed up, a terrified look on his face.

"Don't, Mitch!" Lindsay cried, stepping forward

herself, realizing that if Mitch chose to beat Peter to a pulp, she would be powerless to stop him.

Mitch clenched and unclenched his fists, but he didn't raise either of them. Lindsay breathed a sigh of relief at the same time that Peter shuffled backward, adding to the distance between himself and Mitch.

For a long, pulsating moment no one said a word. Only the sounds of the night could be heard over their labored breathing.

Finally Peter turned to Lindsay and spat, "Let's get the hell out of here."

"You...go ahead."

"What? Have you lost your mind? I'm not leaving you out here alone with this bastard."

"Don't push your luck, Ballinger," Mitch said in a deadly tone.

Lindsay flinched inwardly, visions of another confrontation looming large. "Peter, just go. Please. I'll be fine."

His hostile gaze bounced between them. "Suit yourself." With those succinct words, Peter wheeled around and strode toward the house.

Lindsay didn't let go of her jammed-up breath until he completely disappeared. She just prayed he wouldn't decide to go back inside rather than home. Moments later, she heard the distant purr of his car engine.

Feeling Mitch's gaze on her, she turned and faced him.

"You okay?" he asked.

She licked her lips, then nodded.

"He's lucky I didn't break his neck."

This was a side of Mitch she'd never seen—cold and deadly. But then, she didn't really know this man at all, she reminded herself, looking harsh reality in the face.

"I'm okay, Mitch, really I am. He didn't hurt me."

"He might have."

Lindsay shook her head. "No. You're wrong. He's not that kind of man."

Mitch gave a bitter laugh. "Could've fooled me."

"He isn't," she stressed. "But it doesn't matter. In this instance, you're right. He was out of line." Lindsay's voice faltered; she was suddenly feeling so tired that she could barely remain upright. "But it's over now, and he's gone."

"And the other verse to that song is that he'd best stay gone."

"You...scare me when you talk like that, in that kind of tone." She knew her voice sounded as weary as her body felt.

As if he sensed something was wrong, Mitch took her gently by the arm and led her toward the gazebo, where he urged her to sit down. She needed no further encouragement. She was trembling both inside and out.

He sat down beside her, and for a while no words passed between them. Yet Lindsay was aware of him beside her with every fiber of her being. She sneaked a look in his direction.

He was staring straight ahead, appearing uncoiled, even lazy, as if he no longer had a care in the world. She knew better. He was anything but uncoiled. At any given moment, he was prone to strike. Was it that dangerous side of him that drew her to him, that made her want to reach out and touch that sun-kissed arm so close to her own?

"If you don't stop looking at me like that," he warned in a guttural tone, "I'm liable to take you right here."

And she would probably let him, heaven help her. But she wasn't going to tell him that. Besides, she was flirting with danger even by having stayed behind. Soon Cooper was bound to wonder why she and Peter hadn't returned. She wouldn't put it past him to check on their whereabouts.

"I'd better get back inside," **she** said in a sudden, desperate tone.

Mitch faced her. "Look at me."

His husky voice drew her to him like a magnet. The moon bathed his features in its glow, allowing her to see into his dark, enigmatic eyes.

"I'm looking," she whispered, licking her bottom lip.

He groaned. "Lindsay, please, don't push your luck. I want you so badly right now, I'm sick to my stomach." Before she could respond, he grabbed her hand and placed it on his crotch, his eyes never wavering.

Lindsay's breath caught as she felt his hard strength even through the thickness of his jeans. "I want you, too," she whispered with no shame.

With a shuddering sigh he removed her hand. "What I *don't* want is pretty boy's hands on you ever again."

"Me, either."

"Then why don't you dump him, once and for all?"

"I've tried," Lindsay said. "But you know Cooper. Or maybe you don't."

"I know that he's hell-bent on you marrying that SOB. I'm sure he's discussed his plans for remodeling the south wing—which I'm not about to do."

"And I'm not about to live there."

"Then you have to tell him. Now."

Her eyes widened. "I'm not sure that's a good idea."

"Are you ashamed of me?" His words were bitter.

Lindsay cut him an incredulous look. "No, of course not."

"Then what's the problem? We're two grown, consenting adults who want to be together."

"It's a bit more complicated than that," Lindsay responded in a tight voice.

"Only because you're choosing to make it that way."

If you only knew why, Lindsay thought. But he didn't know, and she couldn't tell him. Not yet, anyway. Maybe never. A chill darted through her, and it was all she could do not to shiver visibly.

"I'm tired of this charade," Mitch said. "I don't want to have to sneak around to see you anymore."

"You know Cooper will go ballistic if he finds out."

"So fucking what?"

"Oh, Mitch," she said, her thoughts returning to his baby growing inside her and the possible fallout from that. "What if he fires you?"

"I was looking for a job when I found this one."

"It's not that easy, Mitch."

"It sure as hell is. Just tell him."

"I'll think about it."

She flinched against the expletive that shot into the humid air.

"That's not good enough," he said tersely. "This game of hide-and-seek is wearing thin. And I'm not good at playing games."

"Just give me time, okay? You know how Cooper is, how protective he is of me."

"How possessive, don't you mean?"

Both frustration and sarcasm lowered his tone, giving it an angry edge. Lindsay shivered inwardly, touching her stomach. What would he do if he knew about the baby? For a second she was tempted to blurt it out. But that temptation quickly passed.

She had no idea how he would react. And she didn't want to find out, especially not tonight—not when she was too exhausted to even think, much less think straight enough to tell him something of such magnitude.

"Look, I have to go."

She stood, only to have him grab her hand. Without taking his eyes off her, he lifted that hand to his lips, trapping her middle finger and sucking it. A shaft of desire stabbed her so hotly between her legs that they nearly buckled. She whimpered against the onslaught, which seemed to fuel his own desire.

"Mitch, I—"

He dropped her hand and stood. "I know, you gotta go."

She raised her eyes to his, and for another long moment they simply stared at each other. She ached for him to kiss her, but he didn't. Instead, he caressed one side of her face with his knuckles and continued to stare at her as if he were starved for her.

"Oh, Mitch," she said in a broken voice.

"You'd best skedaddle," he finally said.

She turned and had taken two steps when he said in a husky tone, "Know that you'll be sleeping on my side of the bed tonight."

She halted, the bottom dropping out of her stomach. But she dared not turn back around or she knew she'd never leave. Stiffening her shoulders and her resolve, she made her way toward the house.

"You look like hell."

Peter gave Cooper a look. "I feel worse."

"What happened to you, for God's sake? Whose fist did you run into?"

"Your estate manager's."

Cooper knew he looked as stunned as he felt. "Mitch Rawlins?"

"So that's the bastard's name," Peter muttered.

Cooper blinked, trying to make sense out of what Peter had just said. It had been a couple of days since Peter had dined there and taken a stroll outside with Lindsay. Cooper had wondered why they hadn't returned to the parlor and joined him for drinks.

The following morning he'd questioned Lindsay, at which point she had made an apology of sorts, saying she'd been tired and that Peter had left. Cooper had wanted to ask her if they had discussed the baby and Peter's taking responsibility for it, but she hadn't given him a chance—nor had she since.

He figured she had purposely avoided him. That

was why he'd called Peter and told him to get over here ASAP.

Now, as he continued to stare as his prospective son-in-law, a perplexed frown knit his brows. "Let me get this straight. Mitch Rawlins gave you that shiner."

"You're damn right he did."

"Why? He must've had a reason."

Peter flushed.

"What the hell happened?" Cooper asked in a heated tone.

"Lindsay and I were talking about the baby."

"Go on."

"Anyhow, I told her I'd marry her regardless, but she wasn't the least bit interested. In fact, she was downright insulting."

"You didn't handle her right, then."

The high color instantly drained out of Peter's face. "I did the best I could."

"Finish about Mitch," Cooper ordered impatiently.

"Well, Lindsay was in a huff and turned to walk off. I grabbed her by the arm and swung her around." Peter paused and took a quick breath. "She told me to get my hands off her, which, under the circumstances, made me madder than hell."

"What happened next?" Cooper asked in a cold tone.

"This Neanderthal seemed to appear out of nowhere. Before I knew what was happening, I was on my ass, his ugly mug looming over me."

"For chrissake, Peter—"

"You know what I think?"

"Regardless, I'm sure you're going to tell me."

Peter pursed his lips. "There's something between those two."

Cooper tossed back his head and laughed an empty laugh. "You're crazy as hell."

"No, I'm not. I saw the way he looked at her."

"And just how did Lindsay look back at him?" Cooper was amused and didn't bother to hide it, even though he knew he was insulting Peter.

"Like she could eat him up."

"Why, you bastard," Cooper spat. "I'll have your hide if you repeat that outside this room. My daughter doesn't cavort with the hired help."

"I disagree," Peter said in a tone that bordered on belligerence. "I'll even step farther out on that limb and say that I think this Rawlins character could be the father of her child."

"Damn you! Don't you ever say that again, you hear me? That's just jealous garbage coming out of your mouth. And if you ever repeat it, you'll have me to answer to. And I swear, I'll do more than blacken one of your eyes."

"Cooper, you didn't see them together, and I did."

"I don't give a tinker's damn what you saw." Cooper was breathing far harder than he should. "I know my daughter. She would never stoop that low or defy me to such a degree."

"She already has." This time it was Peter who was amused.

"You'd best watch your mouth."

Peter merely shrugged.

"Granted, I don't know who fathered her child, but it's not Mitch Rawlins."

"Whatever you say."

"Well, I'm saying it. When you leave this room, you just remember that. Now get out."

Peter stomped to the door, where he swung around. "Do we still have a deal?"

"Not if you don't get some balls and persuade my daughter to marry you."

Peter gave him a sharp look, along with a curse, then slammed the door behind him.

Cooper didn't know how long he stood there with a helpless feeling washing through him. He wiped sweat off his forehead, even though the air conditioner was spitting out cold air. How dare Lindsay defy him to such an extent?

How dare she?

Twenty-Two

"Hey, sis, are you ill?"

Lindsay gave a start as Tim's blunt words singled her out. All eyes seemed to jump to her. She managed a smile, then said with forced vigor, "I guess I'm not as hungry as I thought, though the dinner's delicious."

"It is that," Eve said in her soft, Southern-accented voice. "I have to say, Dolly outdid herself for my birthday."

Lindsay thought so, too, though she had eaten sparsely. Her stomach was not in the mood for food, hadn't been since she found out she was pregnant. Her mood wasn't festive, either, and she was sorry about that, as well.

It was the first time the family had been together since Cooper's accident, and she had so wanted to enjoy the evening. Instead, she was not only physically unfit, but mentally unfit, as well. Questions over what to do about the baby and Mitch preyed heavily on her mind.

Still, she was trying not to think about her dilemma at the moment. Instead she concentrated on the lovely flowers in front of her, another way in which Dolly had gone all out for the party. The arrangement of white lilies mixed with Waterford crystal candle holders made for a smashing centerpiece. In addition, the table was set to perfection with the family's best china and silver.

"Lindsay."

Her daddy's gruff voice pulled her back to the moment.

"You have to eat," he said.

She hated being the center of attention, especially when it was Eve's evening. And her sister-in-law looked smashing, too, in a midnight-gray dress that was just a shade darker than her eyes.

"I'm fine, Daddy," Lindsay finally said, forcing a brighter smile. "Don't fuss so. That's what you're always telling me."

Cooper gave her a long, pointed look, but didn't say anything further. Thank God. She regretted having told him she was pregnant. It had been a knee-jerk response on her part, and it had only provided him with additional ammunition to use to try to control her. Although he hadn't said anything more to her about her condition since she'd sent Peter away again, she knew that wouldn't last.

An all-out confrontation loomed, and she dreaded it.

"So what have you been up to, sis?" Tim asked, taking a sip of wine.

"Oh, just my usual charity obligations," she said off-handedly, once again trying to divert the attention elsewhere.

"That's not what I've heard," Eve chimed in, smiling at Lindsay.

"And just what have you heard?" Tim asked.

"That Lindsay's working on a project that will benefit abused women and children. It's supposedly a one-of-a-kind facility." Eve paused. "And I think that's wonderful."

"Well, I don't," Cooper said harshly. "That's not at all what I want her involved in."

Eve flushed and for a moment seemed at a loss for words.

"Don't mind Daddy," Lindsay said lightly, trying to ease the growing tension. "He doesn't want me doing anything that takes me away from his dinner parties."

Tim winked at Lindsay. "I hear you. At least he's on your case now, instead of mine."

"I suggest you two stop while you're ahead."

Although Cooper's lips wore a half smile, Lindsay knew he wasn't amused. His eyes were hard as stones.

"Let's change the subject, shall we?" she said, averting her gaze. "Let's toast Eve one more time."

Tim stood abruptly. "I think that's a great idea. Then I'll give her my gift."

"I told you not to get me anything," Eve said, her tone a bit anxious.

"Oh, come on," Tim said. "You know better than that." Once the toast was done, he leaned over, picked up a beautifully wrapped box off the floor and handed it to her. "Happy birthday, my dear."

Eve was clearly flustered and not very excited, Lindsay noticed, watching as her sister-in-law stripped the package of its ribbon and paper.

This time all eyes centered on Eve as she opened the box.

"Oh, Eve, that's gorgeous," Lindsay said, flashing her brother a curious look, then switching back for a closer look at the diamond tennis necklace that Eve was still staring at, her mouth open.

For someone who was always broke, Tim had purchased an extravagant gift, Lindsay mused. Dare she hope that he had indeed straightened up and gotten his financial act together?

Apparently Eve was thinking along those same lines, because her face was white and pinched as she focused her attention on her husband. "I thought we were broke," she said in an accusing tone.

An abrupt silence descended over the room. Finally Tim broke it. "Can't you just say thank you?" He bit out his words, and a muscle bunched in his jaw.

Lindsay knew he was furiously embarrassed and was trying to hang on to his temper.

"Under the circumstances, no," Eve said, her chin beginning to quiver.

"I don't think this is the time or place to discuss your finances," Cooper interjected, his gaze pinging back and forth between Eve and Tim.

Eve stood. "You're exactly right. This is something that should be discussed at home, which is exactly where I'm going." She added, "Thank you for a lovely party."

She walked out then, leaving a heavy silence behind her.

"Daddy, I'm sorry about that," Tim said, shifting in his seat as if he were sitting on a bed of fire ants.

"Instead of being sorry," Cooper retorted, "I suggest you get your wife in hand."

Lindsay had had enough. She stood. "If you'll excuse me, I'm going to my room. It's been a long day."

"Good night," Tim muttered darkly.

Cooper's gaze touched on her, then he said, "We'll talk later."

That was what she was afraid of, Lindsay told herself as she made her way up to her room, where she quickly stripped off her clothes and slipped on a robe.

What a mess her family was, she reflected a little while later. What a fiasco dinner had turned out to be. She could imagine what was going on between Eve and Tim about now. Most likely World War III. Was any one of them normal—especially herself? Tears welled up and burned her eyes.

A baby was growing inside her. Wondering what to do about that was tearing at her, making her crazy. Suddenly Lindsay panicked, feeling as if the walls were once again closing in on her. She practically ran to the French doors, threw them open and walked onto the balcony.

Fresh air.

Humid though it was, the air felt good. She sucked it deeply into her lungs until she felt her heart stop racing. Yet the panicked feeling didn't totally subside. It wouldn't until she made a firm decision.

Should she have the baby?

Dear Lord, she wanted it, but she was afraid, afraid it would be damaged goods, like herself and her mother. What if Emily had passed some defective gene on to her. Would she in turn pass it to her child?

There was always that chance. Was she willing to

take it? Hot tears continued to burn Lindsay's cheeks, but she didn't try to stop them. Should she tell Mitch? She didn't know what to do. She wanted to, but she was afraid of that, too. So what was the answer?

An abortion?

A wave of dizziness hit her so hard that she almost lost her balance. Grasping the railing, she clung to it until the world righted itself. Although that thought was repugnant to her and went against everything she held dear, she had to consider it. She had no choice.

If only she knew how Mitch would react to the news that he was going to be a father. Unfortunately, she had no idea. In so many ways, he remained an enigma to her. She couldn't imagine him as a parent. But then, she couldn't imagine herself in that role, either.

But together, with love, they might be able to make it work. No doubt she loved him, had loved him from the first moment she'd seen him, though at the time she had thought it was just lust.

Did he love her? She didn't know. That uncertainty alone was enough to keep her mute about the baby. She wouldn't marry a man who didn't love her, not even to give her child a name.

How could loving someone hold so much pain?

She continued to grip the railing, feeling the gentle breeze caress her cheeks and dry her tears. She didn't know when she first realized he was there, close by, in the inky blackness, watching her. But she knew.

Should she say anything, or wait for him to make the first move? What madness this man—the father of her child—worked in her. She couldn't begin to figure out why, nor did she want to. All she wanted was to dash down the balcony stairs and run to him.

She ached for him. She needed him. Now. Tonight. This second. Her hand clutching at her stomach, she called out his name.

He stepped out of the shadows, and though she couldn't see him clearly, she imagined that his blue eyes were fixed on her.

"I'm here," he said in his low, husky voice.

"I know."

He walked toward the balcony, then stopped and peered up at her. "Are you all right? It's awfully late for you to be outside."

"I couldn't sleep."

"Neither could I."

Silence.

"Maybe if we tried it together?" he suggested.

"Think that might work?" Her heart was laboring so hard, she thought it might burst.

"We won't know till we try. Come on down."

Lindsay didn't wait for a second invitation. As if her legs were detached from the rest of her body, she threw caution, logic and everything else to the wind and headed for the stairs.

Mitch met her at the foot. But he didn't take her in his arms. Instead, he grabbed her hand and led her to his cabin.

"I hope we don't get caught," she whispered, halting at the front door and gazing up at him through slightly dazed eyes.

"You can always say no."

"I don't want to say no."

"I think I'd die if you did," he rasped.

The sounds of the night suddenly pulsated around them, but she heard nothing but her heart.

"Lindsay…" His voice was filled with such agony that it broke her heart.

She placed a hand over his lips. "Shh." Then, opening the door, she walked inside.

The bedroom was cast in a muted glow, which allowed him to see her face. What he saw robbed him of his breath. There was sorrow and bruising in those lovely planes and angles. And dried tears.

Something was wrong, terribly wrong, only he didn't know what. He feared she wouldn't tell him, either. Maybe that was best. Right now, she seemed only to need him to hold her, to *love* her.

Stifling a groan, he stared into those ravaged eyes as he untied the sash of her robe, slipping it off her shoulders. He stopped breathing again at the sight of such perfection. He yearned to touch, to kiss, to lose himself in that perfection.

Unable to wait another second, he stripped off his own clothes, then eased her down onto the edge of the bed, with every intention of gently pushing her back against the spread.

Only she stopped him. "Not yet," she whispered.

Before he could respond, she reached out and cupped his buttocks, drawing him toward her. When her tongue dipped into his navel, he jerked as if he'd been hit with a high current of electricity.

"Lindsay, my sweet Lindsay," he muttered irrationally as her tongue deserted his navel and traveled lower. When she reached his burgeoning penis, she opened her mouth wide and licked his flesh.

His head fell back, and his knees almost buckled at the unexpected emotion this tender and wonderful worshiping of his body brought on. It hit his soul, and sobs of ecstasy broke from his throat.

"Enough," he ground out at last, pushing her down, spreading her legs and thrusting into her.

She cried out and lifted her buttocks so as to take all of him.

Using his hands to brace himself on either side of her, he moved in, then out of her, creating another kind of friction—hot and frantic.

"Please!" she cried again, locking her legs around his buttocks, trapping him inside her.

He covered her. Then, taking her with him, as close as two people could get, he rolled onto his back so that she was now atop him, where he speared high and strong into her.

Digging her hands into his shoulders, she began to ride him hard and fast. Another moan erupted from his lips as he reached his peak, then watched as Lindsay began to spasm. At the end, into the scared darkness, she whispered one word.

"Mitch."

Twenty-Three

Lindsay blinked until her vision cleared. She surveyed her surroundings. It finally hit her where she was and who she was with. She swung her head around and found Mitch propped on an elbow, staring at her.

For some idiotic reason, she felt herself blush all over. Instinctively, she reached for the sheet.

His hands stilled hers. "Don't you think it's a bit late for that?"

"I guess you could say that." Her tone was as breathless as his was teasing.

Suddenly his eyes changed. Something flared into them that she couldn't identify.

"Lindsay—"

"Don't say anything," she whispered in a broken voice. "Not yet, anyway."

He swallowed convulsively. "Why not?"

"I'm pregnant, Mitch."

He didn't so much as move a muscle, except the one in the left side of his jaw. It jerked several times. Her heart faltered. He wasn't overjoyed; that was for sure. But what had she expected? After all, she'd just dropped something akin to a grenade in his lap and watched it explode in his face.

"It's mine."

Because those two words were a flat statement of fact, Lindsay didn't take umbrage. How could she, with Peter in the picture and Cooper's all-out push for her to marry him?

"Yes. I've...never slept with Peter."

"Oh, God, Lindsay." Mitch struggled to get another breath.

She bit down on her lower lip so hard she tasted blood. "I know. It's a mess, isn't it?"

"Does your father know?"

"Yes," she said again.

Mitch muttered an expletive.

"But he doesn't know whose it is," she said in a rush.

He was so close to her that she immediately felt some of the tension drain from his body. "Are you going to keep it that way?"

"For now."

"I had no idea you weren't protected."

"If I'd been sleeping with Peter, I probably would've been."

His eyes darkened as he continued to peer into hers. "Even when I convinced myself you were, I couldn't stomach the thought of him touching you. Maybe that was one reason I took so much pleasure in decking the SOB."

"Oh, Mitch."

He was quiet for a long moment, then he asked, "How do you feel about...the baby? I mean—"

"I know what you mean. But I don't really know. First I was numb. Now I'm sick."

"Sick?" His voice was suddenly thick with concern.

"To my stomach, which is pretty normal."

"How are you doing emotionally?"

"Not very well," she admitted. "Actually, I'm scared for so many reasons." She paused. "What about you? How do you feel?"

"Scared shitless."

"At least you're honest," she said bleakly.

"Do you want this baby, Lindsay?"

Unexpected tears gathered in her eyes. "I want it, but I'm afraid to have it."

"Ah, hell, don't cry, please." He sounded as if it hurt him to talk, as if he were strangling. "I can't handle that."

"Well, this is something to cry about."

"You're right, it is."

"Daddy thinks my marrying Peter will solve everything."

"Over my dead body," Mitch spat.

"Over mine, too."

"Thank God."

Lindsay turned away and didn't say anything else for a long moment. She was desperately trying to organize her tormented thoughts into words he would understand. If only he loved her, then maybe there would have been a chance for them and their baby. But he didn't, and she knew that, had known that all along.

While that broke her heart, she didn't condemn him for it.

"So what are you going to do?" Mitch finally asked into the drumming silence.

"I'm considering an abortion." There. She'd said the ugly word out loud, gotten it out in the open. But it didn't make the choice any more palatable. In fact, she felt as if someone had taken a knife and was jabbing her heart.

"It's your call," he said in a neutral tone.

Lindsay stared closely at him, trying to read what was going on behind his eyes, what he really felt. But she couldn't. If he had any fiery thoughts on the subject, he was keeping them to himself. But then, he was a master at disguising his emotions. Still, his apparent indifference brought on another jab of that knife.

"Don't you want to know why?" she asked, her voice trembling.

"Only if you want to tell me."

She struggled for breath. "I'm afraid that my— our baby won't be whole, that it—" Tears clogged her voice and she couldn't go on.

"Shush," he said, pulling her to him and holding her close. "It's okay. I understand. But you have to know that I don't think you're defective in any way. I pretty much think you're perfect."

"Mitch, Mitch," she whispered, remaining against him for a moment, feeling her hot tears mingle with the thick hairs on his chest.

"Please, Lindsay, don't cry. I only want what you want."

Then ask me to marry you. But he didn't say those words, and she didn't expect him to. Pulling back, she forced herself to look deeply into his eyes once again. "Will...will you go with me?"

"To a clinic?" His voice was as bleak as his features.

She nodded, her throat too full to speak.

"You know I will."

She swallowed hard. "I should go now."

"Yeah, you should."

"I'll make the arrangements and let you know."

"Whatever," he said without emotion.

Lindsay rolled to the side of the bed and reached for her robe, stood, then slipped it on. When she turned back around, Mitch had also gotten up and was stepping into his jeans.

She tried not to stare at his backside, at his muscle-hard buttocks, but she couldn't help it. Even now, after hours of passionate lovemaking, she felt a new influx of heat at the apex of her thighs.

Suddenly he swung his head around, and their eyes met. Fire leapt into his before his entire face tightened. "You're pushing your luck, Lindsay," he said tersely. "I can only take so much."

She wasn't sure exactly what he meant, but she wasn't going to stay and find out. It would be daylight soon. She couldn't take a chance on getting caught fleeing from his cabin.

At the door, she swung around, then whispered, "Mitch, I'm sorry."

Mitch regarded her through narrowed lids. "Yeah, me, too."

He couldn't believe it.

He slammed the shutters closed, then turned and began pacing the floor. Peter had been right, after all, a fact that he couldn't bear to acknowledge. But he had no choice.

The evidence had been thrown in his face.

How could she? How could his own daughter humiliate and embarrass him like this? Neither one of them would get away with it. He would see to that.

But he would bide his time, and when it was right, the ax would fall. For now, he would hold on to his temper and the desire to tear that bastard limb from limb.

He needed Rawlins to oversee the south wing, now more than ever. And he was damn sure going to use him, like he'd used Lindsay. The thought of them together, coupling like animals, sickened him. To think his grandchild belonged to a man with nothing—no money, no education and, most of all, no heritage.

A nobody.

Livid. That was what he was. Livid at the injustice of it all.

Well, when it suited him, he would deal him more misery than he'd ever bargained for.

"You're fucked, Rawlins," Cooper muttered. "And royally, too."

"Boss, are we calling it a day?"

"That we are, Jesse."

"Don't mind if I brag, but that new fence around the north pasture looks damn good."

"Thanks to you."

Jesse waved his dirty hand. "Not me. You're the one who did most of the work."

"It was a team effort."

"You think the doc's gonna like it?"

"What's not to like, Jess?"

The smaller man grinned, then scratched his head. "Nothing."

Mitch gave him a fleeting smile. "See you tomorrow at the crack of dawn."

A short time later, Mitch was in his quarters, performing his nightly ritual of taking a shower, fixing a bite to eat and drinking a beer.

Tonight he was actually having several beers. But short of getting stinking drunk, beer would do little to temper his raging thoughts. They were driving him mad. He had considered drinking scotch straight out of the bottle to deaden his mind and his emotions. But he'd figured he would be wasting his time. Nothing short of a miracle would dissolve the painful lump lodged in his throat.

Would she decide to have an abortion?

That question had dogged him ever since she had told him she was thinking about it. He hadn't even had time to digest the fact that his child was growing inside her. Now he was grieving over its loss.

Mitch got up with his beer in hand and walked out onto the porch. His eyes turned heavenward, where he watched the moon peek through what looked like storm clouds.

He had never thought of himself as parent material. When he and Wendy married, it had been a given there wouldn't be any children. She hadn't wanted any, and neither had he. Good thing, too, he thought ironically.

So why did he suddenly feel differently? Why now, of all times? He didn't know why, only that he did. He didn't want her to get rid of his child which surprised the hell out of him. He had thought he was immune to this kind of emotional upheaval.

Love. That word again. Was love what this turmoil was all about? Or was he just a masochist hell-bent on punishing himself for wanting her so much? But love aside, he would still marry her in a minute, if only he thought the marriage would work.

It wouldn't. Even if Cooper had no objections, Mitch's own inadequacies would nix that. Having chosen not to practice law, no way could he give her the kind of life she was used to, and no way would he take any favors from her old man, either.

Yet he didn't want to be without her. He adored her laugh, respected her intelligence, admired her penchant for doing good. Most of all, he lusted after her body. But his pain went deeper than his need for her body. It cut to his soul.

I'm considering an abortion.

The enormity of those words came crashing down on him again with such force that he almost went to his knees.

He felt weary and incredibly sad. Hanging his head, he grabbed hold of the post and clung to it, his insides suddenly wracked with silent sobs.

Only after he raised his head did he realize his face was drenched with tears.

"Oh, God, Lindsay, are you sure you know what you're doing?"

"No, Mary Jane, I don't."

"Then why don't you give yourself more time?"

Lindsay had met her friend for a quick cup of coffee before she was to meet Mitch at the clinic. Her time was about to run out.

"I can't handle thinking about this anymore, M.J. It's tearing me apart on the inside. I've cried until I can't cry anymore. So the sooner I get it behind me, the better it will be."

"At least health-wise, anyway. You look like you would break under a puff of wind."

"It's my mental health I'm thinking about," Lindsay said, her breathing shallow. "I can't bear the thought of going back to that mental hospital."

"Oh, honey, that's not going to happen."

"It might, if I don't make a final decision and stick to it."

"Does Cooper know?"

"No, and he's not going to until after the fact."

"Is he still pushing you to marry Peter?"

"Actually, he hasn't said anything lately, which has me worried. It's almost like he's suddenly gone into denial about the baby."

"Well," Mary Jane said, "you can forget that. Knowing your father, he's got something up his sleeve."

Lindsay shivered. "Just as long as he doesn't know that Mitch is the father."

"I suspect Mitch can take care of himself."

"That's not the point," Lindsay said in a small voice.

"How's he taking this?"

"I don't know. He keeps his emotions behind closed doors. He told me it was my call."

"I'm proud of him for that. He could have caused trouble."

"No, you're wrong. You have to love someone to do that."

"So have you seen him since you told him?"

"No, and it's been three days now. But I've been purposely avoiding him. I slipped a note under his door asking him to meet me at the clinic."

Mary Jane cocked her head. "If he had asked you to marry him, what would you have said?"

"Yes...then probably regretted it the rest of my life."

"You love him, don't you?"

Lindsay sighed. "Yes, but he doesn't love me."

"God, Lindsay, I hate this for you."

"I take full responsibility for my actions. You warned me that I was likely to get burned, and I did."

"Still, I'm grieving for you. I can't imagine going to that clinic."

Lindsay forced herself to stand, though her heart was slamming against her rib cage. "Me, either, but I'm going."

"Promise you'll call me," Mary Jane said, her eyes anxious.

"I promise."

She didn't know how long they had been sitting in the car, nor did she care. When she had driven into the parking lot of the clinic, Mitch had been waiting in his vehicle.

He'd gotten in beside her, then asked, "Are you okay?"

"No," she'd said simply. "But I will be."

"Yeah, right."

Those were the only words that had passed between them. The silence had stretched from seconds into minutes. She sneaked a look at his profile. It looked molded out of stone—cold and remote.

Biting her lip, she turned away, but not before a whimper passed unchecked through her lips.

"Lindsay, look at me."

She turned and caught her breath. He looked the way she felt—like he'd been gutted.

"Is this what you really want?"

Her chin quivered as her eyes locked on his. "No."

"Then why the hell are we here?"

"Because it's the only way." The huge lump in her throat made her voice barely recognizable.

"It certainly isn't."

Suddenly and without warning, Lindsay began to sob.

"Don't," he pleaded, drawing her into his arms, frantically kissing the tears off her face.

She clung to him.

"Do you really want to destroy our baby?" he asked against her lips.

"No!" she cried. There. She'd finally admitted out loud what her heart had known from the beginning. No matter what, she couldn't get rid of the baby. With that silent declaration she felt the block of ice around her heart finally melt.

"Then let's get the hell out of here."

"Where are we going?"

He paused. "To get married. If you'll have me, that is."

Lindsay pulled back and stared at him, while the very air seemed to hold its breath.

"So what's it going to be? Me or an abortion?"

Lindsay's heart filled to the bursting point. *"You."*

Twenty-Four

Lindsay Rawlins.

She had done it. She had actually married Mitch. Even now, several days later, Lindsay still couldn't believe that he had asked her to marry him out of the blue and that she had accepted. But she had.

Although she didn't have a ring that she could wear, she had a marriage license, or at least Mitch did. She had been afraid to keep it here in the house for fear Dolly or one of the maids might accidentally stumble on it while cleaning.

She didn't quite know how to react, because their union was certainly not a normal one. Since they weren't living together, no one knew they were married. She had to adjust to the sudden change in her life before she could share it. One minute excitement coursed through her, the next fear stabbed her. As for Mitch's feelings on the subject, they hadn't discussed it.

Lindsay dropped her towel, then peered into the long mirror in her bathroom, wondering if there were telltale signs, if it was obvious just how drastically her life had changed in the past few months. Did her eyes reflect it? They had a somewhat dazed look to them, she thought critically. And her body, how about that?

Her mouth turned down as her gaze dipped to her tummy. It now had a slightly rounded appearance, where before it had always been flat as a board. Still, she figured it would be a while before it was a dead giveaway that she was pregnant. Because she was so thin, people might think she was simply gaining weight, which she could definitely use.

Lindsay drew in a quivering breath and walked into the bedroom, where she began dressing, only to stop halfway through the process and sit on the side of the bed. Here she was, preparing for the day as if it were any other day, only it wasn't. Her days would never be the same again.

She was married.

Dear Lord, what had she done? For starters, she had given her baby a name. But what about herself? Until this morning, she had functioned as if she'd been drugged with something that had deadened her body and her emotions. Now the numbness was beginning to wear off and everything was coming back to life.

And she was frightened, almost as frightened as she'd been after she'd found her mother dead. When Mitch had asked her to marry him and she'd said yes, he had taken matters into his own hands. He had driven them to a city over a hundred miles away, where he obtained the license, then called a preacher acquaintance of his who agreed to perform the ceremony.

Grasping hands tightly, they had driven to a small chapel, met the minister and exchanged vows. Afterward, Mitch had taken her to dinner, though neither had eaten much.

Mitch hadn't been as in control of himself as he would have liked her to believe. The lines in his face seemed to have deepened, and his eyes had been wary. For some unexplainable reason, that had made her feel better. If he hadn't been somewhat disconcerted by what happened, he wouldn't be human.

And he *was* human. A semblance of a smile crossed Lindsay's lips as she thought back on the first thing he'd said to her after they had given the waitress their order.

"If you're sorry, don't say it."

His unexpected words took her aback, yet she smiled. "The same goes for you."

He relaxed then, right in front of her eyes, as if a heavy burden had been lifted from his shoulders. He smiled, and though it was short-lived, it lasted long enough to warm her heart.

"I'm glad to see you've got some of your spark back."

Her eyes clouded. "I'm not sure how long it's going to last."

"We're in this together now, Lindsay," he said, reaching for her hand and toying with it.

Her pulse instantly went off the charts. God, all this man had to do was touch her, and she melted inside. At this juncture, she didn't know if that was good or bad. What she did know was that it was scary that someone had so much power over her.

"I still can't grasp that we're married," she said at last, her tone husky.

His gaze was warm as it wandered over her face. "Well, we are, and we're going to have a baby."

Her lips parted. "That's also hard to grasp."

"You're telling me." He withdrew his hand and took a sip of water, though his eyes continued to hold hers.

"I couldn't go through with it, Mitch." She choked on the sudden lump that lodged in her throat. "I couldn't let someone destroy my...our baby."

He reached for her hand once again and squeezed it. "I couldn't bear it, either. After we talked, I tried to drown my thoughts in booze, only it didn't work."

"So what now?" she asked, expelling a shaky breath.

"I want you, Lindsay, in every sense of the word, which means sharing more than a bed with you."

A pulse quickened in her throat. "You mean live together?"

"I could handle that."

"But—but we can't."

"Why the hell not? We're married."

"Daddy doesn't know."

Mitch's mouth tightened. "That's easily remedied. We'll tell him. Together, if you'd like."

"No." She licked her dry lips.

"What do you mean, 'no'?"

"Please, Mitch, just trust me on this. Now is not the right time to tell him."

"So what are you suggesting?"

Lindsay averted her gaze. "That we keep it between us for now."

He leaned across the table. "What's the point? He

knows about the baby. Don't you think he'll be glad it's legal?''

"He might be glad about that, but he won't be glad I—'' She aborted the remainder of her sentence when his expression turned dark and suddenly menacing.

"He won't be glad you married *me*, right?''

She nodded.

"Well, that's too fucking bad. He'll just have to get over it.''

"Please, Mitch, let me do this my way and in my time.''

"All right, you win. For now.'' He paused, and when he spoke again, his tone was hard. "After all, you only married me because you were pregnant, right?''

Her heart almost stopped beating. Dare she tell him the truth? No. Fear of rejection kept her silent. "Right.''

"That's what I thought,'' he said harshly.

"Look, I don't want to fight with you,'' she whispered, her chin beginning to quiver. "Not today, anyway.''

His features suddenly softened. "I couldn't agree more. In fact, I don't ever want to fight with you. I just want to make love to you.''

She flushed. "I'd settle for a kiss.''

"My, but you're easy to please, Mrs. Rawlins,'' he drawled, getting up and crossing to her side, then leaning over and giving her a hot, wet kiss.

When he pulled back, her head was spinning.

"I'm hungry.'' Then he added, for her ears alone, "But not for food. Whattaya say we haul ass?''

Lindsay grabbed her purse.

Now, she realized, there was still a smile on her face when she focused on what had happened next. They had gone to a swanky hotel, checked in and made love.

She jerked her thoughts back to the present. Today, it was back to reality, to the sad fact that she was married to a man she barely knew. A virtual stranger.

It was with a heavy heart that Lindsay walked out of her room a few minutes later.

"Pregnant? Lindsay?"

"Not so loud," Cooper said to his son in a low, clipped tone. "If I wanted everyone in the restaurant to know, I'd stand up and announce it."

Tim rolled his eyes. "Funny."

"There's nothing funny about any of this."

"You're right, Dad, there isn't." Tim rubbed his clean-shaven chin. "Are you sure she's pregnant? I mean, is *she* sure?"

"That's what she said, and I have to take her at her word."

"I hear you."

"I'm at my wits' end as to what to do with your sister. It seems as if she's gone totally off the deep end."

"Ah, come on, that's not fair. As far as her mental stability's concerned, she's never been better."

Cooper's eyebrows shot up. "Really? You call getting knocked up out of wedlock 'stable'?"

"You know what I mean. She's not depressed and in that funk like before."

"Well, she should be depressed. I sure as hell am. And humiliated. And the list goes on."

"Well, I'm not exactly jumping through hoops myself." Tim paused, his eyes narrowing. "Do you think she's considering an abortion?"

"If she won't marry Peter, then I hope she does. In fact, I'm going to insist on it."

"Peter's not the father?"

"No."

"Then who?" Tim frowned. "I had no idea Lindsay was involved with anyone else."

"Me, either."

"Did she tell you who he is?"

"No, but I know."

Tim's jaw went slack. "You do?"

"Yes."

"Well, tell me."

"It's not necessary that you know."

"I beg to differ. It affects the entire family."

"Not for long. This man is someone I will not allow her to marry—under any circumstances."

"For chrissake, Dad, you can't control the world."

Cooper's expression turned fierce. "When it comes to my children, I can."

Tim's face drained of color. "Was that a direct slap at me?"

"After that escapade at dinner the other night, you're damn right it is. I don't know what's going on with you and Eve or your finances, but you'd best get it all straightened out."

High color crept back into Tim's face. "I'll have you know everything's under control."

"I hope you've told your wife that good news," Cooper said sardonically.

"How the hell did we get off on me? We were talking about my sister, which is a helluva lot more serious."

"I agree. I was hoping she'd said something to you, that you could shed some light on what that girl's thinking about. First that crazy project for abused women, now getting pregnant by some—" He stopped short, drawing his brows together in a scowl.

"Tell me who he is, and I'll defend my sister's honor."

"There's nothing humorous about this."

"You're right, there's not. And I wasn't joking. I'd love to beat the hell out of him for taking advantage."

"I don't know who took advantage of whom, but that's not the issue. Like I said, no daughter of mine is going to be ridiculed by my friends."

"What can I do?" Tim asked.

"Try and talk some sense into her while I'm gone."

"Gone?"

"Patty and I are leaving town for a few days."

"I can't promise anything, but I'll talk to her. Suppose you tell me what to say."

"Encourage her to marry Peter."

"I'll give it the old college try. What if she tells me to stuff it?"

Cooper's lips twisted and his eyes turned cold. "Then I'll do what has to be done."

Twenty-Five

"How did it go?"

Lindsay heaved a relieved sigh, then grinned at Rita Thomas, the shelter's director. "Absolutely great. Beyond my wildest expectations, actually."

Rita lifted her head up, shaping her hands into a prayer-like gesture. "Thank you, Lord."

Lindsay and several hundred more people had attended the banquet that had been in the works for some time now—a banquet for the purpose of jump-starting the golf tournament that would officially kick off the fund-raising for the new facility.

She had met with the two largest investors privately, along with several board members of the local junior college where she hoped the facility would be built. In fact, a possible site had been mentioned, one that she hadn't yet seen.

"So what's next?" Rita asked, breaking the short silence.

"Visit the site. If it looks promising, I'll take you."

"Think we can be choosy?" Rita asked, her rounded eyes on Lindsay.

Lindsay smiled. "Not really, but I haven't shown the board members the scaled drawing yet. It's still at the architect's. So they don't have a definite sense of my vision.''

"So the lot might not be large enough? Is that what you're thinking? Or maybe too large, huh?''

Lindsay shook her head. "Not a chance it would be too large, my friend. In my mind, I envision this project taking off and booming, as in expansion, expansion. The possibilities are endless.''

Rita's eyes glowed, and her voice contained unsuppressed excitement. "Wouldn't it be the cat's meow if that happened?''

"It's going to happen. You just wait and see.''

"How 'bout some more hot tea?'' Rita asked, standing and heading toward the cabinet.

They were in the tiny kitchen at the shelter. Lindsay had planned on spending the majority of the day here, which she hadn't done in a while. She liked to keep abreast of what was going on with the women and their children.

With Cooper being out of town and no dinner parties in the offing, she had time on her hands during the day. Of course, the nights were a different matter. Her heart suddenly skipped a beat.

She planned to spend them with her husband. Just thinking about him in that context made her giddy.

"Do you mind me saying something personal?''

Lindsay reluctantly pulled her thoughts off Mitch and gave Rita her undivided attention, noticing that the director's face was filled with unnatural color. "Of course not. What is it?''

"You're different,'' Rita said bluntly, her color burgeoning. "I don't know why, but it's a fact. There's a special glow about you, a vibrancy.'' She paused, tilting her head to one side. "Maybe it's as simple as the project and the euphoria associated with that."

Careful, Lindsay warned herself. Unless she was prepared to announce to all of Garnet that she was married and pregnant, she had best contain her feelings.

However, in defense of herself, that morning was the first day she'd felt worth a darn. Nausea had plagued her from day one of the pregnancy. Even now that queasiness was threatening to return; her stomach was beginning to poke her again.

"You bet it is," Lindsay said hurriedly, realizing Rita was giving her an even stranger look. In order to cover her partial lie, she added, "I think you're right. I'm on an adrenaline high now that the project is finally off the ground."

"Well, you definitely have a sparkle that hasn't been there before. I'm so glad for both of us that it's going to work."

"Actually, neither of us should get too excited yet, or at least I keep telling myself that," Lindsay said. "I don't think I could handle it if something went wrong."

"You could handle it, all right," Rita countered without hesitation. "But, like you, I'd be devastated—"

"Can anyone join this party?"

Lindsay froze, then swung around, her heart in her throat. Mitch lounged in the doorway, dressed in jeans, boots and a sports shirt. Her gaze was drawn irresistibly to the display of sleek muscles rippling under the thin material of his shirt. And he smelled good, too, the subtle scent of his cologne invading the cramped quarters.

What on earth was he doing here? She couldn't imagine, but she was suddenly so shocked and tongue-tied that she couldn't say anything.

And he was her husband, for crying out loud.

Rita stood, a perplexed smile on her face. "Can we help you, sir? I'm Rita Thomas, the director of this facility."

Mitch smiled an easy smile that upped Lindsay's heartbeat even farther as he returned the introduction.

Lindsay heard Rita's sharp intake of breath before she cut her eyes in Lindsay's direction. "I take it you two know each other," she said. Then, as if realizing how inane that must have sounded, Rita gave a hyper little laugh.

"I guess you're wondering why I'm here," Mitch said, his grin spreading across his entire face, catching like wildfire.

"As a matter of fact, I am," Lindsay said in a somewhat breathless voice. It was then that she noticed he was carrying a picnic basket—the one she'd carried to his cabin.

"Compliments of Dolly," he said, walking over to the table and placing the basket on it. "Fresh baked cookies."

Rita's eyes widened, then ping-ponged between the two of them. "Who's Dolly?"

"Our housekeeper," Lindsay muttered, still sounding as if she was having trouble breathing—and she was. God, but he oozed a sexual charisma that was all his own. She had never seen it duplicated, nor would she. That was what made him so addictive, at least where she was concerned.

"How nice of her to think of us," Rita was saying, her gaze on Mitch.

His grin intact, Mitch leaned against the cabinet and crossed his tanned arms across his chest as if he wasn't in any hurry whatsoever.

"I'm just the gofer."

Lindsay ignored the fact that her insides were quivering like jelly and forced herself to stand. "Oh, really?"

"Yeah, really," he said easily, his eyes resting on her, though they gave nothing away. "I had to order some supplies, so Dolly asked me if I'd drop these off."

"Well I can't thank her or you enough."

Rita's tone held awe and admiration, both of which Lindsay could understand. Mitch was a hunk who would affect any normal red-blooded woman. And he was hers. For a moment that thought made her delirious enough to shout. But then she reined in her emotions and took control.

"I'll walk Mitch out," Lindsay said.

He shoved himself away from the counter. "Great." Then to Rita, he said, "Take care, you hear? Perhaps I'll see you again."

"You're welcome anytime," Rita said in the same hyper voice.

Another grin flirted with Mitch's eyes and mouth. "As long as I bring cookies, right?"

Rita giggled like a schoolgirl.

Suddenly Lindsay wanted to kick his backside.

She had to get him out of there before she did just that. "I'm ready when you are," she said pointedly.

Mitch strode to the door, then turned and winked at Rita. "See ya."

Once they were alone in the hall and out of earshot, she glanced up at him. "You big flirt."

He looked as if he could eat her up. "Jealous?"

"Of course not," she responded quickly.

His eyes glittered. "Ah, heck."

"What are you doing here?" she asked, feeling her face turn scarlet.

"I wanted to see you. Dolly provided me with an excuse."

"I wanted to see you, too, only not here."

"I know, but I've missed you." He stopped suddenly and grazed one side of her cheek with the knuckles of his right hand, while his voice dropped a degree lower. "How 'bout we step into the nearest closet and let me show you just how much?"

Unconsciously, her gaze drifted below his belt. When her head came back up faster than it went down, he chuckled. "See what you do to me."

"You're awful," she muttered.

"When am I going to see you again?"

"This evening."

His eyes probed. She could read the unasked question in them, and she responded, "He's out of town. He will be for two days."

"Thank you, Jesus."

"Now will you get out of here?"

"I'd kinda like to see the place, actually." The playfulness had left his voice and his face.

Lindsay blinked. "Are you serious?"

"Yeah," he said softly. "Especially since this is another of my wife's passions."

This time *she* blushed like a schoolgirl. *His wife*. Would she ever get used to that? Or would this marriage end before it ever had a chance to begin?

Now where had that question come from? Suddenly her good humor fled, uneasiness taking its place.

"What's wrong?"

"Uh, my stomach," she lied.

"The baby's okay, right?"

"It's fine."

He looked relieved. "So show me around."

She did, and she could tell he was impressed with the way the facility was run. He even had kind words for the handful of women he met, which Lindsay really appreciated. Would she ever get to know the real Mitch Rawlins? He was proving to be more complex than she'd ever imagined.

Once the tour was completed, she walked outside with him. "Thanks," she said, her earlier thoughts still making her feel a bit off center.

"For what?"

"For taking an interest."

"Hey, I think what you're doing is great. But then, I've already told you that. Sometime I want to see all the plans."

She smiled up at him. "That can be arranged."

His eyes darkened. "You don't know how much I want to kiss you right now."

"I'll see you later," she whispered, her tongue deliberately circling her bottom lip.

He groaned. "You'll pay for that."

* * *

Her moist body clung to his as she arched up and pressed her breasts into his chest. His flesh was on fire at the feel of her jabbing nipples. He took tiny bites of her shoulder and heard moans erupt from deep within her.

He nudged open her thighs, and, without coaching, she encircled his hips with her legs. It was in that instant that he pushed himself inside the heated folds of her flesh.

Her eyes opened wide, and he saw himself reflected in their depths, which sent him into a frenzy, bringing muted gasps from her as he emptied himself inside her.

Later they lay entwined, their hearts continuing to beat as one.

"How many times have we made love already?" Lindsay asked, her warm breath fanning his face.

"Who's counting?"

"Me."

He chuckled. "Go right ahead, but you'll get tired. I promise."

"Don't misunderstand, I'm not complaining."

"Good, because all I have to do is touch you and my body goes from a simmer into a full boil."

"You know just which buttons to push to turn me on," she said, her eyes glazed.

"I keep thinking that while I'm inside you, I just might feel our baby. Crazy thought, huh?"

"Actually, I think it's a wonderful thought."

He leaned over suddenly, his tongue drawing a circle on her stomach. She watched him with a question in her eyes.

"He's somewhere in there, right?" Mitch asked, looking up at her.

"How do you know it's a 'he'?"

"I just know," he responded simply.

"Does it matter?"

"Not one iota. Just as long as he's healthy."

"Then we're together on that."

"Forever," he whispered, his lips meshing with hers once again.

That was when he heard the knock, followed by a big, booming voice. "Rawlins, open the door."

"Shit," Mitch muttered as he pulled his mouth off hers.

"Who is that?" Lindsay asked.

"Someone who's in big trouble." He rolled off the bed and reached for his jeans. "I'll be right back."

"Where are you going?"

"Outside to talk." He gave her another quick, hot kiss. "Keep my spot warm."

Once he was out in the warm night air, his expression changed. It turned fierce. "Avery, what the hell are you doing here?"

The big, burly man shrugged. "You won't talk to me on the phone, so I had no choice but to track you down."

"Like hell!"

"Look, Mitch, you've got to help me out."

"That's not going to happen, so take your fat ass off this property."

Avery smirked. "I'm immune to insults. You oughta know that."

"I'm through. Finished. Why can't you get that through your thick skull?"

"Because I don't believe it. People like you and me don't ever get through. It's in our blood."

"I've changed, dammit!"

"No, you haven't," Avery drawled. "And when you're ready, you'll call me."

Mitch scowled. "I wouldn't hold my breath if I were you."

"Ah, hell, Rawlins—"

"And don't ever come back here," Mitch added.

Avery merely smiled, then disappeared back into the darkness.

Twenty-Six

What was going on?

Although Lindsay hadn't followed Mitch out of the room, she'd been tempted. But something had held her back. Though she was more than mildly curious as to who his untimely visitor was, the thought of purposely eavesdropping was distasteful to her. She would much rather her husband volunteer the information.

Maybe he would do just that when he returned. Of course he would, especially if she asked, which she intended to do. Despite the unconventional circumstances, they *were* married. That alone should prompt him to confide in her.

Meanwhile, she would just have to be patient. She frowned up at the ceiling, the moon drawing patterns across it, when it hit her once again just how little she knew about her husband.

She didn't know a thing more now than she had before she married him. That had to change. She had shared her secrets; now it was his turn.

Suddenly feeling a sneeze coming on, Lindsay looked around for a box of tissues. When none was obvious she leaned over and opened the bedside table drawer.

Her eyes widened with shock, and her lips formed an *O*. Then, finding her voice, she whispered, "Oh, my God."

A gun.

A bolt of terror shot through her as she stared at the lethal weapon lying next to a package of tissues. At first she recoiled; then she did something that was totally foreign to her. She reached out and touched the cold metal. With increasing boldness, she carefully lifted it from its hiding place.

Shuddering, she dropped it on the bed beside her and waited, her heart pounding in her ears.

"Now, where were we?" Mitch asked in a husky voice after opening the bedroom door and striding in.

"Not where we left off, that's for sure," Lindsay said, her voice tight.

Mitch halted, the sudden change in her obvious. His gaze flickered over her before settling on the weapon. He made no effort to hide how he felt. Fury twisted his features.

"What the hell do you think you're doing?" he asked, sounding as if he were strangling.

"I was about to ask you the same thing."

"I don't have to explain anything to you," he said, his tone now coated in ice.

Lindsay flinched as though he'd slapped her. "Why, you...you bastard!"

Mitch's eyes reflected his tone. "I may be, but that doesn't change anything."

"Well, it does for me," Lindsay lashed back, lunging off the bed and grabbing her robe.

"Running away won't solve anything. If you'll just calm down—"

"No! I don't want to calm down." She was trembling as if a tiny tornado had just struck her system. "I want to go home."

"Back to Daddy." His words were wrapped in sarcasm.

Lindsay's eyes flared. "That's right. That's obviously where I belong."

"Suit yourself."

"Believe me, I will."

With that, Lindsay dashed out of the room and out of the house, but not before a string of Mitch's expletives assaulted her ears.

He shouldn't have talked to her that way. After all, she was his wife, for God's sake. She deserved to know about his past. She had asked a fair question and deserved a fair answer. But he hadn't given her one.

He'd acted like an ass.

And he had paid for that reaction ever since. He couldn't sleep, nor could he eat. It was as if his emotional self had shut down. His physical body, however, had remained in top condition. He'd worked long, backbreaking hours, refusing to quit until sweat covered every inch of him and his muscles jumped convulsively.

Yet even when he fell exhausted into bed, thoughts

of Lindsay continued to burn through his mind, until he got a painful erection and began to tremble.

He had to make things right between them. But he was so damn confused. Had he fallen in love? Or was he still confusing lust with love? He didn't think so—not anymore. His soul was involved.

However, as long as she insisted on keeping their marriage a secret, he could not be one hundred percent sure. Any kind of normal life they might have together would remain out of reach.

No matter. He couldn't bear this rift between them, knowing it was his fault. He wasn't sure he was ready to spill his guts to her. But he had to do something so that he could see her again, *touch her* again, even if they had to sneak around to do it.

It was as if he were having a clandestine affair with his own wife.

Nonetheless, he was hopeful he would run into Lindsay when he went to see Cooper, who had demanded his presence in the inner sanctum.

A smirk toyed with Mitch's mouth as he knocked on the side door, guessing Cooper wanted to talk about remodeling the south wing again. He would do the work, all right, but Lindsay and that lowlife Peter wouldn't be living in it together.

A part of him dreaded the day the old man found out about him and Lindsay, but he wasn't going to take on that worry now. His main thought was patching things up with his wife.

Once Dolly answered the door and they exchanged pleasantries, he made his way toward Cooper's study, all the while keeping an eye out for Lindsay.

She was nowhere in sight.

Forcing his disappointment aside, he knocked on the heavy door.

Moments later he was facing his boss from across his desk. "Mornin'."

Cooper didn't return his greeting. Instead, he raked his eyes over him, his lips curled. "You're through here, Rawlins."

Mitch forced himself not to react, though his insides were a cauldron of fear and anxiety. "As in fired, you mean?"

Cooper's features turned into a sneer. "What do you think?"

Mitch shrugged, still keeping his emotions under wraps. So the old man had found out. How? It didn't matter. What mattered was how he was going to fix something that was obviously broken.

"Pack your shit, then get out."

"I don't think so," Mitch drawled, deciding to call his hand.

Cooper stood, his face purple with rage. "You'll do like you're told!"

"I'll leave, but not without Lindsay."

"You're not taking my daughter anywhere, you hear? Just because you took advantage of her and got her pregnant doesn't give you homestead privileges."

So he didn't know the rest of the story, after all. Well, he was about to. "But a marriage license does."

"You're lying!" Cooper said in a choked voice.

Mitch looked him over with contempt. "You know better than that."

"No way would my daughter marry the likes of you!"

"If you don't believe me, ask her," Mitch said with a nonchalant shrug.

Cooper was quiet for a long moment, then asked, "How much?"

"This is not about money, Cooper."

Cooper laughed an ugly laugh, as if the devil had invaded his system. "Everything's about money."

"Not with me it isn't."

As if Mitch hadn't spoken, Cooper went on. "So how much will it take for you to walk away from my daughter and the...baby?"

"You're wasting your time."

"I ought to have you horsewhipped for taking advantage of my daughter."

"You probably should."

"So why don't you do what's right and leave them be?"

"I can't. Where I go, they go."

"By God, that's not going to happen!"

"Daddy! What on earth is going on?"

At the unexpected sound of Lindsay's voice, Mitch swung around. But her gaze was on her father, not him.

"Tell me you're not married to this man."

Mitch met Lindsay's stunned gaze. With the silence beating around them, they simply stared at each other.

"Lindsay!" Cooper raged on. "Answer me!"

"We are married, Daddy."

Mitch heard the tremor in her voice and drew a harsh breath, aching to knock Cooper on his ass for his behavior as well as his archaic attitude. He didn't care about himself; he could handle his father-in-law. But obviously Lindsay couldn't. Cooper could still intimidate the hell out of her.

"How could you?" Cooper gasped. "How could you do this to me?"

"Let her be," Mitch said tersely.

"You stay out of this, Rawlins. She's my daughter."

That tore it. Mitch leaned across the desk and got in the older man's face. "She's *my wife*."

"Stop it!" Lindsay cried. "Both of you. Right now."

Both men's eyes swung in her direction.

"I won't have you bickering over me like two dogs over a bone."

Mitch stepped toward her. "Lindsay—"

She held up her hand, her face ravaged by tears. He wanted to hold her and make all this go away. But he couldn't. He feared he might never hold her again.

"Don't touch me," she said. "Just go. I can't handle anything else right now."

Her words cut him to the quick, and he reacted accordingly, speaking to her alone. "There's nothing to handle, Lindsay. When you make up your mind whether you want to be my wife or Daddy's princess, you can let me know."

* * *

Somehow Lindsay managed to get through the next few days without running into Mitch. She figured he was avoiding her, as well. Yet she knew something had to give. She couldn't continue to live like this. She missed him terribly, but she was also angry at him—angry at his penchant for privacy, and angry that he had divulged their secret.

When she had walked in on him arguing with her father in the study, she'd panicked. Once Mitch had stomped out, she had headed toward the door herself, though Cooper had done his best to stop her.

"Where do you think you're going, young lady?" he'd demanded, his color still high.

"To my room."

"I refuse to condone this marriage. You have to know that."

"I do know that, Daddy. But if Mitch goes, I go with him."

"I'll never believe that," he sneered. "You'll come to your senses. Until then, I'll allow him to stay."

"I'm sick to my stomach. I'm going to my room."

"Then go," he snapped, turning his back on her. "We'll talk later."

That "later" hadn't come as yet, but she knew it would. She told herself that when it did, she could handle it, handle *him*.

Now, Lindsay shivered as she made her way downstairs toward the kitchen for a cup of tea. It was late afternoon, and she'd been in her room most of the day, working on the project. She hadn't felt well, either. Her stomach had been on the warpath. Being pregnant *and* stressed made for a lethal combination.

Maybe that was all the more reason to seek Mitch out. Perhaps she had been too hard on him concerning his desire for privacy. Maybe if she hadn't come on like gangbusters, he might have confided in her. But she didn't think so. There was something about the way he'd looked when he'd walked back into the room, even before he saw the gun, that made her think he was upset.

His facade had slipped for one second, and what she'd glimpsed in those eyes had frightened her. His visitor, whoever it had been, had gotten him riled to the point that he'd become more of a stranger than he was before.

As for that fiasco with her daddy—well, Mitch shouldn't have blurted out that they were married. Maybe it was his defense against getting fired. What ever Mitch's reasoning, his high-handedness still smarted.

Now, as she made her way past Cooper's study, she heard voices—Cooper's and Peter's. Oh dear, she thought, Peter was the last person she wanted to see. She would not have lingered so much as a second—especially since the door was cracked and she could have been seen—except that she heard her name mentioned.

She paused, out of harm's way, and listened. Although she couldn't hear all the conversation, she heard enough.

Her hands flew to her mouth, covering it so she wouldn't cry out loud. Instead, she cried silently,

Why, Daddy? How could you? How could you do this to me?

For a moment Lindsay was tempted to barge into the room and confront him on the spot—only she didn't. Two against one weren't odds she liked. And when she finally spoke her mind, she wanted to be geared for battle, to be at her fighting best. Right now, she wasn't geared for anything.

Heartsick, she turned and made her way back upstairs.

Twenty-Seven

"Are you sure you're all right?"

Lindsay gave Dolly a wan smile. "I'm just tired."

"That's why I brought you this pot of hot tea and this plate of tea cakes."

"You're a dear, Dolly. I don't know what I'd do without you."

Dolly snorted. "I don't, either. You look so thin a good hard wind could pick you up and blow you clean away."

"Do I look that bad?"

"I didn't say 'bad,' honey. I said 'thin.'"

"I'm pregnant, Dolly."

The beloved housekeeper's eyes widened, and her jaw went slack. "You're...what?" The maid sputtered as if she had run plumb out of steam.

"'Pregnant' is the word." Lindsay mustered up another smile. "You can say it. It's no longer a secret."

Dolly snorted again, then said, "Lordy mercy, child, how did that happen?"

Lindsay laughed outright this time, and it felt good. These past few days had been a living hell for her as she tried to figure a way to work things out between the two men she loved. It had been like knocking her head against a brick wall, especially since her daddy had left before dawn on a fishing trip with Tim.

"Honey?"

Lindsay gave Dolly a startled look. "Sorry. I was woolgathering."

Dolly's expression was soft and warm. "Is there anything else you want to tell me? You don't have to. I mean, if I'm overstepping—"

"Oh, for Pete's sake, Dolly, you're family. Of course I want to confide in you."

"Well, no matter what, I love you," Dolly said with a bit of defiance. "And I'll always love you."

Lindsay left her desk chair and gave the housekeeper a great big hug. "The same goes for me."

Dolly dropped her arms, stepped back, then pointed her finger at Lindsay. "From now on, you're going to eat right—and a lot of it, too."

"Now, Dolly, don't start."

Dolly placed her ample hands on her hips and glared at Lindsay. "I refuse to let you have a puny baby."

Lindsay chuckled. "All right, all right. I give up."

"Good. I'll pour you some tea."

Lindsay let go of a sigh as she watched Dolly putter. "Mitch Rawlins is the father."

Dolly straightened as if she'd been shot, then whipped around. "Lordy, if you don't stop shocking me, I'm gonna have a heart attack."

"And we're married. So you can rest easy on that score." What Lindsay didn't add, but wanted to, was that she hoped they would stay married. The way the situation was now, she had no idea what to expect.

Dolly sat down in the nearest chair and started fanning herself with her right hand. This time Lindsay hid her smile, though she knew Dolly was putting on a show. What she had just been told was heavy stuff, especially because it was unexpected.

"Then why isn't Mr. Mitch living here with you?"

Lindsay put a trembling hand to her head. "Daddy just found out himself and went berserk."

"Lordy me. What did he have to say?"

"You can imagine. He fired Mitch, then backed down when I told him I would leave with him."

Too bad Mitch hadn't been around to hear that part of the conversation, she thought. He had already stormed out of the house when she'd told Cooper that, so he didn't know she'd defended him. Anger and pride had kept her from telling him.

Dolly made a clucking sound. "My, my, what a mess."

"That it is, especially when I'm trying to keep peace between two hardheaded men."

"You've taken on an impossible task, my dear."

"Oh, don't say that," Lindsay wailed. "I have to work this out. I just have to. I don't want to live without either of them, though I'm not happy with either at the moment, especially Daddy."

Her mind suddenly turned back to what she'd overheard between him and Peter—an issue that hadn't been resolved as yet. But it would be. As soon as Cooper returned home.

"You just take care of yourself," Dolly was saying.

"I plan on it." Lindsay put her hand on her stomach. "I want this baby, Dolly. I didn't know how I felt at first, but now I've never been more sure of anything." Her features took on a pinched look. "Though I'm worried that it won't be normal, that it'll be—"

"Don't you dare say that," Dolly warned in a huff. "What's more, don't even think it. Just because your mamma was sick, don't mean your baby will be."

"What about me, Dolly? I was sick like her."

"It's what you saw that made you sick. You have to believe that."

Lindsay hugged her again.

"You just think on being happy with Mr. Mitch, you hear?" Dolly grinned. "He's a real nice man."

"I kinda think so, too."

Dolly's grin faded. "But it's not right, you two not living together. You'd best get that straightened out." She paused, her gaze shifting to the clock. "Lordy, I gotta get out of here and get back to work."

Once Lindsay was alone, she sampled one of the tea cakes and took a sip of tea, thinking it tasted good, which was a plus. Since her stomach had been so queasy, food was not tops on her priority list.

For some unexplainable reason, her eyes drifted to her mother's trunk, and she wondered what Mother would have thought about her having married Mitch. Would Emily have encouraged or discouraged such a relationship?

Lindsay sighed, got up and walked over to the chest, then eased onto the floor in front of it. Once the lid was raised, she stared at the contents and touched several of the items, her eyes misting over.

Would she ever get over having lost her mother?

Her gaze finally settled on the small stack of letters. She picked them up, untied the ribbon holding them together, then began flipping through them.

It was when she came to an unopened envelope that she paused. The letter was one Emily had written to a friend—a letter she obviously hadn't mailed. Lindsay's curiosity getting the better of her, she slid a finger under the tab, pulled out the flimsy paper and began reading.

Moments later, she sat rigid, a feeling of anger and hopelessness washing over her. She wished now that she hadn't read the letter, hadn't experienced her mother's heartache and pain through the written words. If only her daddy... No. She wouldn't do this to herself. She couldn't stand any more jolts to the heart. Besides, what was done was done.

Staving off the tears, Lindsay stuffed the letter back in the envelope, closed the lid of the chest and scrambled upright. Maybe if she ate another tea cake it would quiet her stomach. But the treats no longer appealed to her, suddenly looking like lumps of sawdust.

Making a face, Lindsay walked out onto the balcony, hoping for a glimpse of Mitch, certain his presence would be a balm to her sagging spirits. He was nowhere in sight, though she knew he was still working somewhere on the estate. She had seen him yesterday, without him seeing her.

Even though Mitch didn't love her, he hadn't deserted her, either, and that in itself gave her hope.

But she was still miffed at him for keeping secrets from her when she'd been so honest with him. Somewhere there had to be a middle ground, and she had to find it—for both her own and the baby's sake.

She didn't want to live without Mitch in her life.

A tap on her door pulled her out of her reverie. "Yes?" she said.

Dolly stuck her head around the door. "It's Mr. Peter. He's downstairs."

"Oh brother," Lindsay said, pulling a face.

"What do you want me to tell him?"

"That I'll be right down."

Dolly nodded, then shut the door. Peter was not high on her priority list, either, but now was as good a time as any to speak her piece, once and for all. She had a score to settle not only with her daddy, but with Peter, as well.

Moments later, Lindsay walked into the den and faced a smiling Peter, who held a huge bouquet of flowers.

"Hello, Peter," she said.

He stiffened, having picked up on the chill in her voice. "Still miffed at me, huh?"

She ignored his whining and asked, "What do you want?"

The bouquet slipped out of his arms onto the nearest chair. "To patch things up between us."

"There is no 'us.'"

He rubbed the back of his neck, then blew out his breath. "I didn't come here to argue with you, Lindsay. These flowers are my way of saying I'm sorry."

"You're wasting your time and money on me. You have to know that."

He blanched. "I won't accept that. I still want to marry you. And under the circumstances, I think you ought to take me up on my proposal."

"Mitch and I are married."

That small bombshell had the desired effect. He turned visibly green. "I don't believe you."

"I don't give a damn what you believe."

"Does Cooper know?"

"Yes, he does."

Peter clenched his jaw so tightly that Lindsay thought it might shatter.

"So now you'll have to find another gravy train to hitch on to. This one's no longer in operation."

He glowered at her. "I don't know what you mean."

"Oh, I think you do. I overheard you and Daddy talking the other afternoon."

He gasped. "You mean you eavesdropped."

"Not intentionally. I just happened to be walking by when I heard my name mentioned. Naturally I was curious."

"Naturally."

"Look, I don't owe you anything, Peter, except my deepest contempt."

His features turned menacing. "Getting rid of me is not going to be that simple."

"Don't you dare threaten me."

His nostrils flared. "Cooper owes me, and I aim to get what's coming to me."

"If you don't leave me alone, you *will* get what's coming to you, all right. From Mitch."

He released an ugly laugh. "This was all *Daddy's* idea from the get-go. In case you didn't hear that."

"Get out!" She gritted her teeth. "Now! And don't ever come back."

"I'm going, but it's not over till the fat lady sings. And she ain't even started yet."

"Get out!" Lindsay cried again.

The second he sauntered through the door, Lindsay sank onto the sofa, her breathing coming in tiny spurts.

"Are you all right?"

She glanced up at Dolly, who stood in the doorway, her face wrinkled with concern.

"No, but I will be when I get over being mad as a hornet."

Dolly sniffed. "That man's no good."

"You're right, he isn't. Contrary to what he said, we *have* seen the last of him."

Dolly nodded, then shuffled off. Lindsay, however, remained on the sofa for a while longer. If only her daddy hadn't left before dawn that morning, she would definitely have confronted him right there.

Tears stung her eyes. How could Cooper have done such a thing to her? How could he have so little respect for her? Pushing those unwanted questions aside, Lindsay got up and made her way toward the stairs, her thoughts shifting back to Mitch.

Suddenly it seemed so important that she make things right between them. He might not love her, but he cared enough to have married her.

And that was a start.

Twenty-Eight

Her stomach!

It felt godawful. Lindsay eased onto her side in the bed and curled into a fetal position, then took deep, ragged breaths. Neither remedy proved to be helpful. The nausea kept coming in waves.

She felt clammy all over, too. Maybe that was her problem, she told herself. Maybe she was hot and that was contributing to her nausea. Exerting as little effort as possible, she tossed back the top sheet.

Moments later her teeth began chattering, and she grabbed the sheet again as another wave hit her, flip-flopping her stomach.

"Ohhh," she moaned, splaying a hand over her abdomen and massaging it. What was wrong? Since day one of her pregnancy, she'd been sick, but never like this—never so ill she couldn't seem to function.

If only she could throw up, then maybe whatever had her in its grip would let go. She just prayed the baby was all right, that this malady that had struck her didn't have anything to do with the pregnancy.

She squeezed her eyes shut and felt tears on her face. "Oh, dear Lord, please help me," she whispered, even as another pain assaulted her.

Food poisoning? Could that be the culprit? She'd

had it once before, and if she remembered correctly, what she was feeling now was similar to what she'd felt then. But, she couldn't be sure. At the moment her brain was fogged up, and her mouth was devoid of saliva, so dry she couldn't swallow.

And her belly... God, it hurt. She lifted her knees higher and tighter until they were pressed against her stomach. That gesture didn't help curtail the growing pain and nausea, either.

Suddenly she lurched out of the bed and dashed to the bathroom, barely making it to the toilet. Once there, she lost everything inside her. It was when she realized she was gagging with the dry heaves that she knew she had to get help.

The baby!

She had to think of the life growing inside her. If she didn't stop this, she might do her and Mitch's child irrevocable harm. Mitch. She wished he were there beside her, that he were holding her in his strong arms. A pain of another kind socked her, but this time it went straight to the heart.

A sob ripped through her, and her head spun.

Spreading one hand against the wall to steady herself, Lindsay waited for the room to settle before she took a step. Dolly. Now that she'd lost the foul contents of her stomach, she felt better. She could call for help.

Five minutes later Dolly was hovering, having placed a damp, cool rag on Lindsay's forehead.

"As soon as I can, I'll make you some hot tea," Dolly said. "But first we need to call the doctor, since Mr. Cooper's gone."

"Maybe you're right," Lindsay responded, her tummy starting to gurgle again. "Although I hate to bother him at ten o'clock at night."

Dolly snorted. "Well, I don't. That's what he gets paid those big bucks for."

If Lindsay hadn't felt so badly, she would have laughed. Leave it to Dolly to tell it like it was.

"Anyhow, you need something to settle your tummy. You have the baby to think about, you know."

"I know." Lindsay lifted dark-circled eyes to Dolly, who had pulled a chair up beside the bed. "Of all the times for Daddy to be gone. And Tim, too. Either one could've given me something."

"Only they're not here. So tell me who to call and the number."

Once Dolly had placed the call and the doctor had answered, Lindsay reached for the receiver.

A few minutes later she had the name of a prescription that was safe for her to take. The problem was the only pharmacy open at this time of night was not close. Thinking Tim might have the medication at home, she told Dolly to call Eve. After all, her brother owned several pharmacies and kept samples of all kinds on hand.

"Ms. Eve's taking a look-see," Dolly said moments later, getting up and rewetting the rag. "How do you feel?"

"Like someone's using a blowtorch in my stomach."

Dolly frowned. "That's not good."

Another sharp pain took Lindsay's next breath. Surely she wasn't going to throw up again. She decided not to bet on that as the nausea made its presence known once again.

"Honey chil', breathe deep," Dolly cooed, pressing the rag back in place. "That'll sure 'nough help."

Lindsay did as she was told. The pain did subside momentarily, for which she was grateful, though not nearly as grateful as she was when she saw Eve standing in the open door, a hesitant look on her face.

"Please, come on in," Lindsay whispered, her eyes darting to her sister-in-law's hands. Eve was holding a small sack.

Dolly stood, then swung around. "Oh, thank goodness. Did Dr. Tim have them?"

Eve crossed to the bed, her dove-gray eyes brimming with concern as she peered down at Lindsay, taking her hand. "That he did, so we're in business."

"Thanks, Eve," Lindsay said, taking the pill and glass of water that her sister-in-law gave her.

"Now maybe you'll feel better," Eve said, stepping back. "God, you had me scared. And from the looks of you, I had a right to be."

Dolly resumed her seat, after having pulled up another one for Eve, who perched on the edge of it, her eyes flicking around the dimly lit room.

"I'm hoping it's just a virus and not anything to do with the baby," Lindsay said in a voice peeled raw from vomiting.

Eve's expression softened. "By the way, congratulations on both the baby and getting married."

"As you probably know, things are not good."

"Tim told me Cooper was having a conniption."

"That's an understatement." Lindsay suddenly winced again.

Eve stood abruptly, her gaze swinging to Dolly, then back to Lindsay. "Look, I'm going to go so you can rest and the medicine can take effect."

Lindsay managed a brief smile. "Thanks again for coming to my rescue."

"When you're better, we'll have lunch. I'm so excited about the baby."

"Me, too," Lindsay said, taking Eve's outstretched hand briefly, then letting it go.

"I'll see my way out," Eve said to Dolly, who had risen. "You stay with Lindsay."

Lindsay's eyes followed her sister-in-law to the door; then they fluttered shut at the same time that her belly unclenched. Sighing, she closed her eyes and drifted off to sleep, only to awaken a short time later.

"Honey chil', are you sick again?"

"Oh, Dolly," Lindsay wailed. "That blowtorch is back in my stomach, and it's killing me."

"Enough is enough," Dolly muttered. "I'm going to call 9-1-1."

"No. Please. I don't want to have to go to the emergency room. Maybe I should take another one of those pills."

"You're not due another one for several hours yet."

Lindsay's stomach spasmed again, and she cried out.

"That does it," Dolly said. "I'm—"

"Call Mitch," Lindsay whispered, writhing in pain. "He'll know what to do."

* * *

Mitch ran like a marathoner who was in the lead and smelled the finish line. Still, he wasn't going fast enough to suit himself. If something happened to Lindsay before he reached her, he would never forgive himself.

The truth hit him then, as if he'd been slammed by a freight train. He loved her, loved her as he'd never loved anyone in his entire life.

And things between them couldn't be worse. That train suddenly hit him again, almost sending him to his knees.

Earlier in the evening he'd been like a whipped dog in body and spirit, having taken to the sofa, where he nursed his wounds, all the while wishing he had the balls to seek out Lindsay and apologize for behaving like an ass.

When his phone had rung, he'd been tempted not to answer it, thinking it was either his ex-boss or his ex-wife. They were the only two people who ever called, and he hadn't wanted to talk to either of them.

Yet the ringing hadn't let up. Finally he'd picked up the receiver and growled into it. Once he recognized the housekeeper's voice, his head cleared.

Now, as he bounded toward the house, he couldn't help but feel a growing seed of encouragement. She had asked Dolly to call him, which was a damn good sign. So maybe he would have a chance to make things right between them, after all.

Not if she dies.

How could he even think such a thing? Nothing was going to happen to her. She was going to be just fine. After all, she was just sick to her stomach. How serious could that be? Hell, he didn't know, especially since she was pregnant.

The baby! *His baby.*

Perspiration pricked his face and body, feeling like the invasion of tiny needles. Of all the times for Cooper to be gone. By the time Mitch reached the house and dashed up the stairs, he was drenched in sweat.

He knew he had arrived in record time, though it seemed like an eternity before he finally made his way into Lindsay's room and saw her pale face bathed in agony.

"Thank God you're here," Dolly said, standing and wringing her hands. "I'm really worried."

"Has she taken anything?" Mitch demanded, his gaze pinned to Lindsay.

"Yes, what her doctor prescribed. Ms. Eve brought it over."

Mitch frowned. "Who's that?"

"Dr. Tim's wife."

A warning bell went off inside Mitch's head, but he had no choice but to ignore it. Now was not the time to give in to misplaced suspicions.

"I'm taking her to the emergency room," Mitch replied in a low, clipped tone, barely able to speak past the lump in his throat.

"I was hoping you would," Dolly responded, shoving the chair aside so he could get to the bed. "She's ready to go. Robe, slippers and purse, with the medication she took."

"It's Mitch," he whispered leaning over Lindsay and gently lifting her into his arms.

Her eyes fluttered open for a moment, then fell shut again. It might have been his imagination, but he thought he felt her body become less rigid, though silent tears coursed down her cheeks.

"I'm going to get you some help," he said, his voice husky and urgent. "You'll feel better soon."

With a nod in Dolly's direction, he walked out, holding the precious cargo close to his chest—a chest heavy with fear.

What was taking so long?

Mitch stood at the window in the emergency waiting room and stared without focus through the open blinds into the inky blackness. He had been allowed to remain with Lindsay in one of the cubicles until a little while ago, when Dr. Mason had arrived and asked him to step out while he examined her.

Mitch had been tempted to argue, hating like hell to leave Lindsay's side. But he hadn't, picking up on the steel in the doctor's voice. But God, he felt helpless, a feeling he despised, thinking of it as a show of weakness.

He couldn't stand seeing her so pale, so lifeless. He shuddered, staring at his watch, wondering what the hell was taking so long. The longer he was away from her, the more uptight he became.

Without her he felt lost, empty and without purpose.

Both Lindsay and the baby *had* to be all right, he reassured himself. They just had to be. He wouldn't have it any other way. And when this nightmare was all over, he and Lindsay would live together as man and wife. He would do whatever it took to make that a reality.

He had no idea if she loved him or not. Love had

never been discussed between them. He winced. They had been too busy lusting after each other. But hey, he wasn't without hope. He hadn't even known how he felt about her until now. He would give her all the slack she needed. The only thing he wouldn't give her was distance.

He wanted her with him, wanted to wake up with her beside him every morning for the rest of his life. He wanted to watch her stomach grow big and heavy with their child, wanted to watch the baby suckle at her nipples...

An emotion that had nothing to do with sex shot through him, almost doubling him over. To think he was going to have a family—something he'd never had before. He couldn't wait.

"Mr. Rawlins."

His head came up and around as if he'd been jerked by a chain. Dr. Mason stood behind him, a grave look on his face.

Mitch's heart raced with dread, and when he tried to speak, his tongue felt twice its normal size. Finally he forced himself to ask, "Is Lindsay all right?"

"She will be."

"Thank God." Mitch's chest was hurting so painfully that he clutched at it. "And the baby?"

"I'm sorry. She lost the child."

Twenty-Nine

Mitch's voice, when he finally spoke again, was low and strained, as if his vocal cords were in a bind. "Does she…does Lindsay know?"

"No. She was asleep." Dr. Mason paused. "I thought you'd want to be with her when she was told."

A white line formed around Mitch's mouth. Then he muttered, "Thanks."

Minutes later he was back in the emergency room cubicle, facing his wife, who was awake now, and whose shadowed eyes rested on him for a second before darting to the doctor.

"The baby? Is…it all right?"

Mitch stepped next to the bed and reached for her hand, his mouth working. "No, Lindsay. You lost the baby."

For a while no one spoke. Mitch couldn't take his gaze off Lindsay, though his own mind was still having difficulty fully processing the devastating news.

But it was Lindsay about whom he was most concerned. She placed a hand on her stomach, and he watched her shoulders beat in time with her sobs. The muted wailing sounds filled the room with an icy chill.

"Why?" she whispered, lifting her tear-ravaged face.

Mitch couldn't say a word. At that particular moment, he was struggling to keep from drowning in his own misery. God, he didn't know how badly he'd wanted this child until it was lost to him.

As for Lindsay—he couldn't begin to know what she must be feeling, especially since the baby had been part of her flesh. He lifted his head and took a deep breath, then lowered his gaze back to Lindsay. He had to be strong. They couldn't both fall apart. And she had earned the right.

"We don't know why, my dear," Dr. Mason was saying. "Sometimes we never know. But if there is a reason, we'll find it." He paused again and patted Lindsay's arm. "I'll be back shortly to check on you."

The heavy silence was all-consuming as Mitch eased down on the side of the gurney, still holding her frail hand in his. "I'm so sorry," he whispered, feeling his Adam's apple bob up and down.

"Oh, Mitch!" she cried, diving into his arms. "Why did our baby have to die?"

"I don't have that answer, my darling," he whispered, burying his face in the sweet fragrance of her hair, hiding his own tears.

He held tightly as she continued to weep against his chest, her slender body convulsing against him.

For a moment he thought he couldn't bear to hear those pitiful sounds coming from her throat, but he had no choice but to listen. She needed him. And he couldn't let her down.

When the siege was over and she pulled back, he

wordlessly and tenderly wiped the tears from her cheeks.

"I want to go home," she said, her eyes having taken on a disturbing vacancy.

Mitch knew where home was, and while that request kicked him in the gut, he would cut his tongue out before he'd say anything to the contrary. As it was, she didn't need any more grief. If she wanted to be with her daddy, then so be it.

Besides, maybe that was the best place for her, though he would take her to the cabin in a heartbeat if she were to say the word. But he had his own healing to do, and in his own way.

The wreckage inside her was visible; it showed in her eyes, in her face, in her voice. But he couldn't let his grief out that way. He wished he could. He wished he could break down and sob, just the way she had done. But his pain was a huge, hard knot deep inside his gut that threatened to spread and poison every vital organ in his body.

"I'll be right back—that is, if you'll be all right." Mitch stood, then eased her back down on the stark white sheets, noticing there wasn't much difference between their color and that of her face.

She turned on her side and stared into space out of those wide, empty eyes. His heart wrenched as he peered down at her for another long moment before turning and striding out, his mind a sudden hotbed of unsavory thoughts and unanswered questions.

He found the specialist out in the hall and didn't mince time or words. "Doctor, from all accounts her pregnancy was normal, right?"

The man didn't hesitate. "Right."

"So why did she lose the baby?" Mitch didn't try to contain the desperation gnawing at him. "There has to be a reason."

The look in Dr. Mason's eyes bordered on pity, and when he spoke his tone was almost too sympathetic. "I'm sorry, but there doesn't. Sometimes we just have to accept what fate deals us."

Mitch's piss factor shot into the danger zone. "That might be the way you work, but not me. I don't deal with fate."

Dr. Mason frowned. "So what are you suggesting?"

"That you find out why my wife miscarried our baby."

"I don't think you heard—"

Mitch interrupted. "I heard every word you said, but I want a definitive answer."

"What if there isn't one?"

"I can't accept that."

"Do you know something I don't know, Mr. Rawlins?" The doctor's gaze pinned Mitch. "The way you're pushing this thing makes me think you do."

Did he? Or was he looking for a scapegoat, someone other than nature to blame for the loss of his child? He didn't know, but what he did know was that the conversation he'd heard between Tim and an unknown party concerning Mexico and prescription drugs had once again reared its ugly head.

And the fact that Lindsay had taken medicine from Tim's supply at home made that thought even uglier.

Of course, there was probably no connection, he reasoned, nothing to get bent out of shape about. But the suspicion was there nonetheless, and he had to act on it. Much to his chagrin, he was finding that old habits did, indeed, die hard.

"Mr. Rawlins?"

Mitch heard the impatience in the doctor's tone and jerked his thoughts back in order. "Run some tests on the medicine she took, okay?"

"The medication will show up in her blood work, which is being done, of course, and I'll be reviewing it."

"When you do, let me know."

With that, Mitch turned and went back to Lindsay, his face grim and his heart in shreds.

"Oh, Lindsay, I'm so sorry!" Mary Jane cried into the receiver.

"Me too," Lindsay replied in a dull, listless tone.

"I won't ask if you're all right, because I know you're not."

Lindsay stifled a shudder as Dolly strode into the sunroom with a fresh pot of peppermint tea. Lindsay had just come downstairs and settled on one of the cushioned sofas when she got the call from Mary Jane, demanding to know why she hadn't heard from Lindsay.

Lindsay had told her about the baby.

"Oh, God, I'm so sorry," Mary Jane repeated. "I wish there was something I could do."

"Me too—only there's not."

"How did Mitch take it?"

"Not well, or at least I don't think so. The whole way home from the hospital, we didn't talk. He looked beat and totally unapproachable. I haven't seen him since."

"And Cooper?"

Lindsay sighed. "I told him this morning. He seemed more angry than sad."

"That figures," Mary Jane said in a huffy tone.

"I don't know if I can pick up the pieces this time, M.J.," Lindsay said in a broken voice.

"Sure you can, my friend. You have no choice. So don't let me hear you talk like that again, you hear?"

"All right."

"You still have Mitch, and the fact that you love him hasn't changed."

"You're right about that."

"Then you should be with him. To hell with what Cooper thinks or says."

"I don't know how Mitch feels about me."

"It's time you asked him," Mary Jane told her bluntly.

Lindsay felt her eyes fill up with tears again. She blinked them back.

"Look, I'll see you soon," Mary Jane said. "And we'll talk some more. Meanwhile, know that I love you."

Once Lindsay pushed the off button on the cordless phone, she stared through the window. Not a cloud in the sky, she thought, watching a bluebird bathe himself, and with such fanfare, too.

A smile almost curved her lips, but it never quite made it. Her heart couldn't even muster up the energy to pull off so simple a gesture.

Her baby was gone. She had to accept that. Somehow she knew that she would. But she had to go through the grieving process in order to heal from the inside out.

If only Mitch were here. Suddenly she ached for him, ached to smell him, to hold him, to sink her soul into his. But she didn't know how to tell him how she felt, for fear of rejection.

Now that the tie that bound them—their baby—had suddenly been severed, he might want his freedom back. He might want to end their marriage.

Yet he'd been so tender, so caring, when he'd held her in the hospital, she would swear he cared deeply for her. If so, why hadn't he told her?

But then, she hadn't told him how she felt, either.

Cooper's face rose sharply to mind. If she chose Mitch over him, her daddy would never forgive her. Her heart balked. Although she was angry and felt betrayed by her daddy, she couldn't imagine not having him in her life.

But Mitch was her husband, and she loved him and wanted to be with him.

And she had no doubt that he, and he alone, was the panacea she needed to help fill the void that losing her baby had created. Somehow, she had to find the courage to tell him.

"Great," Mitch muttered savagely.

He saw Cooper making his way toward him. Still, he kept right on working. Another tree had succumbed to the wet ground and toppled over behind the greenhouse. The crew had sawed it into big logs; he was now splitting those into more firewood.

The backbreaking task had helped him vent his pain over losing the baby and the hopelessness concerning his relationship with Lindsay—a hopelessness that was an invisible malignancy threatening to devour him.

God, how he loved her, how he wanted to hold her, absorb her pain, make her healthy and whole again. How he wanted her to love him, to make another baby with her.

"Turn around, damn you."

Cooper's sneering voice was behind him now. Slowly Mitch turned and, with features devoid of expression, faced his father-in-law. "What can I do for you?"

Cooper's eyes held a steady glower. "I want you to know that I'm holding you responsible for what happened to Lindsay."

"And I accept my share of that responsibility."

"If you hadn't pursued her," he ranted, "she would have married Peter, and none of this would have happened."

"That might be true—only we'll never know, will we?"

A vein in Cooper's neck was beating furiously. "If it weren't for my daughter, I'd do whatever it took to get you off this property."

"Remember, if I go, Lindsay goes with me."

"I wouldn't be too sure about Lindsay, you cocky bastard."

"Cooper—"

"I'm not finished. Because of you, Lindsay will likely suffer another breakdown and won't be good for anything or anyone."

Mitch almost choked on his fury as he struggled to keep from strangling the older man. "If you weren't such an old fart who didn't know when to shut up, I'd mop this dirt up with your ass!"

Thirty

Tim walked into his office at home and looked around.

He didn't want to be here. But he'd pushed his luck as far as it would go, having managed to escape an extra day, though his daddy hadn't exactly been thrilled, pointing out that he had patients who needed him. But Tim hadn't cared. Although fishing wasn't the great love of his life—not by any stretch of the imagination—it had been an excuse for getting away from the office.

It was times like these, when his insides were in an upheaval, that he wondered why he'd ever followed in his father's footsteps. Caregiving hadn't turned out to be his strong suit. In fact, the more he was around his whiny patients, the more he disliked his job.

Money. That had been the reason he stuck it out. He'd known he had the potential to make megabucks, just like his old man. But for various reasons his pot of gold hadn't materialized. Maybe his patients could see through him, sense that his heart wasn't in what he was doing, that he *was* only in it for the money.

Tim sighed suddenly, tossing those unwanted

thoughts aside. Until his pharmacies started making big money, he had no choice but to keep practicing medicine. Even though his finances were looking up, his creditors were still lined up, waiting their turn to get a chunk of his ass.

Plopping his bag onto the nearest chair, Tim headed toward his desk. He wondered where Eve was. He had expected her to be there, seeing as she'd known he was due home.

He was actually looking forward to drinks and a quiet dinner with her. Maybe she'd left him a note. His eyes scanned the top of his desk. That was when he saw it.

An open box of sample drugs stared back at him. He frowned in confusion. What the hell?

"Tim?"

"In here."

Moments later, Eve walked into the room, her features sober. When she paused in front of his desk, making no effort to kiss him, he knew something was wrong.

"Have you been home long?" she asked.

"Nope. Just got in."

"Then you haven't heard."

Chills feathered his spine. "Heard what?"

"About Lindsay."

"What about her?"

"She lost the baby."

"Good God."

"She got really sick to her stomach and ended up in the emergency room."

"When?"

"Last night."

"Is she okay?"

"Yes, at least physically. Mentally, she's pretty torn up."

"I can imagine." Tim fiddled with his glasses. "Do you know any of the details?"

"Actually, I was the one who took her the medicine."

"What?" Tim demanded, his eyes narrowing.

Eve pointed to the box on the desk. "Since she was so sick and time was of the essence, Dolly called to see if you might have the drug her doctor prescribed. Luckily I found it in the closet and ran it over there."

Tim sat down, a funny feeling settling in his lower belly. "Yeah, that's a good thing."

Eve cocked her head. "Are you all right?"

"Just a little tired, that's all."

"I think it would be nice if you paid your sister a visit. Things are not great for her right now."

"That's an understatement," Tim said, trying to rein in his scattered thoughts. "Under the circumstances, I imagine Daddy's fit to be tied."

"Don't you know it."

"He asked me to try and talk some sense into my sister, but as it turned out, I would've been wasting my breath. She was already married." He paused. "I'm still reeling from the fact that Rawlins got her pregnant and that she married him."

"It shocked me, too," Eve said. "But then, that's her business."

Tim rubbed his mustache, then responded tersely, "No, it's family business. Any time there's a scandal, it involves all of us."

"Please don't get started on that. Like I said, Lindsay needs your support, not your censure."

Tim leaned back in his chair and released a harsh breath. "I know."

"So how soon will you be ready for dinner?"

"As soon as I clean up."

Eve nodded, then left the room. But Tim didn't move. That funny feeling in his belly had turned into something else—full-fledged panic. Could the drug she'd taken be in any way responsible for what had happened?

What if the black market medications he'd started selling in his pharmacies were not the real thing? His panic burgeoned, and for a moment he couldn't seem to get his breath.

Could his supplier have duped him?

No, he told himself, refusing to admit that his ticket out of his financial hole could have caused a death, much less that of his sister's baby.

Just the thought of it turned his stomach to such a degree that he lunged out of his chair and strode out of the room. However, he couldn't outrun his tormented thoughts.

They tagged along beside him.

"I thought I might find you here."

Lindsay had watched Mitch ride up on horseback as she sat on the grass, propping her back against a huge oak draped in moss. She had come to her favorite place once again, and for much the same reason as before: to find solace.

Now, as Mitch dismounted and came toward her, Lindsay suddenly realized that his unexpected presence had done what solitude and nature hadn't been able to do, and that was perk her up.

As always, Mitch appeared so big, so hard, so in control. On closer observation, however, he wasn't as much in control as she'd thought. The grooves around his mouth were deeper, and shadows lurked in those eyes that hadn't been there before.

What if he'd come to tell her it was all over, that he wanted his freedom?

"Dolly told me you were here," he said in a soft but husky tone. "I hope that's all right."

"Of course it is," she said, peering up at him. "You're my husband." Now why had she said something stupid like that? She felt color invade her cheeks as he plopped down beside her, though he didn't touch her.

"Mmm, I like the sound of that word," he told her, removing his hat and laying it on the ground.

She felt her color deepen as his eyes probed hers. "You do, huh?"

"Yeah, it has a nice ring to it, sorta like 'wife.'"

Lindsay felt her pulse quicken, and for a moment she couldn't say anything, especially when the heat that suddenly flared between them became almost palpable.

Finally she asked in a halting voice, "Does that mean you want to stay married?"

"Only if you do," he said, reaching out a hand and brushing strands of hair off her face.

That wasn't exactly what she wanted to hear, but she guessed it was better than nothing. Lindsay swallowed against the intensity of the heat.

"I'm...so sorry about the baby," she said, tears blurring her vision.

"Hey, it's not your fault."

She sniffled. "What if it is? What if it was something I did?"

"Don't say that." This time his voice sounded encased in steel. "You didn't do anything wrong."

"Oh, Mitch," she sobbed, "I can't seem to pull myself back together. What if I have another breakdown?"

"That's not going to happen."

He pulled her against him then and held her, pressing her face into his chest. She could hear the loud beat of his heart in her ears as she burrowed even closer, feeling some of the pain inside her ease somewhat. This was where she belonged. When his arms were around her, she was no longer afraid; the demons couldn't overtake her. If only he didn't ever have to leave her.

"I'm so afraid, Mitch. I feel so alone, so—"

"God, Lindsay, don't say that. You're not alone like you were when your mother died. You have me. I'm here now, and I'm not going anywhere."

She drew back and looked at him. "I wish I could believe that."

"Well, believe it," he said fiercely, "because that's the way it is."

He kissed her then, a deep soul-kiss that almost stopped her heart, not to mention what it did to the rest of her body. Fire pooled between her legs just as he withdrew his mouth and pulled back.

Her eyes widened in surprise as his features suddenly changed from passion to anger.

"When this is all resolved, we're going to start all over."

She intended to ask what he meant by that, but when his mouth found hers again, all rational thought fled.

She clung to him, taking refuge in his lips and tongue as they probed and sucked deeper than ever.

"Thanks for seeing me."

Dr. Abe Mason nodded his head, gesturing for Mitch to sit down. Mitch did so, but wasn't sure how long he could stay there. He was so uptight, he felt every nerve in his body.

"What choice did I have?"

Although the tone of his voice was neutral, Mitch sensed that Dr. Mason was uptight, as well, which was not a good sign. However, he would reserve judgment until he heard what the good doctor had to say.

He had left Lindsay in her hiding place, though grudgingly. He'd wanted to make love to her, which hadn't been possible. After having had a miscarriage, she had been too fragile physically and mentally.

He had just held her. And while he'd taken a hard-on with him, he didn't regret his decision.

Lindsay had needed compassion, not passion. For once he'd done something unselfish, even if it made him uncomfortable in the process.

"You're here about the blood test, I take it," Dr. Mason said, relieving the silence.

"That's right," Mitch said without mincing words.

"It was the medicine."

Mitch tensed. "What about it?"

"It was the wrong drug."

Mitch wasn't surprised by what the doctor told him. Still, it kicked him in the gut. Again. Hard. So hard, he flinched visibly. "What the hell does that mean?"

The doctor drew an unsteady breath. "It means that the packet was mislabeled. Instead of getting the anti-nausea drug I prescribed, she took a drug that is designed to cause a miscarriage."

"Jesus."

"It's a drug that's illegal in the States but that's widely used in Europe."

"You're one hundred percent sure about that?" Mitch asked, his tone rigid as iron.

"It causes a woman's progesterone level to decrease drastically, which shows up in the bloodstream."

When Mitch remained quiet, he added, "We've already started an investigation into the matter."

"How about the police? Have you brought them in?"

"Yes."

Mitch rose, though his legs felt as if they had a thousand-pound anvil tied to them, holding them in place. He extended his hand. "Thanks, Doctor. I'll be in touch."

Dr. Mason gave him a strange look. "Are you all right?" Once he asked that question, he cleared his throat and added in an apologetic tone, "Sorry. Of course you're not all right. How could you be, when you found out your baby didn't have to die."

Mitch thought he would choke on the words before he got them out, fury laced with unbelievable pain raging inside him. "And I'm depending on you to find out who's responsible."

He wasn't, of course. He had flat-out lied to the doctor. He aimed to do his own investigating, and he was already a jump ahead. Lindsay's brother was a bona fide member of the guilty party.

Mitch had decided not to share that tidbit with the doctor. He was holding that trump card for his own use. Sure, the hospital would investigate, but he had his doubts that anything would be linked to Dr. Timothy Newman.

Hard cash had a way of greasing the right palms, and Cooper Newman certainly had enough cash and influence in town to know which palms to grease.

Mitch gripped the steering wheel a few minutes later. Only when he heard his knuckles pop did he loosen his hold. His unborn child was dead.

That made the tragedy personal, and he intended to go for the jugular.

Everything inside him rebelled at what he was about to do. But the way he looked at it, he no longer had a choice. Too much was at stake. Holding on to his dream had to take a back seat to settling this score. What damage his decision would do to his and Lindsay's future remained an unknown factor. And while that figuratively brought him to his knees, he couldn't back down. If he didn't go with his conscience, he wouldn't be fit to live with.

Picking up his cell phone, he punched out a number. Seconds later, he muttered, "Okay, you win, but only if it's favor for favor."

Thirty-One

Something had finally gone right. For that, Lindsay was grateful. The site for the prototype facility had been finalized, and the money to start the project was in the bank. In fact, construction was due to begin today. She had just returned from the meeting where the green light had been given to the contractor.

Now that the dream had become a reality, the next phase of hard work was about to begin—finding the right staff, gathering furniture and supplies, screening applicants. But as in every step thus far, she'd had the best of help in volunteers who were as enthusiastic as she was to see the project through to the end.

Still, she had to stay on top of things, which was good, in that it gave her stability, stopped the ground from shifting so badly beneath her feet. Within the past week, her life had been turned upside down yet again. Not only was she trying to come to grips with the loss of her unborn child, but she had her future to deal with, as well.

Her relationship with Mitch had to be addressed and dealt with. She couldn't continue to live in limbo any longer, especially where her heart was involved.

Since their marriage was no longer a secret, she didn't have to sneak around to see him anymore. If she so desired, she could waltz right up to his front door and knock.

And that was exactly what she intended to do this evening, after he finished work for the day. Peering at her watch, Lindsay noticed she didn't have long to wait. Her meeting had taken most of the day.

Now thoughts of Mitch took precedence over everything else. What if he...? No. She wouldn't think like that, not after their conversation the other day. She would rather think he cared enough to want to make their marriage into a real one, the same way she did.

Suddenly a chill darted through her, reminding her again how little she knew about the man who had fathered her child and whom she called her husband.

Was he always going to be a question she couldn't answer?

Lindsay shivered visibly, then forced herself not to dwell on the dark side. But then, she'd been living in the dark for so much of her adult life that old habits were hard to break. Mitch had touched her life with sunlight. Having felt that warmth, she didn't ever want to return to that prison of darkness that had held her captive.

Instead she wanted to spend the rest of her life with Mitch, learning who and what he was. Exciting? Absolutely. In fact, she could hardly wait for him to return to his cottage.

Holding that thought, Lindsay changed her designer suit for a pair of jeans and a T-shirt. She had just slipped into some sandals when it occurred to her to do a repeat performance of their first time alone. She would have Dolly pack another picnic basket—this time with just fruit, cheese and wine.

Almost giddy with anticipation, Lindsay dashed downstairs, only to pull up short. Her daddy was coming toward her. On seeing her, Cooper also stopped abruptly, his brows knitting together in a frown.

Since her loss of the baby, she hadn't seen much of him. She knew that hadn't been accidental. It was as if they had both planned it that way.

"Hello, Daddy," she said, feeling some of that same awkwardness she'd felt after her mother had died.

"We have to talk," he said rather brusquely.

"I know."

"But now's not a good time for me."

Lindsay breathed a silent sigh of relief. She hadn't wanted anything to hamper her efforts in going to Mitch. It appeared as if that wasn't going to happen.

However, that conversation she'd overheard between him and Peter had created a wound inside her—a wound that continued to fester. And while she was tempted to blurt out her anger and resentment on the spot, she didn't, especially with Daddy in a dither to leave.

She wasn't prepared to settle for anything less than his undivided attention.

"I'm on my way out the door to a dinner engagement," Cooper added, when she didn't respond.

"I'll see you later, then," she said, not looking at him.

"Oh, by the way, I expect you to see a lawyer and start divorce proceedings immediately."

Though his words cut to the quick, Lindsay didn't dare give him the satisfaction of knowing that. She kept on walking, though she held her breath until she heard the front door slam.

"Lord amercy, child, you look plumb sick," Dolly said when Lindsay crossed the threshold into the kitchen.

"I am."

Dolly's lips curved down. "I heard you and your daddy."

"How could you not?"

"I'm sure he didn't mean to hurt you," Dolly said in a soft tone.

"Well, he has."

"Oh, honey chil', what a mess. I wish there was something I could do."

"There is. Pack me a picnic basket, please."

When Lindsay tapped on his door, she was both excited and frightened. Don't be silly, she told herself. He was her husband, for heaven's sake.

Still, she waited with suspended breath for a response. When none was forthcoming, she frowned, then eased open the door. She knew he was there, though she didn't see him. His scent filled the air. Was he in the shower? Her stomach went a little crazy. If so, maybe she should join him.

For a moment, just the thought of doing something so brazen made her dizzy, but then she began to wonder how he would react. Realizing she was holding on to the picnic basket for dear life, she crossed to the table and put it down. She turned, and that was when she saw him.

"Oh," she gasped, throwing her hand up to her chest, feeling her face suffuse with color. "You scared me."

He stiffened visibly in turn. "Anything wrong?"

"Does anything have to be wrong," she asked in a stilted tone, "for me to come here?"

Though his expression was unreadable in the waning sunlight, he didn't seem glad to see her. His big body remained taut, as did his voice. Her spirits took a dive, along with her confidence.

"You're not overjoyed to see me." It was a flat statement of fact.

Mitch cleared his throat, then said with obvious impatience, "You know better than that."

"Do I?"

"Yes, dammit."

An awkward silence descended over the room. At the moment he was more of a stranger than ever. What was going on? Had he crossed paths with her daddy, after all? Had they duked it out? Was that why he was so uptight?

She voiced her thoughts. "Did you run into Daddy?"

"No, why?"

Another feeling of relief surged through her. "Uh, just wondering."

"Are *you* okay?"

He crossed deeper into the room but kept his distance. Her spirits dropped even lower, though she tried not to let him know that. A person could only stand so much humiliation; she'd already received her quota for the day.

Struggling for a clear breath, she turned her back and headed toward the door.

"Hey, where are you going?"

She turned, her chest constricting with anger. "Back where I came from."

"I saw the basket on the table," he said.

She smiled without warmth. "Stupid me. I thought you might enjoy my company and a little something to eat, to boot." Her voice faltered, but she would be damned if she'd cry. Besides, she didn't think she had any more tears left.

Mitch's mouth worked, and his eyes darkened with an emotion she couldn't identify. Was it need? This time it was her heart that faltered.

"I don't want you to go," he said thickly.

Then why don't you hold me and kiss me? she wanted to cry. But pride kept her from doing anything other than standing mute and continuing to stare at him through naked eyes.

"What's going on, Mitch?" she finally asked in a soft, shaky tone.

Wordlessly, he made his way to the bedside table, opened it and withdrew the gun. Her eyes widened, and she sucked in her breath and held it while he jammed the weapon down into the waistband of his jeans.

"I don't understand!" she cried at last.

He closed the distance between them, grabbed her and kissed her hard and long. Only after they were both panting did he let her go and step back.

"There's something I should've told you right off, but I didn't."

"What?" She could barely force the word out.

"I used to work for the FBI."

She gave him an incredulous look. "The FBI?"

He nodded.

"You're an FBI agent?"

"Ex," he said harshly.

She shook her head violently, as if that gesture would help clear it. "Then why do you still have that...gun?"

"Remember that visitor I had the other night?"

"Yes."

"It was my ex-boss, Ken Avery. He's after me to do a special job for them."

"God, Mitch." She spread her hands, trying to find the words to express what was going on inside her.

"I know I should've told you, only—" He broke off, then added, "Hell, I have no excuse."

"This is crazy!"

"I'm going to help them out, but only because they're helping me in return."

Not only was Lindsay stunned and perplexed, but her mind was reeling, as well. How could she not have known her husband was a government cop? How could her *daddy* not have known? Was it because he had never seen Mitch as a threat? That must have been the case; otherwise, Cooper would have had him investigated in a heartbeat.

In her own defense, there was no way she could have known unless he chose to tell her, which he hadn't. Now she knew why she'd always thought he had a dangerous side to him.

Her eyes targeted the gun and stayed there. Had he ever killed anyone?

"Lindsay, after this is over, we'll be together."

She heard the desperation in his tone—a desperation that matched her own, but for different reasons. "After what's over?" she finally managed to choke out, still staring at him through wide eyes. "The job you're doing for them?"

"That and the investigation of your brother."

If he had pointed that pistol at her and cocked the hammer, she couldn't have been more shocked. Or outraged.

"What?" she shrieked.

"Tim's dealing in black market prescription drugs for the sole purpose of turning a fast buck."

"What!" she shrieked again. "But how...I mean—" She couldn't complete the sentence. The words simply couldn't pass the lump in her throat.

"Because of that greed, we lost our baby."

"That's crazy! *You're* crazy if you think that."

"Wait'll you hear the facts, then make your judgment."

Lindsay almost strangled on her fury. "I don't believe a word you've said. Tim may be many things, but he isn't a criminal."

"If that's the case, then he has nothing to fear from me or the law." Mitch's tone was unyielding.

Lindsay blinked, feeling as if she was outside herself looking in. "The law? You can't be serious."

"Oh, I'm serious," he said in the deadliest of tones, looking beyond her into the distance, his body rigid. "Trust me on that."

Thirty-Two

Lindsay walked out on the balcony, then back inside. She couldn't be still in mind or body. She felt as if something live was crawling through her brain and over her flesh.

Shivering, she grabbed the railing and looked off into the distance, chewing on her lower lip, her thoughts locking on Cooper. She couldn't imagine what her daddy would do when he found out who Mitch was, and that he had a vendetta against Tim.

The crawling sensation worsened. Lindsay let go of the steel railing and flung her arms across her chest. But mentally or physically, there was no way to protect herself against the blowup that was sure to come.

Once Mitch had dropped his verbal bombs at the cottage, the true confession she'd been prepared to share with him had been destroyed in the blast.

She had moved in a daze, like the walking wounded, toward his front door.

"Please," he'd said hoarsely. "Don't go."

She had swung around, her features pinched with sadness. "Under the circumstances, I think it's best."

He sighed and rubbed the back of his neck. "It was my baby, too, Lindsay."

"I know," she whispered, beginning to tremble. "But you're wrong about Tim."

"That remains to be seen. But what if we don't talk about him right now?"

"That doesn't mean I can stop thinking about the things you said—your accusations." She paused, and a pregnant silence fell between them. "And what about your little secret, the fact that you're an FBI agent?"

"Was."

"Oh, please."

"Lindsay, I want you in my life."

"You have a strange way of showing that," she said with a tremor.

"Don't you want to know what happened to your—our baby?"

She drew back as if he'd slapped her. "I know what happened. Nature took its course, and while I'm devastated over that, I'm not looking for a scapegoat like you are."

"That's not what I'm doing. You—"

"Save it, Mitch. I've heard enough. I'm going home."

That time he hadn't tried to stop her. He had merely looked at her through pain-filled eyes. Because she felt as if she were on the rack, being pulled both ways, she hesitated. She loved him, but she loved her family, too.

And she trusted them. From the get-go, Mitch had been anything but honest with her. How could she trust him? It had been that question—minus an answer—that had finally sent her out the door without a backward glance.

Now, as she tried to make sense out of something that made no sense at all, Lindsay fought against an oncoming bout of depression.

No. She wouldn't allow that to happen. She had come too far to slip back into that dark hole. Besides, she had too many people depending on her. For starters, the shelter and the ongoing project. She couldn't let everyone down who had backed it. More importantly, she couldn't let herself down.

This latest debacle with Mitch and Tim was just another curve in the road—albeit a sharp one—that she would have to ride out. Somehow, somewhere, she would find the strength.

As for Mitch—well, her torrid feelings for him would have to be shelved again. Until this was resolved with Tim, she didn't dare put her soul under any more glaring lights.

She still loved Mitch, but love without trust could not endure. Dear Lord, she wept silently, how could things have careened out of control so suddenly, without warning?

Crying over spilled milk certainly wasn't the answer. She knew that from experience. The only way to put Humpty-Dumpty back together again was to find the truth.

As badly as she hated to admit it, Mitch had raised doubts in her mind. He had sounded so convinced that she couldn't ignore what he'd said, even though she wanted to with everything that was in her.

Suddenly Lindsay felt the need to hurt Mitch for making her distrust her brother the same way she had come to distrust him. Yet she had loved her unborn child, and if losing it *wasn't* an act of nature, then she wanted to know that, as well.

Sometimes life sucked. Like now.

Turning, Lindsay went back inside, straight to her desk, and picked up the phone. A few minutes later, her gynecologist came on the line.

"It's Lindsay, Dr. Mason. Lindsay New—er, Rawlins."

"How are you?"

"Better than I was, thank you."

"What can I do for you?"

"Tell me the truth concerning my baby."

"I'll do my best," he said gently.

A few minutes later, Lindsay dropped the receiver back in its cradle, feeling dizzy. And sad. But then she rallied, refusing to wallow in self-pity. Forcing herself to get up, she dressed in a cream silk pants outfit and left the house.

When she arrived at Tim's office, she was afraid he wouldn't be in, since it was a good hour before he was due to see patients. But luck was with her: his car was in its private parking place.

On jelly-like legs, Lindsay made her way inside the building, then up to Tim's plush suite. No one was in the outer office, so she went straight to Tim's door and knocked.

"It's open."

When she walked in, his eyes widened. "Why, sis, what a surprise."

"Hello, Tim," she said with a catch in her voice.

He came around the desk and, after hugging her briefly, stepped back. "I'm so sorry about the baby."

"I know," she whispered, thinking he looked about as bad as she'd ever seen him look. "Frayed around the edges" was an apt description.

"Hey, have a seat."

"Thanks," she murmured, sitting in the chair directly in front of his desk. He took the adjacent one, then asked, "How 'bout some coffee?"

"Not right now. Maybe later."

He jumped up as though it was hard for him to sit still. "Mine's tepid. I'll just be a sec."

She watched him from under thick lashes as he poured the coffee. His hand shook, which was not a good sign. No doubt he was nervous. Was her presence responsible? Or had he been jittery before she arrived?

She didn't know any other way to find out except to hit him with the words that were about to choke her.

"So to what do I owe this honor?" he asked, sitting back down.

His eyes behind his glasses dodged hers, which was not good, either. "It's not a social visit, I'm afraid," she said softly but bluntly.

His entire body seemed to shift into an alert mode. "Uh, that's too bad, since we haven't seen each other in a while."

"You said a few minutes ago you were sorry about...the baby."

"Of course I'm sorry."

"Sorry enough to tell me the truth?"

His thin features seemed to shrink suddenly, calling attention to the prominent bones underneath. "I don't know what you're talking about."

"Oh, I think you do."

"Suppose you enlighten me."

His tone was a mixture of sarcasm and amusement, both of which made her itch to slap him.

"What about the medicine you sell in your pharmacies?"

He didn't so much as move a muscle. "What about it?"

"Where do you get it?"

That question hit the mark. His nostrils flared, and a spark of fear leapt into his eyes. Yet when he spoke, his voice was nonchalant. "I can't for the life of me figure out why that would concern you."

"Oh, for God's sake, Tim, stop it! You're not only playing me for a fool, but yourself, as well."

His color heightened. "Now, see here, Lindsay. You can't talk to me like that."

"I sure can when it comes to the lethal drug I took."

His nostrils flared even more, and a fine line of perspiration broke through his mustache, darkening it. "You're full of shit."

"Oh, really? I don't think so, and not according to Dr. Mason, either."

"Then he's full of shit."

Sweat now filled the fine lines on Tim's forehead. "I didn't come here to trade insults, Tim, but if that's what it's going to come down to, then I'm willing."

"What the hell is this all about?"

"It's about the drug Eve brought me when I was so sick—the drug that came from your supply."

"I know about that, of course. But that's all I know."

So this was how it was going to go down, Lindsay thought, feeling heartsick. He was lying. She knew that with every fiber of her being.

"The medicine I took was mislabeled."

"Mislabeled." Tim rolled his eyes. "Come on, give me a break."

"How about I give you the bare facts?"

"And just what would they be?"

Again he was insultingly amused and sarcastic, which should have made her feel good about sucker punching him in the belly. Only it didn't; it made her sick.

"I'm sure you know there's a drug they sell in Europe that induces miscarriages."

His eyebrows shot up, and the color receded from his face.

"Instead of the packet containing anti-nausca medication, it contained that particular drug."

"Good God!" Tin lunged to his feet. "And you think I'm responsible?"

"It came from your pharmacy."

"So what? I wouldn't hurt anyone—least of all my own sister."

"Not intentionally, I know that. But when it comes to money, I don't have much faith in you. If you could get foreign drugs more cheaply..." She let the rest of the thought hang in the air.

"So what are you saying—that you hold me responsible for your baby's death?"

Lindsay hesitated. He sounded so outraged, so convincing. But the drug had come from his supply. What other explanation could there be?

"Look, I know I'm not the best doctor, certainly

not the caliber daddy was, but I'm a doctor, none-theless, who's sworn to heal, not kill.''

"But the facts don't lie, Tim!" she cried, peering up at him, aching to believe him.

"I don't give a damn what the facts are!" he exclaimed. "I'm innocent. You have to believe that."

Did she? She wanted to. Oh, how she wanted to. But unfortunately, she didn't. However, she realized she wasn't about to get a confession out of him. Continuing to spar with him like this was a waste of energy and time.

"Have you said anything to Daddy?" he asked, ending the short, hostile silence. "And Rawlins—what about him?"

"To my knowledge Daddy doesn't know, but Mitch does."

"Great!"

Lindsay rose.

"Where the hell do you think you're going?"

She took offense at his attitude and his words. "Hey, I don't owe you an explanation for my actions."

"That works both ways," he said in a frigid tone. "Remember that."

By the time Lindsay made it to her car, her stomach was pitching a fit, much as it had done when she'd been pregnant. Her baby. Misty-eyed, she covered her flat stomach with one hand, wondering if she and Mitch would ever create another child.

Then, swallowing a sob, she started the engine and drove off.

"Why, that bastard!" Mary Jane's face turned scarlet. "Sorry, friend. I know he's your brother, but—"

"I've been calling him that and worse," Lindsay responded in a dull voice.

After leaving Tim's office, she had called M.J. from her car phone. As luck would have it, M.J. had the day off. She had insisted Lindsay stop by her apartment.

Now they were seated on the sofa, sipping peach-flavored iced tea.

"So what are you going to do?" Mary Jane asked.

"Hopefully find the truth."

"It won't bring the baby back, you know."

Lindsay made a face. "Are you suggesting that I just drop the matter?"

"Of course not. Only, Mitch is checking into it, right?"

"Yes, but—"

"Then let him handle it."

"But Tim's *my* brother."

"That's all the more reason to let Mitch handle it. You're too close to the situation."

"And Mitch is too angry for too many reasons."

Mary Jane sighed. "Maybe that's not all bad."

"Maybe," Lindsay said, biting down on her lower lip.

"So he's not just a jack-of-all-trades, huh?"

Lindsay didn't pretend to misunderstand. "Obviously not."

"A government agent." Mary Jane shook her head. "Who would've thought it?"

"Not me," Lindsay responded with cloudy eyes. "I shudder to think what else he's hiding."

"Did he give a reason for not confiding in you?"

"None whatsoever." Lindsay's tone was hostile. "But then, secrecy's been his *modus operandi* since I first met him."

"If I remember right, that was part of his charm."

"After we married, things changed. *I* changed."

"Well, kid, I'm so sorry for all the pain this has brought you. I know you love him, but—"

"I'm not sure about anything anymore."

Mary Jane reached over and squeezed her hand. "Still, I want you to promise me you'll let Mitch take care of this mess with Tim. Don't get in the middle."

Lindsay returned the squeeze, then stood. "I can't promise that."

"So what are you saying?" Mary Jane's eyes spoke volumes.

"That I can't let it go." Lindsay's chest heaved, but her voice grew more determined. "I wish I could, but I can't."

Thirty-Three

"Why, hello, Ms. Newman. Long time no see."

Lindsay gave Tim's housekeeper a warm but brief smile. "You're right, Juanita, I haven't been here in a while. It's nice to see you again."

"Same here. Would you like to come in?"

"Is Eve home?"

"No, ma'am, she isn't. She's out of town for a few days, visiting a sick friend."

How convenient, Lindsay thought. Her spirits, which had been pumped up with adrenaline, suddenly deflated.

"Is there anything I can do for you?"

Lindsay realized Juanita was giving her a strange look, which meant she had let her agitation show. "Thanks, but I'll give Eve a ring next week."

"Well, don't stay away so long."

"I won't. Take care, you hear?"

Once Juanita had closed the door, Lindsay slowly made her way back to her car, her mind still in an uproar. Despite Mary Jane's plea ringing in her ears, she had made a definite decision to follow through with her own investigation.

She almost smiled at the use of the word *investigation*. It sounded so sinister, so cloak-anddaggerish, something that was as foreign to her as living in a developing country. Yet the days when she was content to sit idly by and let others tell her what to do and fight her battles for her were over.

Mitch and the ongoing project were responsible for the new Lindsay. She had defied all odds to have both, though the verdict was still out on a future with Mitch.

Would they ever reconcile their differences and live as husband and wife?

The idea that they wouldn't sent a sudden wave of panic through her. She wouldn't think about that now. She wouldn't think about *him* now.

Suddenly she heard the sound of a vehicle coming up the drive. She stopped in her tracks. It was none other than Mitch behind the wheel.

He braked the utility vehicle and got out, his eyes roaming over her. "What are you doing here?"

Both his high-handed attitude and the tone of his voice rankled. She bristled. "I was about to ask you the same thing."

"I came to talk to your sister-in-law."

"Me, too."

His features hardened. "Let me handle this, Lindsay."

"I can't."

"Can't—or won't?"

She shrugged. "Whatever."

"Look, this is not a game."

Lindsay flung her head back. "Don't you think I know that?"

"No, I sure as hell don't."

They stared at each other for another long moment, tension vibrating between them.

"Look, I'm not one of your subordinates you can order around," Lindsay finally said.

Despite her efforts to hold it steady, her lower lip wobbled slightly. She hated arguing with him. She hated their being at cross-purposes, which seemed to have become their way of life of late.

What she really wanted to do was fling herself into his strong arms and have him hold her, comfort her, *make love to her.*

As if Mitch could read her mind, his gaze softened, and his voice, when he spoke, had a gentleness to it. "I'm not trying to hurt you. You've got to believe that."

She struggled for a decent breath. "I want to know the truth myself."

"Then trust me to find it."

"Trust you?"

The rebuke wasn't lost on him; his features contorted. "Okay, I deserved that. But in spite of what you think, I'm not going to attack with guns loaded unless the need arises."

"Somehow that doesn't make me feel better."

"Dammit, Lindsay, if your brother's guilty, then surely you want him nailed."

She rubbed her temple, where a mean headache was intruding. "Right now, all I want is for this nightmare to be over."

His features softened again, which was almost her undoing. Just when she thought they might have a chance to make a life for themselves together, another heartache further weakened an already shaky relationship.

When was it all going to end?

"It'll be over soon, I promise," he said, his fingers balling into fists. His eyes suddenly smoldered, raking over her once more.

Her breath hung suspended.

"You look beautiful," he said, his tone raspy.

"So do you," she whispered, feeling warmth flood through her, settling at the apex of her thighs.

He took a step toward her, then halted. "God, you have no idea how tempted I am to throw you down on the back seat of that car and bury myself deep inside you."

A moan slipped past her lips before they parted slightly. His apparent need of her was like a gigantic magnet, pulling her to him when she didn't want to be pulled, at least not under these circumstances. "This is hardly the time—"

"I know," he muttered harshly. "You don't have to remind me."

Another silence.

"So I'll call you when I know something."

Mitch's words brought her back to the real world with a hard *thud*. Her insides recoiled, and she glared at him. Had he deliberately been using his sexual charm to get what he wanted which was *carte blanche* to hang her entire family along with her brother, regardless of his guilt or innocence? To hang her entire family?

Those ugly thoughts almost made her knees buckle. Surely he wouldn't stoop that low? But what did she really know about this man? He remained a stranger in too many ways.

"I'm making no promises," she said into the thick silence.

His eyes narrowed in confusion. "Why not? I thought we had a deal."

"I don't know where you got that," she said, skirting around him in order to get to her car.

He grabbed her arm. For a heartbeat, everything seemed to stop. She looked down at his fingers, felt their callused warmth penetrate her flesh.

Then her head came back up, and her eyes flashed. "Let go of me."

"Lindsay—"

She jerked away, got behind the wheel and drove off, her heart beating in a frenzy.

Mitch watched Ken Avery's face closely, looking for a twitch, anything that would give him a clue as to what his ex-boss was thinking.

No such luck. Avery's "agent" facade was completely in place, which meant he wasn't giving anything away, leaving Mitch no choice but to tighten the screws.

"Like I told you, it's a favor for a favor."

Avery's body tensed. "I'm not sure we can do that."

"Apparently you've forgotten who you're talking to."

Avery kept his stone face intact. "You always were a royal pain in the ass, Rawlins."

"That's why I was your best field man."

Avery's mouth turned down. "Who told you that?"

"You did."

"Hogwash."

Mitch grinned briefly, then suddenly grimaced. "Some things don't ever change."

"Do you ever have any regrets over walking away?" Avery shifted his big body in the desk chair, making it screech. "Hell, I still can't believe you did it."

"Yeah, you can," Mitch said, his tone unruffled. "You knew when I told you I was through, I meant it."

"Right," Avery replied sarcastically. "I forgot. You're the man who says what he means and means what he says."

"Another right, Bubba."

Avery scowled. "And you're still full of shit. That doesn't ever change, either."

Mitch chuckled, then watched as the agent lumbered out of his chair and strode to the coffeepot in the far corner of the room. Avery refilled his cup before swinging around and holding out the pot, his eyebrows raised in a question.

"No, thanks," Mitch said. "Your memory is getting fuzzy. After midmorning, I don't drink that nasty stuff."

Without responding, Avery replaced the pot and returned to his chair.

During the short silence, Mitch's eyes perused the room, waiting for that old gut-sinking feeling to wash over him, or bite him on the ass.

Thank God he felt nothing except an immense

amount of relief that he no longer had to report to duty in this office, or in this building, for that matter.

"I take it you're not jerking my nuts, Rawlins—that you do have a legitimate case against your brother-in-law."

"With the Bureau's help, that's what I hope to find out."

Avery suddenly appeared uncomfortable. "Look, I'm sorry about your…baby. Despite what you think, I'm not an unfeeling bastard."

When Mitch had called to make this appointment, Avery had pinned him down as to what he expected from the Bureau and why. As briefly and unemotionally as possible, Mitch had explained what had happened. At that time, Ken had made no comment, personal or otherwise.

Now he seemed eager to make amends, which somehow touched Mitch. "Thanks, Ken," he muttered.

"So how 'bout we put a tail on the good doctor, see where he goes and who he sees? Will that suffice?"

Mitch fought down the bitterness that shot up the back of his throat in the form of hot bile. "That's a start."

"Now that that's settled, let's talk about what *you* can do for *us*."

Mitch relaxed his long legs, crossing them at the ankles. "Shoot."

A little while later Mitch walked out into the sunlight, his gut heavy with dread. Hell, he didn't want to leave town. He didn't want to leave Lindsay. But he had no choice.

He'd given his word that he would track down a missing witness, and he would. At the moment, however, he longed to seek Lindsay out and finish what they had started that morning.

God, how he wanted her, how he ached for her. But even more than that, he felt the urgent need to tell her that he loved her, to confess that his only mission in life was simply to love her and shield her from further pain and harm. But right now, approaching her was not an option.

He could only pray that one day it would be.

Thirty-Four

"Hell, Harv, I should've been a shrink."

Dr. Harvey Milbrook peered at Cooper over his small, rimless glasses, his dark eyebrows raised. "Meaning?"

"Meaning you have great hours and no stress," Cooper pointed out, lifting a leg and crossing it over the opposite knee.

The doctor's pen hit the mat on his desk so hard that Cooper wondered if he'd thrown it down.

"No stress? Stress is the name of this game."

Cooper snorted, though a smile of sorts flirted with his lips. "You ought to try maneuvering a knife in and around someone's heart."

Dr. Milbrook frowned. "Jesus, Cooper, what's the matter with you? Somehow I don't think you came here to talk about stress—at least not yours or mine." He paused. "Or did you?"

"Of course not," Cooper said in a sharp tone. "I'm fine and dandy."

"But there *is* something going on—something that you're worried about."

"You must be a pretty good shrink if you can read *me*."

Milbrook smiled. "That's what I get paid the big

bucks for—to read you and anyone else who happens to walk through that door.''

''Hell, Harvey, I'm not sure I like that.''

''Sure you do. That's why you've spent a fortune with me on Lindsay's behalf.''

Cooper blew out a stagnant breath. ''Speaking of Lindsay—''

''That's why you're here.'' The doctor's words were a blunt statement of fact. ''I knew that when you walked in, only you had to tell me in your own time.''

''Ah, hell, you can't stop using your skills on me.''

Milbrook chuckled. ''You're still as feisty as ever, my friend.''

''Bad ticker and all, huh?''

''As long as it's ticking, that's what counts.''

Cooper sobered. ''That it is, and well, too.''

''So what's the problem with sweet Lindsay?''

''She's about as mixed up as I've ever seen her.''

''How so?'' Milbrook asked in an easy tone.

Cooper stood, then sat back down.

''For chrissake, you're as jittery as a dog in heat. Maybe I should put you over on the sofa.''

''Not in this lifetime,'' Cooper muttered savagely.

But Milbrook was right. He was jittery. And mad. Mad as hell. At Lindsay.

''So let's hear what's on your mind,'' Milbrook said, that easy calm still in place.

''Lindsay's way out of control.''

''In your opinion.''

Cooper scowled. ''That's right. And it's my opinion that counts.''

"She's grown, Cooper, and married, to boot."

"Don't remind me," Cooper said darkly. "But not for long, if I have anything to do with it."

"What about the baby? How do you feel about her losing it?"

Cooper heaved a sigh. "No doubt I want a grandchild. In fact, I'm looking forward to that event—only not under these circumstances."

"Then you think Lindsay losing the baby was for the best."

"Absolutely."

"Does she know how you feel?"

Cooper picked a piece of lint off his trousers, then rolled it into a ball. "I don't know, and I don't care."

"So what this is about is control. You're losing control of your daughter."

Cooper shook his head in denial. "No, it's about my daughter playing Russian roulette with the rest of her life. Mitch Rawlins is not for her. He's not good enough for her."

"Don't you mean for you, Cooper?"

Cooper leaned forward, his eyes narrowed to slits. "Whose side are you on?"

"Lindsay's. She's my patient."

"But I'm paying the bill."

"True, but you know the drill."

"Fuck the drill," Cooper said.

"So what do you want me to do?"

"Convince my daughter that she needs to get rid of this guy and get on with her life."

"Are they living together yet?"

"No, which makes me think there's hope that her sanity will return before it's too late. Otherwise…"

"Otherwise what?"

Cooper sank his hands into the soft leather arms of the high-backed chair and met Milbrook's direct gaze head-on. "Otherwise I'll take matters into my own hands."

"Like what?"

"Like having my daughter committed," Cooper said in a cold tone.

Would her plan work?

She hoped so, though she wasn't sure it was the best plan—or even a smart one, for that matter. But for the time being, it was all she had. She had been tempted to go to Cooper, to tell him what Tim was supposedly into. That temptation had only been fleeting, because she knew her daddy wouldn't believe her, especially if he knew Mitch was involved.

Still, she also knew it was just a matter of time until Cooper found out what was going on. If nothing else, Mitch would see to that.

Shrugging those unwanted thoughts aside, Lindsay forced herself to concentrate on what she was about to do. When she had gotten behind the wheel of her car after dinner, she'd had every intention of going back to visit Mary Jane, only her plans hadn't worked out that way.

The evening had started out more dismally than usual. Cooper had gone out to dinner—not that he would have been any company, anyway. They were barely speaking. And Mitch wasn't getting back until late—not that she would have fared any better with him. They weren't speaking at all.

She suspected those factors contributed to this

well-brained scheme to go to the Newman Clinic. Now, as she stood in front of the door, she cast a furtive look around, then jammed the key in the lock and thrust it open. Despite the fact that Cooper had given her a key to the building, she felt like an intruder. Maybe because she *was* an intruder.

She had come here for the sole purpose of scouting for incriminating evidence against her brother, for something solid that would point to his guilt or innocence.

Lindsay desperately wanted to believe in the latter, but she feared the worst. If only he'd looked her in the eye when she'd confronted him, she might feel differently, might give him the benefit of the doubt. Not once, however, had he met her gaze. Thus, this clandestine visit.

Taking a wary breath, she made her way directly to Tim's office, though she had no idea what she was looking for. Even if she found tons of sample drugs, she wouldn't know the defective or mislabeled ones from the legitimate ones.

So what was she doing there?

She had to do something, she rebuked herself. If Tim was in any way responsible for her baby's death, then she had to know it. And he had to pay. That thought filled her with such dread that for a few seconds her limbs felt frozen.

Then she rallied, chiding herself for turning cowardly. She'd had the courage to come here. The rest would be a cakewalk. With that in mind, she crossed into Tim's office and headed straight for his massive desk.

She opened three drawers before she found it. The

black ledger was the only thing in that particular drawer. Feeling herself getting excited over what would most likely turn out to be nothing of importance, she removed it.

She flipped on the desk lamp, sat in his chair and opened the ledger to page one. After a few moments, her emotions were scattered all over the chart. She didn't know which was more clear-cut—sadness or joy.

She had struck pay dirt. Oh, she didn't know exactly what all the information meant, but what little she did understand was definitely incriminating.

Suddenly sadness overrode the joy in her heart. Oh, Tim, she cried silently, how could you? How could you stoop to such a level?

"Damn him!" she muttered, slamming the ledger shut, then blinking rapidly. But she couldn't stop the tears. They trickled down her cheeks, scalding her skin. She reached for a tissue, only to stop mid-action.

Voices.

Tim and someone else whom she didn't recognize. She had to disappear. But where? Frantic, she looked around. Inside the storage closet? Or behind the heavy drapes? *The closet.* It was the only logical place. What if Tim had to get something out of it? Where then? She would be caught red-handed. Still, after surveying the situation, that was her only course of action, because the men were already in the outer office.

If she didn't move *now*, she might as well stay put and suffer the consequences. To hell with that! Tim was the one who was in the wrong, not her.

She had barely made it to her hiding place when they sauntered into the room. Lindsay sucked in her breath and held it while she listened.

"So what has your shorts in a wad?" the stranger asked Tim.

"The fact that you didn't tell me the truth."

His companion laughed a sinister laugh. "Are you really that naive, doctor, or just that stupid?"

"What I am is pissed off and about to own a piece of your ass."

"I don't think so," the man said in a low, controlled tone. "If you'll think about it, it's the other way around."

"You assured me the drugs were okay—that they weren't harmful."

The man laughed. "We do our best, but it's not a perfect world."

"Damn you!" Tim spat. "I just want you to take your sorry goods out of here."

"Greed, doctor. Your own greed is your worst enemy."

"That's beside the point now. You duped me, Freeman. What I want to know is how the hell can I get out of this mess with my hide intact?"

"That's your problem, Newman. But I'm warning you, if you try to involve me and my people, you'll be sorrier than you already are. As far as taking the stuff, you can forget that. It ain't gonna happen."

"Get the fuck out of my face," Tim said, his voice coated in fury.

"No problem," the man said in a smooth tone. "But don't even think about weaseling out of the deal, because that ain't gonna happen either. You're in this for the long haul. Remember that.''

Lindsay didn't hear Tim's response, because both men left the room together. When she thought they'd had enough time to exit the building and the parking lot, she bolted.

Once in her car, she sat still, grasping the ledger against her chest, shaking all over, in such a state that she couldn't even throw up, though the urge to do so was there. Only after she sucked air deep into her lungs was she able to think rationally.

Should she go to Cooper or Mitch? She weighed her options.

If she went to Mitch, Tim would be in serious trouble. And despite what Tim had done, the idea of turning him in was repugnant.

On the other hand, taking the ledger to her daddy would mean the whole illegal mess would be swept under the proverbial rug. Cooper was a master at that.

"Oh, Tim, Tim," she whispered.

With hot tears once again making their way down her face, she started the car and wheeled out of the parking lot.

Thirty-Five

Mitch cursed all the way to the door. He didn't have any idea who his visitor was, nor did he care. He didn't want company. He wanted to be left alone to nurse his anger and frustration.

But when he jerked open the door and saw Lindsay, his own feelings ceased to matter. She looked so broken, so fragile, that for a moment his heart leapt to his throat, almost strangling him.

"God, Lindsay, are you okay?" he finally managed to get out.

"I…didn't know what else to do," she whispered painfully.

He had no idea what she was talking about, but that didn't matter, either. She was here with him, where he could hold her and protect her, and that was really all he wanted to do.

If someone had told him that this would happen to him, that the love of a lifetime would blindside him, he would have laughed in their face. But as sure as God made little green apples, it had happened.

Despite all the odds against them, he loved Lindsay, and he would go to his grave loving her.

"It's all right, darling." He reached for her, enfolded her trembling body in his arms, and simply held her. And while her tremors soon subsided somewhat, her limbs remained rigid, as if she were frozen inside.

He pushed her back a little so that he could see her face, which had been ravaged by tears. Dear Lord, what had happened?

As if she could read his thoughts, she said, "Please don't ask me any questions."

He didn't. Instead, he held her again for several more long, hard-breathing moments, before leaning over and placing his lips on hers, nudging them wider apart until his tongue was inside, surrounded by her heated moistness.

Though she moaned, she returned the pressure of his lips with the same fervor, especially when he clutched the cheeks of her buttocks and ground her against his hardness.

He picked up on an escaped whimper as he felt her body go slack. Removing his lips, he looked into her glazed eyes. They were glazed over, and her head was bobbing slightly.

Realizing that she was on the verge of an orgasm, he jerked open her blouse with one hand, and, without bothering to remove her bra, leaned over and sucked a nipple through the lacy material.

She whimpered again. Louder. That was when he shifted both hands back to her buttocks and increased the pressure of his hips, moving, grinding, until her head jerked back and she cried out with relief.

He took her into the bedroom then.

While he was more than anxious to know what had driven her here, what had put that desperate look on her face and coiled her body, he could wait. He sensed she needed him physically right now more than anything. And he damn well needed her.

It had been too long since he'd been buried in the heated center of her.

That thought suddenly made him nuts, especially when she took the initiative, standing in front of him and unbuttoning his shirt, then slipping it off his arms. Then she parted those delectable lips again, her pink tongue flicking out and targeting *his* nipple.

He flinched, chills dotting his skin, when she teased the nipple into a hard knot. A contented moan escaped her as her fingertips skimmed over the muscles in his arms, shoulders and chest. He felt as if he'd been caressed by the wings of a butterfly.

Yet his flesh burned. And that burning intensified when she undid his jeans, slid them over his hips, then grasped his hard penis.

"Lindsay!"

Every muscle, every nerve, in his body begged for relief. He pushed her down on the bed and practically tore off her clothes. Once her unblemished flesh was exposed, he bent his head over her chest, his lips once again homing in on her nipple.

He sucked. And sucked some more.

He could feel the force of her emotions as she dug her fingers into his back. And it made him all the more determined to keep her with him the rest of his life, no matter what it took.

He pressed her breasts together, then licked up and down the cleavage until she clasped her fingers on either side of his face and held him to a nipple.

"Oh, Mitch," she gasped, "I feel that all through me."

"Me, too, and I can't wait."

He spread her thighs with a gentle hand, and then, with gentle fingers, eased into her. She bucked against that tender assault, her eyes widening on him.

Shifting, he thrust into her, and, knowing what she wanted from him, rose high inside her. Her eyelids fluttered at the same time that she lifted her legs and clamped them against his hips, as if determined to hold him inside her.

Mitch tensed, then let go, every muscle in his body giving way, only to tense again. Though he felt as if the top of his head might explode, he withdrew in order to prolong the sweet agony.

"Oh, please, no!" Her words came out on a gasp as she reached for him, touching the moist tip of him.

Hard spasms racked him as he rammed back inside her, higher and harder than before, filling her totally and completely.

Her cry, followed by his name, sent him over the edge. A fireball of intense heat shook them simultaneously. He expelled an indrawn breath as she sobbed into his sweat-soaked chest.

"Mitch," she whispered, swinging around and watching him.

No response. He appeared to be as deep in sleep as he had been when she'd untangled herself from his warm limbs and gotten up. Using his shirt to cover her nakedness, she had walked to the window, where she now stood.

She continued to stare at him, unable to take her eyes off that hard, muscled body that could do—*had done*—such wicked but incredibly heart-stopping things to hers.

His lips, tongue and hands had investigated every inch of her. A stab of heat suddenly forced her to squeeze her thighs together. How could she still want him?

They had made love for hours, with her giving back as good as she'd gotten, using her own gentle weapons to wreak havoc on his body.

Her misty gaze softened on him as she caught her lower lip between her teeth to head off an oncoming sob. She needed him. She loved him. Suddenly she felt the urge to wake him up with that declaration of love.

Yet the words still wouldn't come—not when there remained so much unopened baggage between them.

In order to fully commit herself to him, she would have to give up her family. And while Cooper and Tim might be unworthy of her loyalty right now, she still loved them, in spite of their failings.

And what about Mitch? He certainly wasn't without blemishes.

But then, neither was she.

God, why did life have to be so complicated?

"Lindsay?"

At the sound of Mitch's voice, she swung back around. She saw him swallow hard as he looked at her.

"Are you okay?" he asked, his voice now thicker than churned cream.

"No," she whispered.

"Do you want to talk about it?"

"Yes, but I can't."

Their eyes held for a long heartbeat.

"You still don't trust me, do you?"

Despite the sad look in those sea-blue eyes, there was no bitterness.

"I—"

"I won't hurt him unless I have to. You have to believe that."

Her thoughts jumped to the ledger on the seat of the car. For a second she was tempted to go get it, to give it to him. But that temptation fled just as quickly as it had hit her.

That ledger was exactly what Mitch needed to hurt Tim, to destroy her family. Sooner or later he would have to know about it, only not right now. For a reason she couldn't identify, she couldn't unburden herself to Mitch.

"Lindsay..."

"I do believe you," she said at last.

He seemed to wilt with relief as well as an emotion she couldn't interpret. Then he patted the place beside him. "Come back to bed," he muttered hoarsely.

Shedding his shirt, she closed the distance between them and dove into his arms.

What a day.

Mitch couldn't say it had been a good one, either. Yet he'd accomplished a lot. First he had located the elusive witness he'd promised Avery he would find—and with relative ease, too. Only problem was, the man was adamant about not testifying.

"You mean you didn't bring him in?" Avery had demanded, his voice rough.

"Nope."

"Dammit, Rawlins, that wasn't the deal."

"Excuse me, but it *was* the deal. You said find the man, and I did."

"Well, just finding him doesn't quite cut it, and you know that."

"Then you'd best get your top negotiator's ass to Texas and talk the man into spilling his proverbial guts."

"That's your job," Avery said hotly. "I had no idea you'd come back without him."

"The man's scared, Ken. After all he's been through, I don't blame him."

"But if he doesn't testify against that gang, then his wife's death will be more meaningless than it already is."

This had been one of the saddest cases Mitch had ever worked. Or maybe he'd just been out of the business too long and forgotten how sick the world was. A gang of boys had surrounded a young couple's car after it had stalled in a not-so-good area of town. While they held a gun to the man's head, they jerked his wife out of the car and raped her, then killed her.

The man, left with two kids to rear alone, had been traumatized, and still was. Yet, like Ken, Mitch knew the man had no choice but to testify against the gang leader, whom the FBI had taken into custody—that is, if he wanted justice done.

But Mitch had done his part. He had found the man, and that was all he intended to do.

"We had a bargain, Ken. You're not thinking of reneging, are you?"

Avery's expression soured. "No."

"Good. So if you don't mind, I'll get the info your boys got on Tim Newman and go about my rat killing."

Avery cut him a look from under thick brows. "You're out of luck there."

"What the hell does that mean?"

"So far the good doctor's as clean as the early morning dew. If he's hooked up with someone peddling dirty prescriptions, then he's steering clear of 'im."

"And your boys never lost sight of him."

A beat of silence followed.

"Well now," Avery said, "I won't swear to that. But if they lost Newman, it wouldn't have been for long."

"Shit!"

"I knew you wouldn't be happy. However, we'll keep tabs on him longer, if you'd like."

Mitch rubbed his chin. "Now that I'm back, I'll take over."

He hadn't let any grass grow under his feet, but had immediately taken care of his second mission. On leaving the Bureau, he had gone to the doctor's office, where he'd picked up a copy of Lindsay's official lab report.

He had waited until he walked into the cottage to read it, then felt the blood pound in his head like the beat of a drum.

Tim Newman's ass belonged to him. And now was as good a time as any to collect that prize.

Thirty-Six

"I'm so proud of you, kiddo."

Lindsay smiled at Mary Jane, whose eyes were filled with admiration. "I can't believe the facility's finally becoming a reality."

"Well, the proof is in the pudding," Mary Jane replied. "Or so they say. And the proof is right here in front of us."

"So it is." Lindsay knew she sounded a bit awestruck by it herself. And she was, even though the project had been her baby from conception to birth.

The land in front of her had been cleared and the slab poured, which was a major milestone. She had hoped this day would come, but until the contractors actually got started, the uncertainty of it all had niggled constantly.

What if she couldn't pull it off?

Now she didn't have to worry about those "what ifs" keeping her awake at night. The money to complete the project was in the bank, with more to come. Of course, the work was just beginning in other areas, but the biggest hurdle had been jumped, and she could rest easier on that score.

She wished the other areas of her life were similarly on track.

"Why the sigh?" Mary Jane asked. "It's a glorious Saturday afternoon, and you should be singing the Hallelujah Chorus over what you've accomplished."

Lindsay shook her head to clear it. "Oh, I am."

"Couldn't have proved it by me. You look like someone just kicked you in the tummy."

"I was just thinking how nice it would be if the rest of my life was this together."

"I can remember when this wasn't."

"Your point, my friend?" Lindsay asked, jabbing Mary Jane on the shoulder.

"Simple. You just hung in until it worked and wouldn't take no for an answer."

"So you're saying I should do the same with Mitch?"

"And your daddy," Mary Jane added.

Lindsay adjusted her sunglasses, then said in a solemn tone, "I haven't told you the latest."

"Then I suggest we head back to my place so you can do just that. I'll make us some tea. Hey, I even have some tea cakes my mom made and sent over."

Lindsay smiled again, thinking how Mary Jane never failed to bolster her sagging spirits. And coming here to the site of the new care facility had also contributed. Yet the pain of what was happening with Mitch and her family never left her. It haunted her dreams at night and dogged her steps by day.

She knew it was only a matter of time—a short time—before she would have to confront the situation head-on herself, and do what she knew was the right thing.

"So what's it going to be?" Mary Jane asked, already starting to inch toward the car.

"You're on," Lindsay said. "Let's go."

Fifteen minutes later, they were in Mary Jane's apartment, curled up on the sofa with two full glasses of mint-flavored iced tea in front of them, along with the plate of decorated tea cakes.

"So what's the verdict?"

Lindsay swallowed a last bite, then said, "Yum."

"Are they as good as Dolly's?"

"Well…"

Mary Jane's lips curved down. "You're right. They don't even come close."

"I didn't say that."

"I did. Mom's not even in the ballpark with Dolly."

"They're pretty."

Mary Jane giggled. "Only they taste horrible."

"You're horrible," Lindsay said, smiling in spite of herself.

Mary Jane took a sip of tea and stared at Lindsay over the rim of her glass, her eyes no longer smiling. When she sat the tumbler back down, she said, "So fill me in."

"I told you the last time we talked, which was here in this very spot, that I couldn't leave matters totally in Mitch's hands."

"That you did."

"Well, I went to my brother's office."

"Oh dear. What happened?"

Lindsay told her. When she finished, tears were swimming in her eyes, and her fingers were balled into fists.

"Holy moly, Lindsay! Have you told Mitch? More to the point, have you given him the ledger?"

"No, although I went to him with that intent."

"What happened?"

Lindsay flushed and shifted her gaze.

"Ah, I get it," Mary Jane responded, a hint of amusement in her tone. "You got sidetracked."

"Sort of," Lindsay admitted in a breathless voice, remembering how hot, passionate and *desperate* their lovemaking had been.

"So what are you going to do? I know you're caught between the rock and a hard place, but if that medicine in any way caused your baby's death..."

Though Mary Jane's voice faded, her meaning was quite clear.

"It did," Lindsay said, a sense of horror infiltrating her tone.

"In that case, Tim will most likely be in trouble with the law."

Lindsay's features were grim. "Exactly."

"Jeez, what's your daddy going to do?"

"Let's not even talk about that."

"What I hope is that when this is all over, there's something left of you and Mitch."

"Me, too, M.J.," Lindsay whispered around the sudden and stabbing pain in her heart. "Me, too."

"Know what? I think you need a hug." Mary Jane opened her arms. "Come here."

Perfect.

Or nearly, Mitch told himself, watching as Tim maneuvered his Mercedes out of the bar parking lot and headed in the direction of his house.

Instead of going home, however, Tim turned in to the driveway of the mansion. Mitch snapped his fingers. *Bingo.* If the old man was there, then Mitch could kill two birds with one stone. Cooper had to know, and the sooner the better, too.

Mitch was itching to get his hands on Tim, yet he wouldn't resort to physical violence. He would do this by the book so as not to mess up the police investigation, which was underway, albeit slowly.

He had spoken to the detective working the case, who had assured him they were looking into the situation.

Don't get yourself all worked up over it, Mitch had wanted to say, pissed off by the detective's lazy attitude. But he'd held his tongue, even though he'd almost had to bite it off in order to keep his mouth shut.

He didn't want to push his weight around, use his Bureau connection to expose Tim and his dirty dealings, but he would. He would do whatever it took to see that justice was done.

Except lose Lindsay.

He prayed he wouldn't have to make the choice. Surely to God she would rally around him, even though exposing Tim wouldn't bring their child back. He suspected that was what she was thinking. And her ties to her family, especially her daddy, were exceptionally strong. And of much longer standing than her ties to him, he reminded himself bitterly.

Still, Tim's pharmacies couldn't be allowed to continue selling impure and mislabeled drugs. When all the dirty linen was aired, he had to believe that

Lindsay would see things his way. If Tim and his cronies were stopped now, no one else would suffer.

He might as well be the one who got the ball rolling.

That thought was uppermost in Mitch's mind when he parked his vehicle, got out and walked up to the house. Tim and Cooper were already outside on the porch, drinks in hand.

A smirk disfigured Mitch's lips. Tim might be drunk; after all, he'd stayed at the bar for quite a while. So if ever there was a perfect time to dangle the poisoned carrot in front of his face and see if he would bite, it was now.

Mitch stepped up to them unannounced.

"What the hell are you doing here, Rawlins?" Cooper demanded, his eyes sparking.

"I came to talk."

"Not to me, you didn't." Cooper's tone was nasty. "You couldn't possibly have anything to say that I want to hear—except that you're finally getting off my property."

"Sorry, no can do. Not without Lindsay, that is."

Cooper's features turned menacing. "As I've told you before, she'll leave with you over my dead body."

Tim cut Cooper a look. "Hey, Dad, take it easy."

"That's good advice, Doctor," Mitch said to Cooper in an easy drawl, refusing to let himself get riled to the point where he was no longer in charge of the situation. "You'd best listen to your son."

"Now, see here, you lowlife bastard," Cooper declared, stepping toward Mitch. "It'll be a cold day in hell before you tell me what to do!" He swung his gaze to his son. "If you were worth your salt, you'd do whatever it took to get his ass off this property."

Mitch felt the icy jab of Tim's eyes.

"He's not worth it, Dad." Then, to Mitch, he said, "Look, obviously you've got something on your mind and aren't going to be happy until you get it off. So spit it out."

Mitch leaned against the rail in a nonchalant fashion. "Glad you picked up on that, Timmy boy, since it has to do with you."

"Enough!" Cooper ranted. "I don't want to listen to anything you have to say."

Tim's face was now a sickly shade of green, and his body seemed suddenly to have shrunk in size. Out of dazed eyes, he stared first at his father, then at Mitch.

"Your son here is mixed up in some pretty heavy stuff," Mitch said.

Tim sucked in a breath, while Cooper swung his gaze to his son. "What the hell is he talking about? If you've gotten yourself in—"

"I haven't," Tim said quickly. "Don't pay any attention to him. He's just got a hard-on, probably because Lindsay's still living with you rather than playing house with him."

"Your boy here is dealing in bad drugs, Cooper."

Once Mitch had lit that giant firecracker and dropped it in the middle of the tiled floor, he sat back and watched it pop, shattering the silence to smithereens.

Cooper jerked his chin up and turned to stare

blankly at his son. "Why, that's the most preposterous thing I've ever heard."

"You're right, Dad," Tim said. "He's just trying to stir up trouble because he's jealous."

"The drug Lindsay took from Tim's home supply was mislabeled. The short version of that long story is that it caused her to abort the baby, and I can prove it."

"That's a lie!" Cooper cried, red-faced.

"The police will be crawling all over his pharmacies and his home before long, checking on all his drugs," Mitch said, having no qualms about lying through his teeth.

A white line had formed around Tim's mouth. "The bastard's lying, Daddy. You've got to believe that."

Mitch could see the desperation clawing at Tim's insides as he practically groveled at Cooper's feet. Sickened by the show, Mitch turned away, only to feel as if he'd been karate-chopped from behind.

Lindsay stepped out of the shadows.

Thirty-Seven

"May I join the party?"

Lindsay hadn't intended to keep her presence a secret. But when she had gotten home from Mary Jane's and stepped out of the car, she had heard the raised voices. Sensing something was up, she had dropped her purse and headed for the porch, only to pull up short and listen.

Then she couldn't move. A sick feeling washing over her had paralyzed her limbs, especially after she heard Mitch hurl accusations at Tim—accusations that *she* could back up with solid evidence.

Obviously Mitch was on a hunting expedition.

But that didn't matter. What did matter was Tim's reaction to her presence. If she hadn't already known her brother was guilty, she knew it now.

He stood wild-eyed, like a deer caught in the headlights of a car. Her daddy wasn't faring much better, though for a different reason. His features were ashen, like something had ravaged his body.

"Oh, God, Lindsay," Tim said in a choked voice, tears running down his face.

Lindsay didn't respond. Instead, she walked over to her brother, reached up and slapped him on the face.

"Why, you—you—" Tim cried in an astonished voice.

Mitch uncoiled his muscles and stepped forward. "You'd best watch what you say to your sister."

Tim didn't react to Mitch's warning. He only had eyes for Lindsay. "Sis, I didn't mean—"

"Shut your mouth!" Cooper blasted his words into the calm night air, shattering it.

Lindsay's jaw sagged.

Mitch swore.

Tim looked dumbfounded.

"Don't say another word," Cooper added. "And for God's sake, stop that sniveling and behave like a man."

Lindsay didn't look at Mitch. She couldn't and still keep her bearings about her. But she felt his eyes on her, delving into her soul, monitoring her every move.

"How could you, Tim?" Lindsay whispered.

Tim cut his eyes at Cooper, then back to her, lifting his chin a notch higher. "I don't know what you're talking about. I didn't do anything."

"Bullshit!" Mitch's choice word hit like another explosive.

"For the last time, Rawlins, get out of my face and off my property," Cooper demanded, his features pinched.

"I'm not going anywhere until this is settled," Mitch responded, rage vibrating in his voice. "I'm not about to let you use your name and influence to sweep Timmy-boy's dirty dealings under the rug so his ass can walk free."

Cooper shook a finger in Mitch's face. "You fuck with me, Rawlins, and I'll ruin you."

"Your threats don't bother me, Cooper. Tim is guilty as hell of selling drugs off the black market, and I'm going to see that he pays." Mitch looked at Lindsay. "How 'bout you? Are you with me?"

"Leave my daughter out of this," Cooper injected loudly.

"Lindsay?"

Mitch's low, throaty tone drew her to him. Their eyes locked for a long moment—his probing, searching. Pale and trembling, Lindsay suddenly jerked her gaze off him and onto Cooper.

However, her daddy wasn't looking at her. He was watching Mitch with disdain. "When are you going to stop living in that dream world? My daughter's not going anywhere with you. I didn't raise a fool. She knows where her bread is buttered."

"Daddy, we have to talk."

"Atta girl," Cooper said triumphantly. "I knew you'd see things my way."

"Look, Lindsay," Mitch said, walking toward her, his eyes pleading now.

"Please," she said in a shaky voice, dividing her attention between him and her brother. "Both of you leave. What I have to say is between Daddy and me."

Mitch didn't make a suitable comeback, but he didn't need to. She knew he was furious as well as hurt, thinking that she'd chosen Cooper over him. She hadn't, but now was not the time to try to make him understand that. She was on a mission, and she had to see it through.

She would make her peace with Mitch later, and she prayed that it wouldn't be too late. She waited in silence while Mitch stalked down the porch steps and Tim scurried into the house.

Once she and Cooper were alone, her daddy took a deep breath and blew it out. "Thank God you came to your senses."

"Is that all you have to say?"

Cooper gave her a puzzled look. "I think that pretty much sums it up."

"Oh, Daddy, you really don't get it, do you?"

Her words obviously hit their mark, for he winced visibly, and his mouth stretched into a thin line. "I don't know what you're talking about."

"Oh, yes, you do."

"I'm tired of playing your little games."

"All right. I'll lay all my cards on the table."

"Please do," Cooper said in a cool tone.

"It's over, Daddy. Your reign over me is through."

He looked blank. "You're still not making any sense."

"I thought we weren't going to play games."

"Will you stop talking in riddles, girl!" Cooper's Adam's apple was working overtime. "My patience is gone."

"So is mine," Lindsay pointed out calmly. "First off, Tim is guilty as charged."

He sputtered, "You don't believe that. It's Rawlins. Why, that bastard's turned you against your own family. Well, I won't have it. You stop talking like that right now, you hear?"

"No, I won't. From now on, I'm going to say exactly what I please."

"Now, see here, young lady!"

"That's what I'm talking about, Daddy!" Her voice was anguished now. "To you, I'm not a person. I'm a robot who's supposed to think and feel on command from you."

"All I've ever wanted was the best for you, Lindsay."

"Oh, Daddy, Daddy, that's the last thing you ever wanted." Tears filled her eyes. "It's your wants and needs that have always ruled this household."

"I disagree," Cooper said harshly. "All I've ever done is love my family."

Lindsay was tempted to laugh. *Love.* He didn't know the meaning of that word, but she wasn't going to tell him that. He wouldn't believe her, anyway. Their definitions of *love* were worlds apart. And though that truth broke her heart, she couldn't let that stop her from finally asserting her independence and making a new life for herself apart from him.

"That's why I won't have you ruining your brother by believing this absurd garbage Rawlins is spitting out," Cooper said into the lengthening silence. "Granted, he's upset that you lost the baby, but—"

"Tim *is* guilty, Daddy."

Her firm but soft words stopped him cold. Yet he rallied and demanded in a fierce tone, "Prove it."

Wordlessly, Lindsay reached for her purse, then pulled out the ledger and handed it to him. "See for yourself."

Moments later, Cooper raised eyes that seemed to

have sunk far back in his head. For a second Lindsay felt sorry for him. But she didn't dare show those feelings, for fear he would use them against her.

"What are you going to do?" he asked without emotion.

"What's right. And you're going to have to accept some unpleasant realities. One, your son *will* be held accountable, which will most likely cause him to lose his medical license."

Cooper cursed.

She ignored those choice words and went on, about to say all the things that had been in her heart for so many years—horrible things that had been stored in the dark. "You also have to accept the fact that I, like Mother, have a problem with depression. While I'm not proud of that, I'm no longer ashamed, either. But you are, Daddy. And because of your feelings, I've harbored that shame all my life. I know Mother felt much the same way."

"You don't know a damn thing about your mother."

"I know that you hurt her terribly with your stable of women."

Cooper laughed an ugly laugh. "Is that what she told you?"

Lindsay felt herself color. "No, but I read a letter to her best friend—a letter that Mother never mailed."

"And what exactly did that letter say?"

"That…that you were driving her crazy because of what you were doing to her, and that she was so depressed she didn't want to live."

Cooper laughed again.

"How dare you?" Lindsay cried.

He loomed over her. "I dare because it's your mother who had the affair. It's your mother who had the lover!"

Lindsay staggered back, her eyes wide with shock. "I don't believe you."

"Well, it's the truth," he muttered bitterly. "She humiliated me, and I couldn't forgive her for that."

"As a result, you became her judge and jury. You sentenced her and punished her."

"You're damn right, I did. She begged for a divorce, but I wouldn't give her one."

"And that's why she killed herself," Lindsay murmured, more to herself than to him.

"She was always despondent, even before she had the affair. I never found the key that opened your mother."

"I'm not excusing what she did. It was wrong. But I'm not excusing you, either. When I look back on things, you never tried to work it out. You made her feel ashamed and dirty for who she was and how she felt. You're doing the same thing with me."

"Lindsay, I—"

"Let me finish." Now that she had started, she couldn't seem to stop. It was as though her heart had been given permission to speak its mind. "I may never forgive you for attempting to bribe Peter into marrying me for fear my mental instability would keep me from finding a suitable husband."

Cooper suddenly looked tired and old. "How did you know?"

"I overheard you and Peter talking."

"All right. I admit to doing what I thought was

best for you. Maybe it wasn't, but Rawlins isn't it, either. I'll stake everything I have on that.''

"I love Mitch."

"I refuse to believe that. He's brainwashed you."

Undaunted, Lindsay shrugged. "If that's what you choose to think, then so be it."

Cooper spread his hands. "Look, let's call a truce, shall we? It's not too late to rethink the situation, especially when it comes to Tim. What's the advantage of exposing him, when the ultimate goal is to stop the distribution of the inferior drugs? I assure you I'll take care of that."

"It's because of those drugs that I lost my baby."

"Turning Tim in won't bring it back."

Lindsay merely shook her head. "As I said earlier, you just don't get it. And that's sad, Daddy, really sad—" Her voice broke. "I pity you."

"I don't want your pity," he spat, and sank into the nearest chair.

"I intend to give the ledger to Mitch—who, by the way, is not the lower-class person you thought him to be." She paused deliberately. "He's an ex-FBI agent with plenty of connections and pull."

Cooper drew in a shocked breath, then stared at her. He was still staring at her when she turned and walked off the porch.

His insides were churning, and he'd never been more frustrated in his life. Would Lindsay ever come to her senses and see Cooper as the manipulator he was? Or had Mitch just handed Lindsay back to her daddy on a silver platter, losing Tim's ass, to boot?

Mitch was afraid to answer either of those hard-hitting questions, but he had no choice. He couldn't ignore the facts as they stood. Lindsay had given him the heave-ho, siding with her daddy, which told him that their marriage was over. His gut twisted.

Not a good day.

Mitch stopped his pacing, then resumed it. He couldn't be still. Hell, he couldn't even drink a beer. He had tried and nearly choked on it. Talk about fucked up.

Hell, they'd never had a real marriage, anyway. In one respect Cooper was right. He had kidded himself into a false belief that Lindsay loved him, or at least cared enough to try to make a life with him.

But he'd been wrong, and that ripped him to pieces. He truly didn't know how he would survive without her. Any minute now, Cooper would have him thrown off the property. He was surprised the man hadn't already sent someone to do just that. Let 'em come. He would go peacefully. If Lindsay didn't want him, then he didn't want her.

Liar.

As long as he took a breath, he would never *not* want her.

At first he didn't realize the sound he heard was someone knocking. He'd been too absorbed in his own misery. Finally, though, it dawned on him that he had a visitor, unwanted or not.

He strode to the door and jerked it open.

"May I come in?" Lindsay asked in a small voice.

Thirty-Eight

"Of course you can come in," Mitch responded in a strangled tone. God, he couldn't believe she was actually standing on his porch, staring up at him with those big, sad eyes.

He ached to jerk her into his arms, to bury his head in her soft hair and lose himself in the smell that was so uniquely hers. Under the circumstances, he was afraid such a bold gesture would drive her farther away, not to mention the fact that she would probably slug him.

Even though she was here, which was a miracle in itself, there remained no doubt whose side she was on. He struggled to contain the bitterness festering inside him and pull himself together enough to make coherent conversation. If not, she might change her mind and disappear.

No matter how she felt, his feelings for her had not changed. He realized that more than ever.

"Mitch?"

"Uh, sorry," he said, moving aside so she could walk past him.

Once she reached the middle of the small living area, he could hear his heart beating at such a rapid rate that he felt certain she could hear it, too. He took a deep breath, hoping to slow it down.

He had to get a grip. But he couldn't get past the idea that she was there to end it all, to tell him to go take a flying leap, to say she was sticking by her daddy and her brother. He didn't think he could handle it. Just the thought made him crazy.

"I have something for you," Lindsay said, again in that small voice.

He sensed she was as uncertain as he was, as skittish as a newborn colt. But he could be wrong. Unfortunately, he knew her body much better than he did her mind, which was not a plus for either of them. If only he could get the chance to know her better.

"What is it?" he asked, unable to take his eyes off her, determined to memorize every lovely detail, in case he never saw her again.

She cocked her head, a frown marring her lineless forehead. "Are you all right?"

Hell, no, I'm not all right, he wanted to shout. I'm anything but all right. "I'm okay. How 'bout you?"

She parted her lips with a flick of that tiny tongue with which he so loved to play erotic tug-of-war. He groaned silently.

"I'm okay, too," she replied in a halting voice, staring up at him through dark, shadowed eyes.

For a heartbeat, Mitch almost lost his resolve and took her into his arms. He wanted her so badly, he could taste it. Taste *her*.

"So what is it?" He shifted his position so as to put more distance between them. In his state of mind and body, he didn't trust himself. This moment in time, with everything hanging in the balance, was suddenly precious, to be eked out, to be coveted.

"This," she whispered, digging in her shoulder bag, then holding out what looked to be some kind of book.

"What is it?" he asked again, reaching for the book, careful not to touch her hands, fearing one spark of her skin would ignite that smoldering fire inside him and force him to do something he would most likely regret.

"It's Tim's ledger."

Mitch frowned. "But how...? I mean...?" Words failed him.

She half smiled at his attempts to complete a sentence. But that smile was short-lived. "It tells you more than you want to know about Tim's involvement in the black market drug business."

Mitch stared at her in stunned amazement. "Why?"

"Why what?"

"Why are you giving it to me?"

Lindsay shrugged her slender shoulders. "It's simple. It's the right thing to do."

"Is that the only reason?" He didn't know why he asked that, nor did he know exactly what he expected her to say. The words seemed to have flown unbidden out of his mouth.

Her response was quick. "Daddy's no longer in charge of me or my life."

For a moment Mitch was too overwhelmed by the various emotions that attacked him from every conceivable side to respond. In fact, his body felt like a war zone. He'd had no idea what he'd expected, but he hadn't expected *that*.

What did it mean in terms of them, of their future? He was afraid to speculate or ask, for fear of what the answer would be.

"You're shocked, aren't you?" Lindsay asked.

"Yeah, I am."

"While I had the stamina and wherewithal to go for it, I got a lot of other things off my chest that had been there for a long time."

"Such as?"

She didn't hesitate. "Tim, of course. And my mother."

"What about her?" Mitch asked gently.

"According to Daddy, she was unfaithful—she had an affair."

He was shocked, but didn't show it. "So how do you feel about that?"

"Terrible for both of them."

"But you have to let your pain go."

"I know," Lindsay said. "There's no way I can fix what was broken."

"No, you can't, my darling." Mitch was quiet for a moment, then added, "I can imagine how Cooper took your sudden show of force."

"Not well, if that's what you were thinking."

A sudden silence ensued, during which their eyes met and held. Mitch struggled just to get a decent breath, still tempted to grab her and kiss her—and to hell with the consequences.

"So how did you get the ledger?" he asked, forcing his mind off the ache in his heart and onto business.

"I went to Tim's office."

An uneasy feeling snaked through him. "Where he just handed it over to you?"

"Of course not."

"How did you get it, then?" he pressed, his uneasiness mounting.

"I found it in his desk."

Since her eyes no longer met his, Mitch sided with his gut instinct, which told him she wasn't telling him the whole truth. He voiced his thought. "So your brother wasn't there?"

She gnawed on her plump lower lip, a gesture that roused his jealousy. He should be the one gnawing on it. Another silent groan rocked him.

"Not at first," she admitted.

"What does that mean?" he asked in a sharp tone, then regretted it. Because he wanted to hold her so badly but was afraid of driving her away, he felt as if he were walking on shattered glass.

"Does it matter?"

"Yes."

She sighed and went for that lip again, which was almost his complete undoing. The only thing that saved him was her answer.

"Tim and another man came in while I was going through his drawers."

"And?"

"I hid in the closet and listened to their conversation."

"About their dirty dealings." His words were a flat statement of fact, a fact that curdled his blood.

She nodded.

"Don't you know how dangerous that could've been?"

"Tim would never have hurt me."

"Yeah, but how 'bout the other creep? You had no idea which way he would've jumped."

"Well, it's a done deal now, and I'm none the worse for having done it."

"I still don't like it," Mitch muttered.

Her head came up, and her eyes sparked defiantly. "You should be proud of me for having the guts to do it."

"I am, but still—"

She slapped the air with her hand, a gesture that effectively killed his sentence. "Just put the information to good use and don't worry about me."

"That's not possible," he said thickly. "I never stop worrying about you."

He saw her swallow hard as the silent seconds beat around them. "Oh, Mitch," she whispered, her mouth beginning to quiver.

Two short strides put him within touching distance. He didn't touch her, though. Instead, his eyes probed deeply into hers, searching for the answer to the unspoken question that hung breathlessly between them.

"Lindsay, my Lindsay," he rasped, reaching out and stroking her cheek with the back of his hand. He watched her swallow again with much the same difficulty as before, even as she leaned and trapped his hand between her face and shoulder.

Instant heat struck his groin, especially when she began moving her head up and down, creating a friction that nearly took the top of his head off.

"God, Lindsay," he rasped again. "Don't play with me."

"I—"

The phone chose that moment to ring. They both froze. Then Mitch cursed, his features twisting in agony. However, it was his insides that took the brunt of the unexpected and untimely interruption.

Lindsay stepped back, breaking all contact.

Mitch turned and glared at the instrument, which kept on ringing.

"Aren't you going to answer it?" Lindsay said in a voice that was barely audible.

"There's no reason not to—now," Mitch muttered, more to himself than to her. The moment was gone, never to be recaptured, at least not anytime soon, he told himself. The phone had brought them down to reality with a *thud.*

Lindsay had retreated back into herself, making her as untouchable as she'd been when she'd first come in. Damn that son-of-a-bitchin' phone.

"Promise me you won't go anywhere," Mitch said brusquely.

"I...promise."

He looked at her for a second longer, then made his way into the bedroom, straight to the phone. He lifted the receiver, all the while feeling Lindsay's eyes piercing his back.

"Rawlins," he snapped into the mouthpiece. He listened, and with each word felt his gut tighten. When the conversation ended, he strode back into the living room.

"What's wrong?" Lindsay demanded, her face seeming all eyes.

"Plenty. Looks like your brother's planning on hauling ass."

Thirty-Nine

Lindsay blinked. "What?"

"Apparently Timmy boy's running scared." Mitch's tone was harsh.

"You mean he's just walking away from everything?"

"According to my contact, that's exactly what he's doing."

Lindsay was speechless. What on earth was Tim thinking? He *wasn't* thinking; that was the problem. Her daddy? Dear Lord, did he know what his son was up to? If so, would he condone Tim's actions? *Had* he condoned them?

Too many questions and no answers. Lindsay felt dizzy and splayed her hand against the nearest wall to steady herself.

Mitch's eyes darkened. "Hey, you're not gonna crash and burn on me now, are you?"

His amused but concerned words were the right combination. Lindsay jerked herself upright and took a steadying breath. "No way. I'm going to see this through to the bitter end."

"Good girl."

"I suppose we're headed for the airport?"

Mitch's lips straightened into a tight line. "As fast as we can get there."

"What if we don't make it?"

"I'm not worried about that," Mitch responded in a deadly tone. "Regardless—he won't be allowed to board the plane."

"Only Tim doesn't know that, right?"

"Right."

Her stomach turned over, and she thought she might have to detour to the bathroom.

Mitch obviously picked up on that, and gave her another intense look. "I can take care of this if you'd—"

"Let's go," she interrupted in a clear, concise tone.

"It might not be pretty," he added, his look intensifying.

"I know that," she said tersely, "but I'm prepared."

He nodded, opened the door and gestured for her to precede him.

The trip to the airport seemed to take forever. From the moment she set foot in Mitch's vehicle, her nerves were on edge. Her mind was also in an uproar, jumping from Mitch to Tim to Cooper. It was as though all three were tied up together in a not-so-neat package, and she couldn't shake any of them loose.

Feeling Mitch's eyes, Lindsay forced herself to remain stoic. She didn't want to appear weak in front of him, for fear he would insist she let him handle this latest crisis alone. That wasn't going to happen. She loved her brother, but she couldn't ignore what he had done. Nor would she protect him any longer, especially when his greed had had lethal consequences.

Their baby had died because of him.

She placed a hand against her mouth to keep from crying out loud. But she must have whimpered, for Mitch whipped his head around and muttered, "Dammit, Lindsay, why don't you let me take care of Tim?"

"No. I'm okay."

"You sure?"

"I'm sure," she said fiercely. "It's just that I can't believe all this is happening, that Tim is involved in something so hideous, so unlike him."

"When it comes to money, you never know about people."

"He's not a bad person, Mitch. You have to know that."

"I'm sure you're right, but that doesn't excuse him."

"That's not what I'm doing. I think he just got in way over his head."

"Probably."

"Poor Eve," Lindsay said. "She's beside herself, I'm sure."

"She might not even know about it."

"Either way, I feel sorry for her."

"You better save some of that sympathy for your brother." Mitch's profile was grim. "When I get through with him, he's going to need it."

Lindsay shivered. When Mitch spoke and looked like that, he frightened her. But then again, she'd always thought him a dangerous man.

"I just wonder how much Daddy knows."

"I wouldn't be surprised if he bought him the ticket."

Lindsay drew a quick breath. "Do you really think that?"

"No. I was just popping off. That's not Cooper's style. He's a fighter. He'd simply hire a name attorney, sit back and watch the show play itself out without getting one ounce of dirt on him." Mitch paused. "On the other side of that coin is your brother, who apparently has a yellow streak a mile long down his back."

"You don't have a very good opinion of my family, do you?" Her voice cracked.

"I have a great opinion of you," he said huskily.

"Thank you," she whispered, suddenly feeling tongue-tied. And foolish. What was wrong with her? He was her husband, for heaven's sake.

Mitch chuckled, then fell silent.

Unexpected heat rushed through her as she cut her eyes toward him. But he wasn't looking at her. He was facing the road, which was good. Now was not the time for them. Later, after this fiasco was over, they would have no choice but to come to terms with their situation.

"We're here," Mitch pointed out, his voice low and controlled.

Without responding, Lindsay opened her door and got out.

A few minutes later, they were in the small airport terminal. Lindsay's eyes darted in several directions at once, as did Mitch's.

"You see him?" Mitch asked.

"No."

"I don't see his tail, either."

"Let's try the bar," Lindsay suggested.

"Right."

They were almost there when Lindsay paused and touched Mitch on the arm. "If he's there, I want to talk to him alone."

"That's not going to happen."

"Yes, it is."

Their eyes collided.

"I don't think that's a good idea," Mitch said with force.

She dug her heels in. "It's nonnegotiable."

"I beg to differ."

"Under the circumstances, I think I should be the one who tells him the party's over."

A sudden glimmer of admiration appeared in Mitch's eyes. "You do, huh?"

"I do," she added emphatically. "You and your cronies can deal with the suppliers, but Tim is mine."

His eyes probed hers for a moment longer, his admiration still intact. "I'll be around, just in case you need me."

Lindsay nodded, then walked around the corner and through the open door of the bar. Sure enough, the first person her gaze landed on was her brother. He was sitting on a stool at the counter, his head tossed back, finishing off the drink in his hand.

Perhaps that was why he didn't see her in the big mirror that lined the back wall of the bar. Lindsay eased onto the stool next to him, certain he could hear her heart. It was pounding so hard, it felt as if it would knock a hole in her chest.

"Hello, Tim."

He froze, then twisted his head around, his face pale and his eyes haunted. "Go away."

"Is that all you have to say?" Lindsay asked in a shaky voice. God, this was so much harder than she'd expected. He looked so gaunt, so frightened, that she wanted to reach out and comfort him, promise him that everything was going to be all right.

She couldn't do that. Everything was *not* going to be all right. Where her brother was concerned, nothing would ever be right again—a truth that broke her heart.

"I said go away," he muttered again broodingly, shoving his empty glass toward the bartender, who silently refilled it.

"Not without you."

He laughed a mirthless laugh. "I'm out of here, sis, in just a matter of minutes."

"It's over, Tim."

"Wrong, sis." He downed his drink. "It's just getting started."

"You're drunk." She didn't bother to keep the disgust out of her voice.

He laughed again. "I wish I were. Then maybe I wouldn't feel anything."

"You should've thought of that before you got involved in black market drugs."

"Don't preach to me!"

"Keep your voice down," she ordered through clenched teeth.

He rolled his glass around on the counter. "Did Daddy send you?"

"No."

Tim smirked. "I bet you're not alone, though. Mitch is with you, right? Of course he is. Hell, he isn't going to let you out of touching range."

Lindsay's heart broke in another place. This was a dark side of Tim she'd never seen before. He seemed hell-bent on taking the most destructive path he could find out of this mess. But at this juncture, only he could help himself.

"You tell that bastard he'd best stay away from me."

"Tim, you really don't think you're going to just walk out of this airport and disappear, do you?"

He slid off the stool and faced her. Though his eyes looked like someone had taken a red pen and drawn lines on them, Lindsay suspected he wasn't drunk to the point that he didn't know what he was doing or saying.

"That's exactly what I'm going to do. Just long enough to let things cool off, that is."

"Meanwhile, dear old Dad can handle things. Isn't that the game plan?"

"What if it is? Hell, he's got the resources, and he's the one with the hard-on about the family reputation remaining intact. I don't care."

"Oh, Tim," she whispered, tears crowding her eyes. "You do care. That's why you're trying to drown your feelings of guilt."

"I hardly think you're qualified to judge my feelings," he said in a jeering tone.

Pain, like quicksilver, darted through her. "Because of your greed, I lost my baby."

Her words hit their mark, and she watched him cringe. Then his whole body seemed to fold up as if she had just knocked the wind out of him.

"God, Lindsay," he sobbed. "I'm so sorry."

"I know you are," she countered softly, tears cascading down her cheeks.

"Then let me go," he pleaded. "I won't ever make this mistake again. I promise."

"I wish it were that simple, Tim, but it isn't. Greed has its consequences, and you have to be held accountable."

He sobbed openly now, despite the fact that others in the bar were staring at them. "I'm so sorry, so sorry. I didn't mean to hurt anyone."

Lindsay didn't have a chance to respond, because Mitch walked up and touched her on the arm, his eyebrows raised. Her eyes flicked beyond his shoulders, picking up two men lounging by the doorway. She knew they were detectives.

"We have to go now, Tim," she whispered, taking his arm. "Come on."

He didn't fight her. Instead, he moved beside her in a zombie-like state.

After Tim was led off by the two detectives, Mitch placed his arms around Lindsay and said, "Let's get out of here."

Once they were back in the close confines of his vehicle, she crossed her arms over her body, hoping to stop it from trembling.

"I'm proud of you," Mitch said. "It took guts to do what you just did."

"It was one of the hardest things I've ever done," she whispered.

He reached over and wiped a smudged tear off her cheek. She peered at him through luminous eyes.

"I'm about to suggest something that will hopefully be one of the *easiest* things you've ever done."

"And what is that?"

Her throat was so lumped up, it took several heartbeats to get the words out.

"That you make your home with *me*."

"Are you sure you want me, especially now that all my family's skeletons are out of the closet?"

She waited with her heart in her throat for his answer. After all, during those times he'd held her, made love to her, he had never once told her that he *loved* her—only that he wanted her.

So had that lust turned into love? Dear Lord, she prayed so, because she wanted to spend the rest of her life with him, no matter what he did or where they lived. Yet she'd been afraid to bare her soul to him, afraid he would reject her.

"Not only do I want you, my darling, skeletons or not, I love you and will for the rest of my life."

"Oh, Mitch!" she cried, diving into his outstretched arms. "I love you, too."

He hugged her tightly, and that was when she felt the tears on his face. Her heart stopped beating as she drew back and met his adoring eyes.

"Do you care where we go?" he asked thickly.

"Home is wherever you are."

He kissed her hard, started the engine and drove off.

Forty

One year later

"**M**mm, you smell so good."

Lindsay propped her head on her elbow and stared down at her husband, who was sprawled naked and damp beside her on the bed. He had just returned from the shower. She reveled in his clean, manly scent, drawing it deep into her lungs.

"What are you thinking?" he asked huskily.

"How good you smell."

Mitch's eyes filled with sudden passion. "You'd better watch out, woman. That kind of talk will get you in trouble again."

"Oh, really?" she responded, grinning. She traced a finger around one of his nipples, then down his belly, to circle his stirring manhood.

Mitch's breath sharpened as his eyes dipped to his now-burgeoning erection, then back up to her. "What can I say?"

"Nothing," she murmured, smiling sweetly. "I love it that your body has a mind of its own."

She leaned down and began nibbling on his lips, while his hand moved over her swollen belly before making its way between her thighs and nestling there.

This time *her* breath sharpened as their lips met in a deep, wet kiss, setting in motion another long session of lovemaking during which his hands and mouth were all over her and vice versa.

Later, when their orgasms peaked at the same time, their muted cries rent the air. Exhausted, they lay close and didn't speak for a long time.

Finally Lindsay pulled back and peered at him. "Thanks to me, you're going to be late for work."

He grinned. "I guess my boss'll be ticked off."

Lindsay playfully pinched a nipple. "Well, since you're that boss, you'll just have to get unticked."

She still couldn't believe that Mitch had decided to practice law after all, even opening his own office. He was doing well, too, opting to defend poor and abused women, many of whom came through the shelter, then ended up in the new facility, which was operating at full capacity.

A plus was that Mitch loved what he was doing.

"Unticked, huh? Guess I will at that, especially since I have such a sexy wife."

"Yeah, right," she said in a down-in-the-mouth tone. "Sexy is the last thing I am."

"That's where you're wrong, my darling. I love your belly swollen with our children."

Lindsay caught her breath in wonder, as she always did when she thought about the twins moving around inside her twenty-four hours a day.

"You're still not sorry we're having two babies?"

"How many times do I have to tell you, I'm ecstatic? Hey, look how much fun we had making them."

"That we did," she whispered, staring at him through eyes filled with love and devotion.

"I love you," he said in a husky tone. "And I know I'll love our children. Yet I can't imagine ever loving them more than I do you." He paused, his eyes narrowing. "I don't ever want to live without you again."

"Oh, darling, you won't have to."

"Well, I'll just be glad when the babies are born. Having twins is always a risk."

"Now, now, we've been over this a hundred times. I'm going to be fine."

"Do you think it'll happen today?"

Lindsay chuckled. "Not a chance. After all, they're not due for another two weeks."

"I know, but—"

"Stop it," she teased. "Just savor the moments to come."

"I'm savoring you, that's for sure."

"Oh, Mitch," she said, laying her head on his chest. "I didn't think I could ever be so happy or so fulfilled."

"It's because things finally worked out for us. And boy, was it ever time."

"After such a rocky start, I guess you're right." Lindsay snuggled closer. "We deserve our share of happiness."

They fell silent and held each other as if they wouldn't get another chance. But that was often how Lindsay felt, regardless of the constancy and certainty of Mitch's love for her.

She had come so close to losing him that she never stopped being thankful, though their life together was not perfect. The estrangement from her daddy had been difficult to deal with.

The fallout from Tim's debacle had been equally difficult, although its outcome hadn't been all bad. He had been found guilty of consumer fraud. Following a probated sentence, he'd been mandated to do four hundred hours of community service.

Eve, who had been devastated by the knowledge that she had given Lindsay the drug that killed the baby, divorced Tim. Before leaving Garnet to begin a new life away from all the bad memories, she had apologized and assured Lindsay she'd had no idea the prescription had been mislabeled.

Lindsay had felt no animosity, and although Eve hadn't asked, she had given Eve money to get a new start.

"I can almost see the wheels of your mind turning, my darling," Mitch said, interrupting the comfortable silence.

"You're right," Lindsay admitted on a soft sigh. "I was just thinking about Tim."

"He's going to make it."

"I hope you're right. I think he's learned a valuable lesson."

"Let us pray."

"Now Daddy—well, he's another story."

"What he is is a hardheaded old fart," Mitch said flatly.

Lindsay smiled, though fleetingly. When it came to Cooper, smiles were in short supply. Since she and Mitch had begun living together as husband and wife, he'd kept his distance. She had tried to reach out to Cooper, but after being rebuffed too many times to count, she had backed off. Still, the breach between them smarted.

"Still thinking about your dad?"

Lindsay forced her mind back on Mitch. She smiled. "Yes, but it's okay. I've managed to find some peace about it."

His gaze softened on her. "That's my girl."

Suddenly she disentangled herself and nudged him with a foot. "I just remembered! I'm supposed to be at the Women's Center in twenty minutes."

Mitch leaned over and kissed her on a turgid nipple. "Then you'd best start steppin' and fetchin', woman."

Lindsay groaned, then gave him a look. "That's not fair."

"I know," he said in a teasing voice, getting up and walking toward the closet.

A few minutes later he was dressed in jeans and a shirt and was putting on his boots. "I'm going to the north pasture to work a while." He patted his beeper clipped on his belt. "If you need me—"

"Don't worry, I won't."

He crossed to the bed, where he leaned over once again, only this time he kissed her on the lips, then murmured, "I love you, Mrs. Rawlins, et al."

Lindsay grinned, then swatted at him. "We love you, too. Now go on and get out of here."

Sweat drenched him, though it was not all that hot. In fact, the weather was just about perfect, the same as his life, Mitch thought with a grateful twinge in his heart.

He wouldn't trade places with a soul. His gaze

traveled as far as possible, and he still couldn't see all the land that belonged to him and Lindsay.

The day after Tim was arrested, they'd moved off the Newman estate and into a rental town house, where they stayed until they purchased these twenty acres, using the money his grandmother had left him. They had a home built on it, and had just recently moved into the house, barely making it before the twins were due to be born.

Twins. He'd been thrilled when Lindsay had told him she was pregnant; finding out she was expecting two had sent him over the top.

He hadn't returned to earth yet.

Mitch threw back his head and laughed out loud. A bird answered with a loud chirp.

"And good morning to you, too," he said, his eyes spotting a robin sitting on the nearby fence post.

Yep, he had the best of both worlds now. He had his own land, where he could dig in the dirt any time he damn well pleased. And he loved his job, even though he was inside a building a lot of the time.

His FBI badge had been permanently retired, something that drove Ken Avery, his ex-boss, wild, which was too bad. But no way could he leave Lindsay for field duty, even if she weren't pregnant.

Despite the fact that he'd never thought he would like practicing law for a living, he found that he did, which was a blessing, especially as it brought him in constant contact with his wife.

Thinking of his wife brought another smile to his lips. Sweet, sexy, hot Lindsay, with her laughter and penchant for living life to its fullest, was a new delight to him each day, a delight he feasted on.

He wondered what she was doing about now—and just then his beeper interrupted. His eyes widened after checking the number.

He swore, then broke into a run.

"What's wrong?" he demanded.

Lindsay was waiting for him at the front door. "My, but you're getting slow in your old age."

"What's wrong?" he demanded again in a breathless voice.

She winked at him and rubbed her tummy. "My water just broke."

"Oh, my God. Does that mean what I think it means?"

"Yes, my darling, it does."

His face drained of color. "Oh, my God," he said again. "What do we do?"

Her smile turned into a wince as another contraction hit her. "We go to the hospital, my love."

Several hours later, Lindsay was watching Mitch as he held both babies, a boy and a girl, in his strong arms.

Suddenly her eyes misted over.

"What are you thinking about?" Mitch whispered.

"I'm just a bit sad that my mother isn't here to see her grandchildren." What she didn't voice was her acute pain over her daddy's absence, as well.

"He'll come around, my darling. You wait and see."

Lindsay smiled through the mist. "I sometimes forget how adept you are at reading my heart."

"That's because it belongs to me."

Those bone-melting words were barely out of Mitch's mouth when the door opened. Lindsay gasped, her eyes on Cooper, who was peeping around the door, looking older and definitely sheepish.

For a long moment no one spoke. Then Mitch grinned and motioned for Cooper to come in. "Your daughter's been a busy girl."

"I see that," Cooper said in a slightly shaky voice, walking deeper into the room.

"Hello, Daddy," Lindsay whispered, the mist in her eyes turning into full-blown tears.

He nodded, his mouth working as he smiled at Lindsay, then whispered, "What are their names?"

"Michael and Abigail."

Cooper cleared his voice. "Abby looks just like you did as a baby. May I...hold her?"

His request touched Lindsay deeply, and she accepted in that moment that he was asking with his heart for what he couldn't ask for with words—forgiveness.

Her eyes sought Mitch. Over her daddy's head, he mouthed, "I love you."

Lindsay closed her eyes for a moment, certain she'd just gotten a glimpse into heaven.

From the critically acclaimed author of
Iron Lace and *Rising Tides*

EMILIE
RICHARDS

Once a struggling community of Irish immigrants, Lake Erie's
Whiskey Island has a past as colorful as the patrons who frequent
the Whiskey Island Saloon. A local gathering place for generations,
the saloon is now run by the Donaghue sisters, whose lives and
hearts have been shaped by family tragedy and a haunting mystery.

Then an act of violence sets the wheels of fate in motion. As an old
man struggles to protect a secret as old as Whiskey Island itself, a
murder that still shadows too many lives is about to be solved—
with repercussions no one can predict.

WHISKEY
ISLAND

Emilie Richards is "a careful storyteller who uses multidimensional
players to lend credibility to storybook situations."
—*The Cleveland Plain Dealer*

On sale mid-June 2000 wherever paperbacks are sold!

Being bad never felt so good…

The Countess Misbehaves

Lady Madeleine Cavendish was a proper, sensible young woman—until she found herself in the arms of devilishly handsome Armand de Chevalier. As their mighty ocean liner sank to its watery grave, the two strangers abandoned themselves to a raging passion. Madeleine never dreamed of a fate worse than death that she'd survive. And that the charming, infuriating Creole rogue whom had once been her lover would find her in the sultry splendor of New Orleans, and insist on reminding her of a passion she desperately was trying to forget…

NAN RYAN

"Beautifully crafted characters, a powerful story and sizzling sensuality have always made Nan Ryan's romances special."
—*Romantic Times Magazine*

On sale in June wherever paperbacks are sold!

MIRA

Visit us at www.mirabooks.com

MNR591

New York Times **bestselling author**

DEBBIE MACOMBER

**Two women—each engaged to the wrong man.
Two weddings—but not the ones they plan.**

Rorie Campbell is living a pleasant, predictable life
and seeing a pleasant, predictable man—that is,
until her car breaks down on an Oregon country road,
and rancher Clay Franklin comes to her rescue.

Kate Logan is devastated when her engagement to
Clay Franklin is broken, and the man she loves
marries another woman. Her impulsive proposal to her
old friend, Luke Rivers, isn't the answer to her broken
heart. But Luke thinks otherwise, and refuses to back
out of the promise of a lifetime.

COUNTRY BRIDES

**"A skilled storyteller."
—*Publishers Weekly***

MIRA

*Available the first week of June 2000
wherever paperbacks are sold!*
Visit us at www.mirabooks.com

MDM626

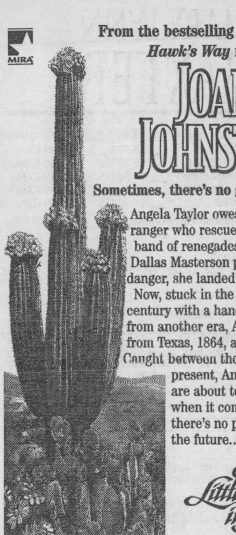

MARY LYNN BAXTER

66523	ONE SUMMER EVENING	___ $5.99 U.S.	___ $6.99 CAN.
66440	HARD CANDY	___ $5.99 U.S.	___ $6.99 CAN.
66417	TEARS OF YESTERDAY	___ $5.50 U.S.	___ $6.50 CAN.
66300	AUTUMN AWAKENING	___ $5.50 U.S.	___ $6.50 CAN.
66289	LONE STAR HEAT	___ $5.99 U.S.	___ $6.99 CAN.
66165	A DAY IN APRIL	___ $5.99 U.S.	___ $6.99 CAN.

(limited quantities available)

TOTAL AMOUNT $_____
POSTAGE & HANDLING $_____
($1.00 for one book; 50¢ for each additional)
APPLICABLE TAXES* $_____
<u>TOTAL PAYABLE</u> $_____
(check or money order—please do not send cash)

To order, complete this form and send it, along with a check or money order for the total above, payable to MIRA Books®, to: **In the U.S.:** 3010 Walden Avenue, P.O. Box 9077, Buffalo, NY 14269-9077; **In Canada:** P.O. Box 636, Fort Erie, Ontario, L2A 5X3.

Name:_____
Address:_____ City:_____
State/Prov.:_____ Zip/Postal Code:_____
Account Number (if applicable):_____
075 CSAS

   *New York residents remit applicable sales taxes.
   Canadian residents remit applicable GST and provincial taxes.

MIRA